A
BEACON
IN THE
NIGHT

Books by David Lewis

A Jewel in the Crown

A Beacon in the Night

Published by Kensington Publishing Corp.

A

BEACON

IN THE

NIGHT

DAVID LEWIS

KENSINGTON PUBLISHING CORP.
kensingtonbooks.com

JOHN SCOGNAMIGLIO BOOKS are published by

Kensington Publishing Corp.
900 Third Avenue
New York, NY 10022

All Kensington titles, imprints and distributed lines are available at special quantity discounts for bulk purchases for sales promotion, premiums, fund-raising, educational or institutional use. Special book excerpts or customized printings can also be created to fit specific needs. For details, write or phone the office of the Kensington Special Sales Manager: Kensington Publishing Corp., 900 Third Avenue, New York, NY, 10022. Attn. Special Sales Department. Phone: 1-800-221-2647.

Library of Congress Control Number: 2025933142

ISBN: 978-1-4967-4912-3

First Kensington Hardcover Edition: July 2025

ISBN: 978-1-4967-4914-7 (ebook)

10 9 8 7 6 5 4 3 2 1

Printed in the United States of America

The authorized representative in the EU for product safety and compliance
Is eucomply OU, Parnu mnt 139b-14, Apt 123
Tallinn, Berlin 11317, hello@eucompliancepartner.com

For my brother,
John Monroe Callas

ACKNOWLEDGMENTS

My novels are mostly about women because they taught me big truths about life, and small truths too, and none of it has been forgotten. In particular, I want to acknowledge: Evelyn Baker, Gwenllian Coleman, Nora Clarke, Elaine Davenport, Paula Dawn, Joycelyn Everett, Joyce Fidler, Bonnie Freeman, Leelya Gary, Karen Hansen, Pat O'Hara, Judi Paul, Polly Peshlakai, Laura Pickard, Linda Ronstadt, Marlene Stringer, Vickie Vining, and Berry Wenegrat.

1

Caitrin Colline stepped out of her taxi into a ruined city. There were no streetlights, and the buildings were blackened shells. This part of London, Whitechapel, was damp and burnt and smelled of dead, half-buried things. She shivered, pulled up her coat collar and asked, "Is this it?"

"No, luv, but I can't drive any farther," the cab driver said, pointing through the windscreen.

The taxi had a single, shuttered headlamp that cast a feeble beam, barely enough for Caitrin to see a bomb crater gouged into the road. Next to it a milk float lay on its side with broken bottles scattered in a congealing gray-white puddle.

"The Blind Stag pub is on the other side of the bomb crater," he said.

"Thank you. I see it."

"You're still thinking of going there? Alone."

"I promised I would."

"All right, miss, have it your own way. Happy new year to you."

"You too. Better than this one, for both of us." Caitrin walked into the darkness as the cab turned and left. She did not want to be in Whitechapel on New Year's Eve, but Florence's invitation was insistent. They were once policewomen sharing an East End beat, until Florence resigned, saying she was not meant to be a copper. Neither was Caitrin; authority and regulations bothered her, and she left the force a few months later.

Bombing had been especially heavy the last few nights, and there were no pedestrians or traffic, only silence broken by Caitrin's shoes on glass shards. If the air in all of London smelled burnt, the ubiquitous sound was of broken glass crunching underfoot. She stopped. Across the road was the Blind Stag pub. It was the only building standing in the street and looked derelict: a blackened fang jutting out of a blasted landscape. The windows were boarded up, and there was no light or sound. A light rain fell. She hesitated and crossed the street. A figure broke from the shadows to block her as she approached the door.

"And now where do you think you're going, sweetheart?" a broad-shouldered man said with a bad Humphrey Bogart accent.

"I was invited to a party at the Blind Stag, but it's—"

"Who invited you?"

"Florence Simmonds."

The man rapped on the door; it opened, and he called out, "Another one of Florence's popsies."

She stifled a cutting reply and entered, pushing through a blackout curtain.

And encountered a different world.

The pub was crowded, but sound struck her first: dozens of voices, loud, laughing; the chime of glasses and a piano somewhere in the smoky distance playing American swing. Oil lamps hanging over the crowded bar and candles burning on every table made the pub a coppered tableau, with the tawny edges and deep shadows of an oil painting by some old master.

"Cat!" Florence called out as she shouldered her way through the throng toward her. "What a sight for sore eyes. You're my only bit of moral support, because I don't know anybody here. I'm so glad you came."

"Me too, Florence," Caitrin lied. She had not seen or spoken to Florence for almost two years and noticed she was thinner, and the spots of rouge on her cheeks had been unartfully applied. "What the dickens are you doing in Whitechapel?"

"Me?" Florence appeared to be startled by the question, a little girl caught being naughty. She recovered. "Didn't mean to be, but I fell in love."

"And who is the lucky man?"

"It'll be a surprise. Do you want to meet him?"

"Of course I do."

Florence's face tightened, and she whispered, "He doesn't know that you and I used to be in the police force, so don't say anything, all right? He doesn't like coppers."

"I understand, and mum's the word."

"I'll go get him," she said and hurried away.

A strange night became stranger when Florence returned with the man she loved. Caitrin recognized him, or at least remembered reading his police record: Daniel "Teddy" Baer.

"Cat, this is my fiancé, Teddy. Teddy, this is my best friend Caitrin," Florence said as she slipped her arm through his.

Caitrin ignored the best friend lie and shook hands with Teddy Baer. She remembered parts of his record. Teddy was the son of immigrant Polish Jews who lived on the west side of Myrdle Street in Whitechapel, facing the immigrant Irish on the east. Naturally, he joined one of the gangs that fought each other, but after the first arrest, he was rarely detained again. Teddy was a smart one, with hair blond enough to make an Aryan envious, and there was a tensile strength to him, as though a much larger man had been compressed to fit in his frame. And no matter how hard Florence clung to his arm and stared lovingly at him, his expression made it clear he was not her fiancé.

"Hello, Caitrin. You're not one of those fur coat and no knickers girls, are you?" he said.

"Why, is that all you're used to?" Caitrin replied as she made an instant mental shift. Teddy was probing, finding her outline so he could fit her into his world. Friend or foe, strong or weak, smart or stupid. He kept his head angled to one side, and she knew why. He was shrewd, charming, and handsome in a way, except for the long red cicatrice of a razor scar down his left cheek. There was a rumor Teddy got striped when he crossed the five Messina brothers, but they ran prostitutes in Soho and Bond Street, and that wasn't his line of work. Those who knew the streets said it was probably Billy Hill from the Camden mob trying to expand his turf. Billy had a reputation for being adroit with a blade, but Caitrin guessed it wasn't him because he was still alive. Teddy was a man who followed his own path. And of all the men in London, what the hell was Florence doing with him?

Teddy took a half step back and inventoried her. Mid-twenties, slim, but by no means thin, a wild mass of red curls, and a confident expression. He pointed to her slacks. "Nice pair of bow-wowsers. Not a lavender lass, I hope? Not going to be competition, are we?"

"Only if you're not man enough to make a woman happy, Teddy."

"We've a right tiger here." He laughed and nudged Florence. "Get your friend a drink. What'll you have?"

"Whisky, please."

"Irish, American, or Scotch?"

"The Irish and Yanks don't make whisky. A dash of water too."

He laughed again, and this time it was genuine. She could not help but like him. Most gangsters were dim bulbs with no idea of a future or horizon past the end of their noses. They lived on

impulse and violence, and most died young the same way. Not
Teddy Baer.

"You a copper like Florence used to be?"

So much for him not knowing Florence's background. "No,
not anymore."

"Gave it all up to fight for king and country, did you? The
honor and the glory?"

"No, because pounding the beat was killing my feet." She
knew you could serve Teddy honor and glory on a gold platter
and he'd sweep them aside—and make off with the gold platter
before they hit the ground.

"What do you do, then?"

"A bit of this and that."

"Sounds like we're in the same line of work."

Florence returned with Caitrin's whisky. To Teddy's admiration, she downed it in one swallow. "Attagirl. Get her another one."

Obedient, Florence went back to the bar.

"I have to take care of a bit of this and that in the back room.
You'll understand. We can talk more later." He left her standing alone.

Florence returned and gave her the whisky. "It's going to be
a good year, isn't it?"

"Couldn't be worse than the last one." She moved closer to
Florence. "What are you doing here, and with him of all people, Florence? You know what he is."

"He's kind to me, Cat, Teddy's not what everyone says.
We've got a flat on Cromwell Street done up just the way I like.
He doesn't want me to work, maybe a spot of volunteering
now and then, as long as I'm always there when he gets home."

Poor Florence, always trying to run away from herself. "Does
he hit you?"

"No." The answer was too swift to be honest.

"Florence, go home to your mum."

"I can't because she's dead," Florence said. "A bomb dropped on her house. Months ago."

"Then—"

"Teddy needs me. I've got to go, sorry." Florence hurried away, Caitrin swallowed the second whisky, and went to the bar for another. Enough of this year. Bring on 1941.

2

Caitrin made up her mind and put down her drink. She had fulfilled her obligation as a friend to Florence, and now it was time to leave. The Blind Stag was growing noisier and smokier, the celebrants drunker, and the thought of being dismissed as one of Florence's popsies was irritating. Had she been invited just to fill out the ranks of friendly females? No matter, it was time for this popsy to go home.

"Are you dancing?" a man said from close behind her.

She turned to face a boy in an RAF uniform. "No, I'm just standing funny."

His mouth opened, but he said nothing. He wasn't a boy, but a young man about her age. He had RAF pilot wings on his left breast, but he wasn't British. The eagle badge on his shoulder showed he was American.

"I have a question. Why do Americans, when they're out and about in London, all have that same bemused expression? As though they had wandered into a zoo by mistake to find strange, unknown creatures."

"I haven't seen anyone like you in a zoo."

"Because I don't like being caged, that's why." The whisky was making her bold. "How the hell did you end up here?"

"We're a neutral country, and I'm not allowed to enlist directly in a foreign military, so I slipped over the border into Canada—"

"Not that bit. I meant how did you end up in the Blind Stag with all the Whitechapel spivs and their painted popsies?"

"My pals got an invitation, and I came along for the ride," he said and gestured to two other Americans behind him being cornered by a trio of giggling girls. *Lambs to the slaughter.*

"Goldilocks Yanks," she said and pointed to his friends. "That one's too tall, that one's too broad, and—"

"I'm just right."

"Or you could be one of the three bears."

"Let me buy you a drink."

"I'll get it. What are you having?"

"Same as you."

"There's no ice. Ever since the *Titanic* went down, the British view ice with justifiable suspicion." She tapped her glass, held up two fingers to the barman and decided not to tease anymore. After all, this handsome man had come a very long way to save the British Empire. "Caitrin."

"What?"

"Caitrin's my name. What's yours?"

"Maxwell."

"From an august American family, no doubt. Maxwell Dupont or Rockefeller?"

"I was named after coffee," he said with an impish grin, and her heart quickened. He could keep up with her. The evening was not over. Maybe it was just starting.

"Please carry on."

"In 1862, Colonel John Overton opened a—"

"Is this a tall tale? 'There was things which he stretched, but mainly he told the truth.'"

"'I never seen anybody but lied one time or another, without it was Aunt Polly, or the widow, or maybe Mary.' Huckleberry Finn."

"Well done."

"Well done you. Can I finish my tale?"

She put a finger to her lips. "Not another word."

"Colonel Overton opened a hotel in Nashville and called it Maxwell House after his wife."

"His wife was named house? Sorry, I really will shut up."

"Teddy Roosevelt stayed there once and tried their coffee. He said it was good to the last drop, so they called it Maxwell House coffee. Mom liked the coffee, and the name, so I'm Maxwell."

"Thank God for you she didn't like Spam."

"Enough of the foodstuffs." He took her hand before she could reply and led her toward the dance floor, a space made by clearing away a few tables near the piano. He wasn't a good dancer, but it didn't matter because pressed in with the other couples there was little room to move, let alone dance. It felt good to be held by a man, the close heat, her hand in his, and she liked that he wasn't shy about eye contact.

"I never finish a dance with a man unless I know his full name."

"Evarts," he said.

"What kind of name is that?"

"Welsh."

"No, it's not."

"How do you know?"

"Because I'm Welsh, and Evarts isn't."

"My grandfather came from Dolgellau."

"Full marks, you pronounced it properly."

"He taught me. At Ellis Island he was one of thousands. They asked for his name and he said Evans, but with all the noise, the immigration officer didn't understand his accent and wrote down Evarts."

"Doomed to be forever an Evarts, Maxwell."

"Max, please."

She stopped dancing and glanced at her watch. An hour and a half left to 1940 that she decided would not be wasted in the Blind Stag. "Let's go."

"Where?"

"The Elephant and Castle."

"The zoo?"

"No, Max Evans Evarts. But we'll need a taxi."

"Not this side of the new year, you won't," Teddy said as he appeared behind his experienced smile. "Large Eric, the doorman, will take you. Leave now because the weather's clearing, and that means Jerry's going to turn up with fireworks."

"Thanks," Caitrin said. "Where's Florence?"

"Too much champagne. Nice meeting you, Caitrin. Hope we can do a bit of this and that together one day." He put out his hand. She took it, and he pressed something into her palm, a condom. "Don't want you getting into trouble now, do we? Happy new year to you both."

"Happy new year to you."

"One be enough?"

She shrugged. "It'll see the year out."

Large Eric was waiting behind the wheel of a CHORLTON'S BAKERY, BREAD & CAKES van with ARP painted in clumsy white letters over the sign on the side. He wore a tin helmet and an ARP armband on his left sleeve and said nothing as he drove them to Mrs. Bardwell's house on Radley Street in the Elephant and Castle. Only once they were out of the van did he speak. "You do know the Elephant and Castle's an aiming point for the Germans to bomb the docks. They drop marker flares and incendiaries."

"I know. That's why all the houses around here are burnt out or flattened," Caitrin said. "Thanks for the lift."

He gave a half-salute and drove away.

"He sounded a bit like Humphrey Bogart," Max said.

"My landlady, Mrs. Bardwell, is visiting her sister Elsie in Dorset. I'm on the first floor—that's the American second." Caitrin looked up. The sky was clear, and a distant siren moaned into life. "Blitz soon."

"Shouldn't we be in a shelter?"

She stepped closer and kissed him. "We could hide down in the Tube station, no privacy and all jammed together on the platform. No toilets or water down there, so it gets rather gamey after a bit. If you like animals, the fleas and lice can be—"

"First floor," he said and kissed her back.

"We could be dead by morning, so we have to cram a life of experiences into a moment and damn the rules." Another siren wailed, closer. Max reacted to the sound; she didn't, except to say, "Blitz soon."

Inside, they kept the lights off, undressed, and slipped into bed. A droning, at first only a whisper, grew louder as the first wave of bombers approached. In complete darkness, Caitrin reached out a hand to find Max, and—

"Ow!"

—poked him in the eye. "Sorry, sorry!"

"It's all right, I have another one."

"Let me kiss it better." Caitrin pulled him closer. "Come here, tell me where it hurts, and I'll kiss it all better."

Bombs fell near the river, and antiaircraft guns barked defiance. A fire engine hurried by, its bell clanging; incendiaries flared at the end of the street; and in the distance, a parachute land mine exploded and made the building tremble. Shell splinters rattled down the roof as a second bomber wave growled overhead.

Luftwaffe Hauptmann Karl Trautloft, in the second wave, preferred to work at night: the city streets were empty, the darkness hid most signs of life, and enemy defense systems were feeble. Witnessing the carnage his bombs had created in the low-level daylight assault on Guernica disturbed him, but Karl could be relied on to get the job done, if he flew at night. His Heinkel 111, named *Lotta* after his mother, always got through to the target; there were never mysterious or unexplained mechanical issues that forced it home early. Karl loved his Heinkel almost as much as he loved his mother. It was a stable machine to fly, but not without faults. The Junkers Jumo engine exhausts were close to the cockpit, and headsets did little to silence the deafening roar. The nose was made almost entirely of perspex, and there was no floor, so the crew could look directly down at the land below. Many aircrew disliked the cockpit because they felt exposed and vulnerable. But not Karl.

This would be a different attack. The X-Gerät radio navigation beams had guided the aircraft from France to London, but on the ground a new beacon, Lighthouse (*Leuchturm*), would pinpoint a particular target. As the main force turned right above the Elephant and Castle toward the London Docks, Karl continued straight and heard the first beacon tones in his headset. It was a faint warbling sound that grew stronger and became a single-pitched tone. Ernst, the bomb-aimer lying prone at his feet, heard the steady tone too, and, at the right moment, triggered the bomb release. The incendiaries struck the fifteenth-century Guildhall; the hammer-beam ceiling caught fire, and the blaze consumed the building. Karl banked hard for home, his work done. The Lighthouse homing beacon, placed earlier on the Guildhall roof by a brave, anonymous German saboteur, had shown the way with great accuracy, while *Lotta* had carried him through another successful flight.

The night's fire-raid would become known as the second Great Fire of London. January 1, 1941, the dawn of a new year, and London was burning again.

3

Winston Churchill had once described Mrs. Bethany Goodman as "a small, middle-aged woman who could climb up and down Kilimanjaro in the morning, have tea with the Queen, and go back and climb the mountain again in the afternoon, with not a hair out of place." Caitrin thought it was a fair description of the woman and wondered what Winston would say about her being a mother superior. Bethany ran 512, an all-female counterespionage unit that was unknown to most people in government circles. As Bethany explained, "Women are either ignored or invisible in our society, which makes them ideal secret operatives." Their headquarters and training facilities at Langland Priory, a secluded country house outside London, was ostensibly a church-run home for unwed mothers. To maintain the subterfuge, staff dressed as nuns for visitors or when they left the grounds, while trainees were young women showing "pregnant" with the aid of a cushion. Caitrin was one of her first and best recruits.

Bethany and Caitrin walked through a woods behind the

house. Neither spoke for a while, until Caitrin said, "Whenever I see you in that habit, I have an urge to ask for confession, or at least to light a candle and feel guilty."

"While I constantly fight the urge to say, 'Bless you, my child' to the milkman. My husband, if he were alive, would be in hysterics to see me in this outfit. Tell me, how is your young American?"

"Max is fine. It's hard to see each other sometimes."

"Flying Hurricanes, right?"

"Yes. He spent months waiting for the RAF to work out what to do with their American volunteers. They created Eagle Squadrons, and he's the old man at twenty-six. Why am I here?"

"Always direct. You are here because I am concerned about our survival. We exist on anonymity and a shoestring budget, which lays us open to being swallowed up by a larger, predominantly male organization. You know of Admiral Canaris."

"He is head of the Abwehr intelligence network and, I'm told, a man who loves his dachshunds."

"Yes, he does. I've heard that when he's away, he calls home daily for a report on their welfare. Gets depressed if they're not well. He is also probably the only man in Hitler's circle who is not a Nazi. Canaris had hundreds of spies, some deep undercover, throughout Britain, but MI5, when they're not tripping over their own laces, along with Scotland Yard and 512, rounded up most of them. It wasn't very difficult. The few we did miss were so incredibly awkward they almost arrested themselves. Canaris sent one spy to Ireland; he promptly got lost, and the IRA stole all his money, so he gave himself up. In a way, we might have worked ourselves out of a job."

"So what's next? Merge with MI5?"

"MI5 are rather amateurish. There are rumors we might be asked to join forces with another agency, but I will not agree if it means fetching tea for the men or typing letters. We women have worked too hard to go backwards now. I received a request from Royal Navy Intelligence and would like you to go to a meeting at the Admiralty."

"Why me?"

"Because you are never impressed with authority," she said and grinned. "And the Royal Navy won't know how to deal with you. Will you go?"

Caitrin flashed a wicked grin. "Yes, Holy Mother."

"Bless you, my child," Bethany replied, with a beatific smile.

At the Admiralty, Caitrin was led down endless echoing corridors and into a small office. The door closed behind her, and there she stood, ignored by a man sitting at a desk. He was reading a dossier and puffing at a briar pipe. Caitrin detested pipes; the smoke constricted her lungs. She silently counted to five before saying, in a loud and clear voice, "I am not a coat rack, nor am I invisible. But I am good at leaving. Watch, and enjoy my absence."

He looked up, startled, and shot to his feet as she turned to leave. He was tall and wore a tailored Naval Commander's uniform. "I'm awfully sorry. Your report was so engrossing I was lost to the world. Forgive me and please do sit down."

Caitrin sat, immediately disliking him because the accent in those few words revealed his background. He was undoubtedly the scion of an old family, which made his progress inevitable in whatever profession he chose. It was a charmed and secure life from birth, complete with an education at Eton or Harrow. In school, it didn't matter if he were less than diligent in his studies; in fact, it was better not to appear too clever, and being good at sports was much preferred. His background contrasted with hers as the daughter of a Welsh coal miner. They were of utterly different worlds. But that was going to change soon; she would make sure it did.

"Would you mind not puffing out so much smoke?" she said. "It's difficult for me to breathe."

"What? Oh, yes, of course," he said, shoving the pipe into a desk drawer. He returned his attention to the dossier. "Your record is quite remarkable. It reads more like a thrilling adventure yarn than a dull operations report. Great fun."

"It wasn't much fun at the time."

"Probably not at the moment, I'm sure, but one day this will make for a gripping adventure novel or two."

"Perhaps."

"Although it might be difficult for readers to accept a, a—"

"A woman as hero?"

"It would, regrettably, be a bit odd. Making it about a man would be so much easier. While art may have its say, the market always dictates the last word." He closed the dossier and tapped the cover. "It says here your service number is five twelve dash double-O seven."

"I was one of the early recruits."

"I see. It is a rather cryptic title for a conversation about our respective intelligence networks. What is your actual name?"

"What is yours?"

"Mine? Oh, sorry. I am Commander Ian Fleming. You are?"

Caitrin, as she had been taught, lied and answered, "Blond, Jane Blond."

"Miss Blond. Pleased to meet you."

"I have a question," Caitrin said. "512 is a small organization operating solely inside the country. Most of us have never been in a boat, let alone aboard a ship. We don't even have ranks, or medals, or uniforms. Certainly nothing as splendid as yours, Commander Fleming, so what good would a partnership be with the mighty Royal Navy?"

As she asked the question, Caitrin knew the meeting was a waste of time, and his next remark, a deflecting one, was confirmation.

"I had expected to meet Miss Bethany Goodman."

"*Mrs.* Goodman is the head of 512, and I imagine she would

have expected to meet Rear Admiral John Godfrey, head of Naval Intelligence." *Rather than you, his pipe-puffing upper-class aide.* As charming as Fleming might be, he and Godfrey were unable to see 512 as anything other than women, who could never be as capable as men. This meeting was nothing more than the opening salvo in a turf war between the various secret agencies, with 512 as the prize—a prize considered a nuisance to be discarded once it was picked clean. She stood and put out her hand. "Pleased to have met you. Goodbye, Commander Fleming."

He stared at her in bewilderment, this confident young woman with the keen eyes and wild red curls. "We haven't finished our conversation."

"Oh, yes, we most certainly have." She stopped at the door and turned to face him. "By the way, I notice your desk drawer is on fire. You might want to call the fire brigade. Good morning."

She left.

4

Max and Caitrin left Tufnell Park Underground station and trudged through a crackling frost to the top of Parliament Hill, where they sat on a park bench and gazed out at London. The sky was a rinsed blue, but to their left, the east, it was stained an ugly brown from fires still burning at the docks.

"I hate the winter," Caitrin said, voice muffled by the scarf around her face. With a woolen hat pulled low and the scarf wrapped high, only her eyes showed. Mittens, an overcoat, tweed slacks, and RAF fleece-lined flying boots, a gift from brother Dafydd, completed her winter outfit. "Once this bloody war is over, we should go from autumn, with its scent of burning leaves, completely ignore winter and jump straight to a bouncing lambs and cheery daffodils spring."

"Do you think Churchill could arrange that?" Max said.

"If he won't, I will," she said, shivered, and sank deeper into the warmth of her clothes. "See the smoke over there? The docks. Bombs struck a timber wharf. The wood's been burning for days. It set barges alight; the firemen cut them free to float downstream, and they drifted back, still burning, on the incoming tide."

Max gazed out at the spreading smoke cloud and said nothing.

"We've lost eight Wren churches and the Guildhall, and your Mr. Lindbergh just had the colossal nerve to ask Congress to negotiate with Germany."

"I assure you he's not mine."

She patted his hand. "I know. You're over here fighting for us."

"Don't worry, Congress won't negotiate."

Caitrin sighed. "Last year, except for November 2, the Germans bombed London for fifty-seven consecutive nights, and the raids often lasted more than twelve hours. Three hundred and seventy deaths one night, four hundred the next. Can you imagine the terror of living in one of those tiny East End row houses, and every night your world is blown apart and people you know, friends, neighbors, die terrible deaths. How is it possible not to go insane?"

"I have no answer."

"Life is one long question with the same answer at the end," Caitrin said and sat up. "Sorry, I'm being grumpy. This is the longest we've been together, a whole two days, so I'll cheer up. At least the other people have gone."

"What people?"

"The others of us."

Max shook his head. "I can fly a Hurricane at three hundred miles an hour, but keeping up with you is impossible."

"Good job I'm not armed, then."

"Explain."

"I will. What attracts you to someone the first time? Is it the hair, eyes, body, a laugh? Whatever it is, it makes you change and put on your best front to attract them to you. Then they change to attract you to them. Until it all settles down, you tell fibs, alter behavior, and add different people to keep it going. Finally, all those people leave and you're left with just the real two of you."

"I got a bit lost there, but I like the real one of you."

"And I like the real one of Max, and promise to try my best never to lie to you."

"Me too."

"Except if you ask me about the color of your shirt."

"Or, does this dress make me look fat?"

"Not sure about that one."

"I have a question. You know what I do. What do you do, your work?"

"I'm a secretary at a home for unwed mothers."

"No, you're not." He pulled down the scarf to reveal her face and said, "And you just broke your promise."

"I can't tell you, Max. I'm sorry I lied. Just don't ask me that question again."

"Okay." He kissed her. "Your nose is cold."

"So is the rest of me."

"Shall we leave?"

"Not yet. I have a question for you," she said and pointed to the sky. "What's it like up there? And don't give me the 'Tally-ho, chaps' routine."

Max thought for a moment and said, "It's terrifying, and I'm scared all the time."

She took his hand, held it.

"When I came here to join the RAF, in initial training I first flew Tiger Moth biplanes. They're so slow sometimes you have to get out and push. Next came the Miles Master, a fast, two-seat monoplane, but after that, you're on your own. There is no Hurricane trainer, so your first flight is your first solo flight. It's powerful, fast, and very responsive. There were lots of accidents in training."

"You don't have to tell me—"

"There is no space in a Hurricane cockpit. Someone said you don't sit in one—you put it on, like a jacket. It's incredibly noisy, and when you fire the guns, everything vibrates." He shivered at a memory. "I was machine-gunned attacking a bomber and watched the holes appearing on my wing, mesmerized. Why are they shooting at me? That's it, that's what it's like, no lies. I'm frightened whenever I take off. We all are."

She kissed him. "But you still go up."

"I don't want to sometimes. It's so strange after you land. You go to the pub, and the locals are talking about cricket, or a fox stealing chickens, and it's all so normal. But an hour earlier, you were so frightened and saw your pal shot down in flames. He's right off your wingtip, burning, struggling, and you can't help. And in the pub, an old guy in the corner's downing his pint and complaining about the missus putting her cold feet on him in bed."

"I can't imagine."

"One day soon, women will be flying into battle too."

"Why should they?"

He was startled by the question, recovered. "Because you want to be treated fairly."

"Why should being allowed to do what men do be considered being treated fairly? We want to be equal, Max, not identical. Men seem to be very good at killing; perhaps when women are equal, we can teach them a different way. I'm sorry, I'm lecturing."

He shrugged, gave that smile that so captivated her, and asked, "Enough of today. Let's talk about tomorrow. What do you want to do once this is all over?"

Caitrin stamped her feet and clapped her hands together for warmth. "That's easy. I'm going to live in a green place with a dog named Fiona, a half-dozen ducks, which will remain nameless because you can't tell one from another, perhaps I'll paint numbers on them, and Derek the donkey. On my own farm."

"No husband?"

"Hadn't pictured one so far."

"Maybe you should."

"Maybe I should. And it has to be a place where I can play the drums without upsetting the neighbors."

"You play drums?"

"No, not yet, but one day I'll be a Welsh Gene Krupa," she said, her flailing arms playing imaginary drums.

"I have a farm, with a big empty red barn." He saw her expression change. "Too soon?"

She laughed and embraced him. "Yes, Max, a bit. But tell me about the farm anyway. Is it sunny and hot there? Tell me it's hot."

"It's just outside Sonora, up in the California Sierra Nevada. Sonora was once a gold-mining town, and it's hot in the summer, and sometimes we get snow in the winter, but not too much."

"Sounds wonderful. Keep going."

"My grandfather rebuilt a ruined nineteenth-century farmhouse and planted an apple orchard. He had a hardware store in town."

"Ironmongers."

"Okay, ironmongers. What's a costermonger?"

"A place where you can buy things at cost. I lie, I lie! It's someone who sells fruit and vegetables from a street stall. Keep going, Sonora sounds lovely, Max, and so does the farm."

"It is, and that's no lie. It's just my dad now."

"What happened to your mother?"

"She died of the Spanish flu when I was little. I was raised by my grandparents. Now they're gone, so it's just Dad and me."

"You must miss him."

"Yes, and I know he's lonely sometimes, but he'd never say

so. Dad desperately wanted a daughter. Anyway, there's plenty of room for a dog, any number of anonymous numbered ducks, and Derek the donkey. And a drum-pounding, female Welsh Gene Krupa could practice all day in the barn. You would love it there and I know my father would love you."

"Perhaps, some time in the not-too-distant future. But we only have today. Let's live this day."

5

Winston was not looking forward to this meeting. Not at all. Men were always easy to deal with because they understood and accepted the hierarchy of command. Men like Brigadier Sir Alasdair Gryffe-Reynolds, who was sitting across the desk from him. Men who were trained from birth to accept the natural order of things, reinforced by the right schooling: Eton in Gryffe-Reynolds's case, rather than Harrow in his. And if they were for any reason recalcitrant, the weight of higher authority soon brought them to heel.

It was not so with women, who seemed to have their own peculiar outlook on life. The junior ones, secretaries and typists, were easy to reprimand, although they often used the frustrating, female defense mechanism of bursting into tears. But there were others, such as Miss, no, *Mrs.* Bethany Goodman, sitting next to Gryffe-Reynolds, whom he found exasperating. She was remarkably intelligent for a woman, and titles and rank did not impress her in the least.

To the whole world, he was Winston Churchill, prime minister of this country and, by extension, the whole British Empire, an empire on which the sun never set. But with Mrs. Goodman he often felt as though he were the lesser and losing opponent in an Oxford debate. With that in mind, he decided to start with a heavy artillery barrage, lit a cigar, and puffed out a great cloud of smoke as he opened fire.

"Rommel is in Africa, commanding the Afrika Corps, and will be a serious opponent. He's not a member of the Nazi party, but is nonetheless a fine general. Swansea, an unlovely town, but don't tell Lloyd George I said that, is now much uglier after three continuous nights of bombing, and U-boats are devastating our Atlantic convoys. If they continue to do so, it will soon become impossible to feed the people."

Gryffe-Reynolds looked suitably gloomy at such bad news, but Bethany Goodman sat straighter and said, "On the other hand, I hear the Lend-Lease bill has been introduced in Washington. Surely, that will change things greatly."

Her one optimistic shot had neutralized his ominous salvo.

"Perhaps, but it might not pass, and then where shall we be?" he answered. "Roosevelt constantly reminds me that Americans are not the English, who sailed off and stayed away. About his country, he uses the odd term 'melting pot' to include the British, Italians, Irish, Scandinavians, and others. The German *Bund* held a pro-Nazi rally in Madison Square Garden not so long ago and attracted twenty-thousand rabid supporters. Roosevelt says Americans are reluctant to involve themselves again in what they see as yet another European squabble."

"If the Lend-Lease bill passes, and I hear it is quite likely, that will get them involved. Surely you, sir, of all people, are not giving in."

"Me? Never!"

"I thought not."

"But we must find a way, apart from Lend-Lease, to bring the Americans into the war. Without them, we will not succeed.

I mention these events because it is time to set aside all personal ambitions and accept sacrifices for the good of the country."

Gryffe-Reynolds looked concerned, while Bethany Goodman appeared . . . he had no idea what she was thinking. But she did ask, "I agree, but exactly what sacrifice or sacrifices did you have in mind, Prime Minister?"

He grunted in annoyance. Yet again, she was ahead of him. "We have a multiplicity of intelligence organizations, and that leads to inefficiency."

"MI5 handles foreigner internment and double agents, MI6 is anti-communist and intelligence, MI9 concentrates on helping airmen escape from Axis countries," Bethany said. "My organization, 512, concerns itself solely with Nazi infiltration and sabotage in this scountry. Sir Alasdair?"

"*Hmm*, yes, as we all know, SOE , Special Operations Executive, is focused on espionage, sabotage, and information-gathering in occupied territories."

Churchill waved his cigar. "While there are still people who are quite certain Lord Haw-Haw is sending coded messages to Nazi spies in England, 512's mandate seems to have outlived its usefulness. We interned over seventy thousand foreign residents—"

"And in doing so, ruined the lives of many innocent Italian waiters and ice cream makers and Jewish tailors," Bethany said.

"Mistakes will happen in war, but it does seem to have had an effect on any fifth-column activity. And the spies we have captured appear to be a motley bunch. The latest one was some poor deluded Dutchman who shot himself in a bomb shelter in Christ's Pieces. So, if this is our greatest saboteur threat, I must ask, why do we need 512 as a separate organization?"

"The country needs 512 because we are small and therefore adaptable to changing circumstances. That has brought us success. The other organizations are much larger and not as flexible."

"We still do jolly well, though," Gryffe-Reynolds said, his feathers ruffled.

"Added to that is our invisibility as women."

"All of those attributes would be just as beneficial in a larger organization. We need fewer but sharper weapons. I will give you a little time, not much, Mrs. Goodman, to prepare a rebuttal. If I am not convinced, we shall reassign your agents, and 512 will cease to exist. Good morning."

He remained seated as they left. That fool Charles Lindbergh had testified before Congress about the wisdom of the United States remaining neutral in what he considered yet another European war. How nice to be so safely shrouded in your own ignorance. And German bombers had attacked Dublin by mistake, which he thought poetic justice for the Irish refusing to let the British use their ports. The deaths of hundreds of seamen were on the collective Irish conscience because the Royal Navy ships could not reach them quickly enough. On a more cheerful note, a hundred and thirty thousand Italians had surrendered in North Africa. But now they were captured, what to do with them? Regardless, the Americans had to come, and soon.

6

The morning train crawled north up the Ebbw Valley in South Wales, often stopping to let loaded coal trains pass south. The valley was noisy and dirty, with every colliery, ironworks, and foundry working overtime. From her compartment window, Caitrin watched the familiar landscape pass. She was coming home to Wales. The last visit had been over a year ago to celebrate her mother's sixtieth birthday.

The train slowed going past the Llanhilleth colliery, and for a moment, she smelled the tang of resin from the great stacks of pine logs used to make pit props. Above the seats in the crowded compartment were black-and-white photographs of holiday villages and seaside resorts: Skegness, Pwllheli, Torquay. The thought of enjoying a peaceful holiday seemed so odd. *Would they ever exist again? Did they ever exist to begin with?*

The train stopped at her station, and she walked uphill to her home. Here was the narrow street where she had lived most of her life. There was Mr. Pullen's barber shop, where she would take her little brothers Dafydd and Gareth. It had a chromium barber's chair in the middle of a black-and-white tiled floor and colored pictures of steamships hung around the walls. Mr. Pullen never spoke when he cut children's hair, so she held Gareth's hand because he was scared. At the other end was Mr. Keyes's corner shop, which sold tinned goods, cigarettes, and sweets, and where he put his prized wirehaired terrier, Kevin, up on the counter to be admired. The stone-walled, slate-roofed row houses were small, and her house was in the middle on the right. Caitrin's mind, body, and soul bore the imprint of the street and this town; it was her home, but now everything seemed foreign.

She opened the front door. It was unlocked—she knew it would be—and entered. "Mam?"

The familiar smells met her, of soap, of ironing, of Mansion Polish. She went through the front room, which was used only for guests and holidays, as if it were part of some great country estate, and into the kitchen.

"Mam?" The kitchen was empty; a coal fire burned in the fireplace, while a plate, cup, and saucer lay on the draining board. The kitchen table took up most of the room, covered with oilcloth from which the pattern had been scrubbed away—linen tablecloth only on Sunday—and through the window she could see the tin bath hanging from a nail in the outhouse wall.

The house seemed to have shrunk. Caitrin's arms lifted from her sides, and her fingers almost touched the walls. There were two small rooms downstairs, and two even smaller bedrooms upstairs, one of which she had shared with her brothers. Five of them had lived in this cramped space, until her oldest brother, Evan, was killed in Passchendaele. Her father died from blacklung a few years past. She now lived in London, the youngest brother, Gareth, was on board a Royal Navy ship somewhere in the Atlantic, and Dafydd was an RAF flight instructor in Scotland. War had disintegrated and scattered the family, and only her mother was left behind. It was quiet, the house holding its breath, guarding its memories.

First the front door, then the kitchen door flew open.

"Caitrin! Oh, my love, Caitrin!" Her mother, Gwen, entered and embraced her. "Mrs. Moore said a strange man went into my house. But it's you."

"Yes, me, wearing trousers," Caitrin said. "And RAF flying boots, courtesy of brother Dafydd."

Gwen took a step back to inspect her daughter. "I hear the clippies on the London buses started the trousers fashion. No wonder, running up and down those stairs all day."

"Probably."

"I'll make tea." Gwen brushed at her tears as she filled the kettle, placed it on the gas ring, and said, "I didn't know you were coming."

Caitrin sat at the kitchen table. "I had some time off, and it was a spur-of-the-moment thing."

"I was over at the Merediths." Gwen placed cups and saucers on the table and sat across from her. "They got the telegram. Their son Idris is missing in North Africa. We know what that means. His mam's going to die of a broken heart."

The war is everywhere; it's a cancer in everyone and everything. "You never know, Mam, maybe he's a prisoner of war. Long after the battle is over, he might turn up; they do sometimes," Caitrin lied. *No, he won't; they never do. Our Evan is still missing from 1917.*

The kettle whistled. Gwen rose from the table and patted Caitrin's head as she went to make tea. It was a mother's gesture of affection for her little girl. "I wish you had been here last week. Gareth was home. He surprised me too."

"How is he?"

Gwen's eyes widened. "Got a tattoo of a Welsh dragon on his chest, and he's very nautical. It's all aye, aye, Mam this, aye, aye, Mam that. Even made his bed shipshape. Imagine that."

"Hard to imagine," Caitrin said with memories of Gareth as a child and his ever-unmade bed.

Gwen sat down and poured tea. "I don't have any biscuits or sugar, but wait until you see this." She rose, went to a cupboard, returned with a paper bag, and took out a bunch of bananas. "Gareth brought these from abroad."

"Oh my goodness, bananas," Caitrin said. "I forget when I last saw one. Before the war, didn't they bend the other way?"

Gwen flashed her an old-fashioned look. "You won't get that one past your mam. He also brought this," she said and produced a dark green, pear-shaped fruit. "He said it was a mungo."

"I think it's called a mango, Mam."

Gwen held the fruit up, rotating it on her fingertips for closer inspection. "Mungo, mango—whatever it's called, I don't know how to cook or eat it."

"Neither do I."

"Oh well, then it will remain a mystery. Our Dafydd's not in Scotland anymore," Gwen said as she put the mango aside, took a shoebox down from a shelf, and opened it. Inside were three bundles of letters tied with ribbon, and each was labeled with her children's names. Caitrin felt a stab of guilt at seeing hers was the thinnest. Gwen undid Dafydd's bundle, unfolded a letter, and read, " 'I'm being transferred from Kinmory to the south of England. I can't tell you any more because I don't know anything. At least that's what I'm supposed to say. All my love, your brightest, best looking, and most modest son Dafydd.' "

Gwen folded the letter, replaced it in the shoebox, and tied up the ribbon. "Our best looking and most modest Dafydd writes often, but he doesn't write much."

"At least he writes to you," Caitrin said. "I haven't done very well, have I?"

"Caitrin, cariad, I love all your letters," Gwen said and took

both her hands. "And that you're here now is the most important thing to me. It's wonderful to have you home."

"I know, but I'll try better in future."

"Hello?" someone called out as the front door opened.

"That's Megan Hughes. She must have seen you, and in a
minute, the whole street's going to be here," Gwen said. "Quick,
hide the bananas."

7

The next morning, when Caitrin came downstairs, her mother had already made tea and boiled the kettle again so her daughter could wash her hands and face.

"Did you sleep well?"

"It was so quiet last night," Caitrin said. "Without my noisy brothers."

"I miss the noise sometimes," Gwen said. "I was going up the hill to visit Dad."

"I'll come with you."

"I'd like that," Gwen said and put a plate in front of her. "Toast, no butter, sorry, but there is a bit of strawberry jam left."

"Sit down, Mam. We'll share. What happened to the bananas?"

Gwen took a banana from a cupboard, sat, and placed it in front of Caitrin. "I saved this one for you. I gave the rest to the Hughes girls. This rationing is hard on them."

"I knew you'd give them away. What about you?"

"They need them more than I do. The younger ones didn't even know what a banana was. They ate them and took the peel home."

"Mam, that banana is yours."

"You gave me an idea. Stay right there," Gwen said, left and returned a few minutes later, wearing a pair of her husband's trousers. "I'm following your fashion. What do you think?"

Caitrin felt tears rising. Her mother was a little girl wanting reassurance about playing dress-up in trousers much too large for her. For the first time, Caitrin saw her as a person, a human being, not just her mother. Her curls were just like hers, but now gray; there were lines grooved in her cheeks she hadn't noticed before, and the floral pinafore was patched and faded. Her mother was finite. "You look smashing, Mam, but I'm not sure the ladies at King Street Baptist Chapel would approve."

Gwen laughed. "I'll wear them on the Whitsun walks and horrify the whole town. They'll need a bit of tailoring first, though."

"Let me send you a few pairs from London instead."

"That would be lovely, but not expensive, though. Now finish your breakfast while I change into something less shocking, and then we'll go. Dress warm; it's perishing out there."

They walked arm in arm down Alexandra Street toward the cemetery. Caitrin had forgotten about living in a small town in which it was difficult to go more than a few yards without someone greeting them. A miner going home from his shift stopped to talk to Gwen. Coal dust in his lashes outlined his eyes so he seemed to be wearing mascara, and there were blue tattooed lines on his face because coal left a permanent mark when it struck skin. His breath from a life of inhaling coal dust was labored, his sentences short, chopped. Farther along, a young woman, not much more than a child, with a shawl wrapped around her to carry her baby, crossed the street when she recognized Caitrin. They spoke for a minute or so, awkwardly, and the feeling of being a stranger in a foreign place rose again.

Gwen sensed Caitrin's discomfort as they walked on. "Tell me about living in London. Is the bombing as bad as they say?"

"Only in some places."

"What about where you live, the Elephant and Castle? I'm your mam, don't forget, so I'll know if you're telling fibs."

"Like most of London, it's been struck a few times," Caitrin said. "But it's the docks they're after." Much of the district had been obliterated, and it was near the docks, but she would never tell her mother that.

They walked the steep incline up the hill, went through the wrought-iron gates and into the cemetery.

"You never mention your work. Is it dangerous?"

"No, not at all."

Gwen stopped, turned, and gently cupped Caitrin's face in her hands. "If I stop asking questions, you can stop telling stories, yes?"

"I'm sorry, Mam. I can't tell you what I do."

"Will it help end this war?"

"I think so."

"Then you told me all I want to know."

They knelt at Caitrin's father's grave. The gravestone read: EMRYS COLLINE, BORN 20 NOVEMBER 1875. DIED 2 JANUARY 1935. (59). Caitrin noticed another name had been added: EVAN COLLINE, BORN 4 MAY 1899. DIED 17 AUGUST 1917, FRANCE. (18).

"I couldn't stand the thought that my son was missing. Children shouldn't vanish from your life, so I had his name put on the stone," Gwen said. "Now Evan is not lost; he's back here with his Dad."

"That's lovely, Mam."

Gwen brought the mango out of her purse and placed it beneath the gravestone. "The flower shop is closed because they can't get flowers anymore, so the mungo mango will have to do. Evan or your Dad would know what to do with it; I don't."

She got to her feet. "I'll give you some time alone. I'll be up at the church."

"Thanks."

Gwen walked deeper into the cemetery and climbed to the top of the hill as Caitrin sat in silence, gazing at the headstone. Emrys and Evan Colline, father and son, two good men who should have lived forever. They deserved better. Not fair. "I'll try my best, Dad, to look after Mam, and make things easier for her. Miss you. Both of you."

She stood, kissed her fingertips, brushed them on the headstone, and went to find her Mam. She climbed uphill, passed the seventeenth-century St. Illtyd's church, and sat beside her on a stile set into a drystone wall. The valley was spread out below, grooved with endless row-house streets and studded with coal mines. Pyramids of black slag dwarfed everything. To their left, a ropeway carried waste from a mine on the valley floor up to the top of the hills. There was no color, only black and gray contrasted with the white of steam.

"I often come here to rest after visiting your Dad, look out at the valley and imagine what it was once like," Gwen said.

"It must have been so beautiful here, before the mines and ironworks came."

"In the late eighteenth century, the parish minister Edmund Jones said: 'The Valley of Tyleri is the most delightful. These warm valleys would make delightful habitations.'"

"That was once upon a long time ago. Not now."

"True. Now we must talk about something much more important."

Caitrin glanced at her mother, unsure of what was coming next.

"I want to know about the man in your life."

"How did you know?"

"Don't be daft. I'm your Mam, not a cabbage. Tell me everything about him. What's his name?"

"Maxwell."

"Maxwell. That sounds posh."

"He's not posh, he's American."

"There are no posh Americans?"

"Mam."

"Sorry. More, please."

"His mother named him after Teddy Roosevelt's coffee."

"That's American for you, and at least he wasn't named after one of Teddy's horses, Jocko Root, or Wyoming."

"How on earth did you know that?"

Gwen tapped the tip of Caitrin's nose. "I'm a valley girl full of surprises. What does he do?"

"He's a Hurricane pilot with the Eagle Squadron."

"And?"

"And what?"

"Do you love him?"

"I . . . yes, I do," Caitrin stopped, blinked, startled. "And hearing me saying that was a big surprise—to me."

"What made you fall in love?"

"I didn't mean to fall in love. We met at a New Year's Eve party. It was noisy and crowded, and we left before midnight."

"Oh, you did, did you?" Gwen said with a knowing smile and Caitrin blushed. "Go on, rascal."

"Max is kind, considerate, and—"

"Swept you off your feet?"

"No, I wouldn't say that."

"Good. If you ever meet a man who sweeps you off your feet, get back up and run like hell because he's not interested in you, only himself."

Down in the valley, a pit hooter blared the end of a shift and the start of another. Caitrin shivered as a wave of cold air rose up the slope. Why did she love Max? What was it about him? Gwen put an arm around her shoulders and drew her closer.

"When I first met Max, I thought he was just a boy. He

looked so young in his uniform. There were no great fireworks or lightning bolts. I liked him, and as time went on, being together seemed so natural, so comfortable. So right. I feel like I've known him forever."

"Is he the one you want to marry?"

"That scares me."

"Why?"

"Because I don't know if we'll be alive tomorrow. He could be shot down, and I could, well, there are lots of ways to die nowadays." Her jaw tightened as she held back London memories. It was normal now in the city to turn a corner and find a bomb-blasted street. Walls had collapsed, shop windows were shattered into pieces across the pavement, and bodies, sometimes bits of them, were being recovered from the ruins. She remembered seeing what remained of a little girl and tried to erase the image.

"That shouldn't stop you."

Caitrin gathered her thoughts. "Growing up here, and working in the London slums when I was a policewoman, I know all about the men getting drunk at the end of a work week and taking out their anger on the family. I saw enough wives with bruises and black eyes on Sunday mornings to make me cautious. And if not that, there are so many kids who get married too young and then wonder what happened to their lives. You and Dad are the only couple I know who were truly in love, and it is so unfair that he died and you were left behind."

"Is that what you're scared of, being left behind?"

"I don't know, Mam, perhaps. I just don't know. How did you know Dad was the right one for you?"

"Like Max for you, being with Emrys felt so right to me. I was only eighteen when we married, and we had almost forty years together. It was hard sometimes, but worth it. I always loved hearing him come through the front door. We had four kids. Gareth, Dafydd, and you are with me; Evan is with him.

Life is fragile, Caitrin, it always is, but don't let that stop you. Go in with eyes wide open, and accept what is, not what might be."

"Where did you learn all this wisdom?"

"In Mam university. You'll get to go there at the right time."

"You are remarkable." Caitrin laughed and kissed her mother's cheek. "If we get married, Max will want to go back to America, to California. That's a long way from Wales. A long way from you."

"So I'll put my name on the waiting list for a telephone and come visit after the war."

"In London, the jewelry shops have either been bombed flat or closed up for the duration. We couldn't get a wedding ring anyway."

"That's a weak excuse." Gwen slipped off her wedding ring, dropped it Caitrin's hand, and closed her fingers tight. "Now you have one."

"No!"

"Yes. I don't need a ring to remember my husband."

"But it's yours. Dad—"

"Your Dad lives forever in my heart and memory. Emrys would love knowing his daughter is wearing the ring he gave me. I know I will. Look at the inscription. It's too small for me to read now, but your eyesight is better than mine."

Caitrin squinted at the ring and read aloud, "Dwy galon, un daith."

"Two hearts, one journey. It's your journey now, Caitrin, together with Max. No matter how long or short it might be, take it and don't be afraid."

The following morning, Gwen went down to the railway station to see Caitrin leave. The platform was filled with soldiers, most of whom she knew: awkward boys in badly fitting uniforms, most of them yesterday's apprentices and shop lads.

When the train finally arrived from Brynmawr, it was already crowded. Everyone managed to squeeze aboard, some of the boys practicing being gentlemen to Caitrin, and Gwen waved to her until the train had disappeared around a curve near the colliery. She stood alone on the platform and raised her eyes from the track to the far hill. Up there, safe above the valley's dirt and clamor, Emrys and the memory of their son, Evan, lay in the silent cemetery. One day she would lie next to them.

But it would not be today.

This coming Whitsun, when all the chapels' congregations were dressed in their Sunday best and parading through the town, with choirs singing hymns and religious banners flying, she would walk with the King Street Baptist women, wearing the slacks Caitrin would send down from London. That should mortify a multitude. Gwen Colline grinned at the outrageous thought and hummed "Show Me the Way to Go Home." All the way home.

8

Mrs. Lilian Bardwell, Caitrin's landlady in the Elephant and Castle, detested the underground air-raid shelters, understandably, because they were crowded places with dreadful sanitation. The night of a heavy bombing, she could no longer take the shelter conditions and fled. She hurried around the corner onto Radley Street and was a few doors from her beloved home when a parachute land mine settled to the ground. Unlike high-explosive bombs, which howled through the air to be buried deep before exploding, land mines floated quietly down and lay still and silent until a delayed-action fuse triggered. Then the detonation was wide and destructive.

The blast instantly killed Mrs. Bardwell, but left her unmarked, while stripping off all her clothing, save for earrings and a shoe. It shattered every window in the street, raked tiles off the roofs, and imploded doors. Burning gas lines made the street an inferno. Caitrin came home to find she owned only what she wore and no longer had a place to live.

In Langland Priory, Bethany Goodman hung her mother

superior habit on a hook behind the office door, sat next to Caitrin on a sofa, and poured them both tea. "There is no sugar, I'm afraid."

"That's all right; at least there is still tea."

"So far. How are you?"

Caitrin's anodyne reply died in her throat, and instead she said, "I don't know."

Bethany sat, waited.

"I can't believe Mrs. Bardwell is dead." Caitrin fought back tears. "It breaks my heart. We used to sit in her kitchen during an air raid because she was frightened to go into the shelters. I couldn't persuade her to leave the house; it was all she had. She must have been scared while I was away, tried going down there but couldn't take it. If I'd been there—"

"You would have died too."

"After the last war, Lloyd George said we should make a fit country for heroes. We haven't done that. Not for heroines either."

"No, we haven't."

"I was looking forward to seeing my mam, but it was so strange to be there. She is well, but the house is empty, and I felt disconnected from the town. I was happy to leave. It was where I grew up, but it felt almost foreign."

"Why is that, do you think?"

"It's because the town's not foreign, I am," Caitrin said. "Because I don't belong there anymore. That was really hard to say."

"Yes, I can imagine."

"Now I'm not quite sure where I belong," Caitrin said and shrugged away the thought. "Mam wants slacks like mine. She'll take great delight in scandalizing the village."

"I heard a rumor that clothes rationing is starting soon, so I suggest buying her scandalous slacks and replacing your ruined wardrobe as soon as possible." Bethany stood, went to her desk, and returned with a folder. She opened it. "My concern about 512 being consumed by a larger agency is well founded. Winston wants a convincing reason why we should still exist."

"With our proven record, we can do that, surely?"

"No is the simple answer, not with our recent performance," Bethany said and glanced at the folder. "We uncovered sabotage at a Spitfire factory, but it was just a girl who was fed up with her job. Another was a man with a drinking problem who left vital screws out of machine guns. There is no organized Nazi fifth column, at least nothing we can find. The Nazi sympathizers, such as Baron Rothermere or Viscount Lymington, have retreated to their estates. Mosley's in jail, and Edward VIII is the most lost of wandering lost souls."

"What are you going to say to Churchill?"

"I have absolutely no idea." Bethany patted Caitrin's hand. "But between us we'll think of a brilliant answer. Tell me about something much more important. How is your young man?"

And for the first time that morning, Caitrin's expression softened. "I have a surprise for him."

Fresh storm clouds grew every day, usually with only a rare and slender silver lining. The Blitz had not abated, but instead spread across the country. Glasgow was bombed, Clydebank nearly obliterated, Plymouth and Bristol were attacked with incendiaries, and London was spared for only a day or so between raids.

Winston Churchill leafed through the evening's report, but there was little encouraging news. Rommel had received heavy armor in North Africa and was attacking, with success, while U-boats were still devastating the Atlantic convoys. But there was some hope: the Lend-Lease bill had finally been signed in Washington. That would release a great flood of supplies, but he knew it was not enough. To prevent invasion and end this war, he needed American troops and weapons. The British were still weak from the evacuation of Dunkirk, had lost most of their equipment, and were unprepared for any great military response.

He growled in response to a knock on his office door, and his secretary, Mrs. Kathleen Hill, entered, holding a folded sheet of paper. "I was asked to give you this right away, sir."

Winston unfolded the paper and read aloud: "Buckingham Palace has been bombed."

"Oh, dear."

He grinned, which she did not expect. "There were no casualties, and the King said he was relieved to have been bombed because now he can look the devastated people of the East End in the eye. That's what I call the English spirit."

"Yes, sir," Mrs. Hill said and left before he could give her more work. It had already been a long day, and she was well aware that Winston was no respecter of other people's time.

A few minutes later, there was another knock on the door, answered by another growl, and again Mrs. Hill appeared, with a second sheet of folded paper. "There's report of another bombing, sir."

He took it and read: "The Café de Paris. Coventry Street."

9

Caitrin and Max came up out of the Piccadilly Circus Underground station against a flood of people going down to shelter from the expected nightly air raid. Most carried cases, bags, and bundles of blankets. One woman had a canary in a cage; a man had a banjo, another a cello.

"I can't imagine what kind of music they would play as a duet, and with a canary chanteuse," Caitrin said as they reached the street.

"Could have been worse—*two* banjos and a canary," Max said.

"Or two harps and a parrot. I detest harps, which is a good reason not to go to heaven, and I'm not that keen on parrots either. Certainly couldn't eat a whole one," she said and put her arm through his as they walked along Coventry Street. Memory battled reality whenever she went out in the city at night. There were no streetlights, no bright shop windows or neon advertisements, and the sporadic vehicles on the road had only single, shuttered headlamps. Some pedestrians carried torches with the lenses taped off, except for a slit in the middle, and a few had colored gels, so they looked like a bobbing swarm of glow worms. The kerbs were painted white, but in such a darkness they barely registered, and she constantly had to remind Max to look right when they crossed the street. It was easy to stumble over rubble from bombed-out buildings, and, as always, the air smelled burnt. Cables holding balloons in place high above the roofs hummed their individual notes, glass crunched underfoot, and always a distant, lone siren wailed. Sometimes she wondered if eventually her pleasant memories would fade away forever and be replaced by this constant, ruined darkness.

"Is there a big one coming?" Max said, looking skyward.

"They're all big to someone, but don't worry, the Café de Paris is twenty feet underground, with the Rialto cinema on top. We'll be fine."

Someone opened the café door—Caitrin assumed it was the doorman, it was impossible to see; they pushed aside the blackout curtain and entered. The air inside was warm, scented with perfume and cigar smoke, and music, energetic American jazz, rose up to meet them. The grand staircase split, curving left and right past one floor, around the bandstand, and down to an oval dance floor in a mirrored restaurant. They were shown to a table at the edge of the dance floor.

"This is a very exclusive place."

"It was, until the war," Caitrin said, and with a wicked smile added, "Now they let anyone in. The hoi polloi, the low polloi—and, horrors, even Americans."

Max ignored her teasing. "It's a replica of the Palm Court on the *Lusitania*."

"I heard it was the *Titanic*," Caitrin said, with an arched, disbelieving eyebrow. "Let's hope the Café de Paris is more unsinkable than either one."

A magnum of champagne arrived.

"Supposedly, that's the only size they have," Max said.

"Then we shall have to do our best and soldier on. Steady the Buffs and all that."

It was nine, and the café was not yet filled, but the debs and their accompanying debs' delights would be arriving well before midnight from the Queen Charlotte's debutante ball at the Grosvenor House Hotel. Many of the tables were taken by American officers, some by British, and a few by elegant couples being English and pretending not to be affected by such vulgar music. Not until they finished their champagne.

"I was hoping for a different table, quieter, because I wanted to talk to you," Max said.

"This sounds serious. Not a confession, I hope. You're not married, are you?"

"No, of course not. But I did want to—"

"Oh!" Before he could finish, Caitrin shot to her feet and raced across the dance floor to a group of men sitting at a corner table. One of them stood and embraced her. She took him by the hand and led him back to their table. "What a wonderful surprise. Max, this is Hecky, Lord Hector. Hecky, this is Max."

"Pleased to meet you," Max said. "My first time meeting a lord."

"His full name is Lord Marlton, Hector Neville-Percy."

"Impressive."

"But his Mum calls him Bobby."

"Bobby?"

"It's a long story," Hector said. "I shan't bore you."

"Max's American and was named after a happy pot of coffee by Teddy Roosevelt," Caitrin said and kissed his cheek. "Sit."

They all sat, Caitrin beaming with delight.

"Why didn't you reply to my letter?" Hector said.

"What letter? I never got it. Mrs. Bardwell's house was bombed, and she was killed."

"I'm so sorry. How do I contact you now?"

Caitrin waved to a waiter, borrowed his pencil and pad, scribbled the Langland Priory address, and gave it to Hector.

He read it. "A home for wayward women?"

"They start as wayward women and end up as unwed mothers, usually with disappearing fathers."

"Don't look at me. Not guilty."

Caitrin shrugged. "We all need to do our bit, and our girls definitely have. We're ignoring poor Max."

"Sorry, Max," Hector said. "When are you two getting married?"

Max sat back, startled. "Keeping up with Caitrin is hard enough, but with two of you, I am outgunned."

"I ask because you are so obviously daft about each other and—"

A shout from Hector's table interrupted him. One of his friends stood, waved, and tapped his wristwatch. Hector waved back.

"You're a very lucky man, Max. Caitrin is a remarkable woman. I was married to her once."

"What?"

Hector's friends shouted again, and one whistled.

"I have to go," Hector said and rose to his feet. He kissed Caitrin. "We're meeting some chaps at the Blue Angel, and I'm off to Scotland in the morning. I'll write you, Cat, and I absolutely insist on being the best man. Boy or girl, name the firstborn after me."

"Which name should we use?"

"Your choice." He shook hands with Max and left.

Caitrin watched him leave. "Now, you wanted to talk to me."

"Yes, but he said you were—"

A crescendo of drums and horns blotted out his words as a lithe young black man, dressed in white and with an impressive grin, leaped onto the bandstand.

"Snake Hips Johnson. Watch him dance," Caitrin said.

The band swung into a faster rhythm, and as he sang, Snake Hips lived up to his name.

"Stay right there; don't move, no more interruptions," Max said, expression solemn. He raised a finger to keep Caitrin in place, went to a table to the left and a little behind the bandstand, spoke to the couple sitting there, and brought them back. "These kind people have agreed to swap tables with us."

"Why?"

"Because it's their wedding anniversary, my congratulations, they want to dance, and I want to talk," he said and aimed his index finger at her. "To you. Alone."

"All right. Happy anniversary, enjoy the champers," Caitrin said to the couple and followed Max to the quieter table.

"That's a bit better," Max said as they sat at the new table. "Now I can hear myself think."

"I can hear you think too, and the answer's yes."

"What?"

"Oh, Max, you can be such a man sometimes."

In the city above, air-raid sirens wailed, and Luftwaffe bombers droned. There were distant explosions, and the band played louder.

"What am I supposed to be? And you never said you were married before."

Caitrin shrugged. "Men are so fragile. We weren't really married. Pretended to be for an assignment and . . . I can't say any more. We never, you know, never shared the marital bed."

Antiaircraft guns fired as the bombers grew louder. Snake Hips was not to be bested and launched into "Oh Johnny." "What makes me love you so? You're not handsome, that's true—"

"You are handsome, and I love you, Max."

Max deflated in relief. "Thank God. I love you, Caitrin."

"If you hadn't proposed, I was going to do it," Caitrin leaned forward and kissed him. "I even come with a wedding ring, see?" She held up her hand to show him her mother's ring. "Made of Welsh gold from the Gwynfynydd mine, near Dolgellau, your grandad's birthplace. Dwy galon, un daith. Two hearts, one journey."

A bomb sheared through the Rialto cinema's glass roof and punched down into the café, but did not explode. The band was shocked into silence, except for the drummer, absorbed in keeping the beat, who stopped a few bars later. Snake Hips clutched the microphone with both hands and, frozen in mid-dance, stared wide-eyed at the bomb, which had broken apart and scattered yellow cordite across the dance floor. There was no movement, no sound. Caitrin's eyes locked onto Max's as he rose to protect her. They both knew bombers never dropped just one bomb. Moments later, a second one followed, and this did explode, directly in front of the bandstand.

"The Café de Paris. Coventry Street. It's underground, isn't it?" Winston said.

"I wouldn't know, sir."

"Used to be a bear-pit once, long ago. What casualties?"

"I don't know, sir; it just came in."

"It's Poulsen's place." Winston grunted. "And was a favorite haunt in the twenties of the Prince of Wales, with his mistress Mrs. Dudley Ward. He called her Fredie-Wedie, if I remember correctly. Usually had his equerry Fruity Metcalfe with him too."

He read further, shaking his head. "London. One hundred and thirty thousand incendiaries and a hundred and thirty tons of high explosives. Fourteen bombs hit Buckingham Palace and Green Park; twenty-three struck Liverpool Street station. This is a new and an unsettling accuracy. What news is there from other cities?"

"We have not gotten the reports yet, sir."

"*Hmm*," Winston said. "That will be all, Mrs. Hill. Why don't you go home?"

"Yes, sir," Mrs. Kathleen Hill said and fled before he could change his mind.

10

Bethany had been driving north in silence for hours. Caitrin, sitting beside her, had hardly spoken since the night of the bombing. Occasionally, she shifted her weight, wincing in pain, and Bethany understood the mental anguish Caitrin was suffering. She had lost her husband, Laurence, in September 1939, at the beginning of the war. He was killed on the bridge of HMS *Exeter* when they were fighting the German pocket battleship *Graf Spee* in the South Atlantic. Too old for children, they still had their dreams. Laurence loved the sea and wanted a cottage on the coast when he retired. Bethany knew that was a dream which would probably not come true, but hoped there would be something for them and hadn't expected everything to end so abruptly. Laurence had died recently, yet so long ago and, to her, so anonymously.

And she was left alone.

That night at the Café de Paris, Max had saved Caitrin's life by moving them to the side of the bandstand, and his body absorbed most of the blast, while the couple with whom they exchanged tables was obliterated. Snake Hips Johnson was decapitated, and most of the band were killed; nearly forty customers died, and dozens more were badly injured. In the chaos, overworked firemen and air-raid wardens struggled to save survivors, and along with them came looters, one of whom stole Caitrin's mother's wedding ring. Caitrin remembered none of this; she knew only that the ring was gone and Max, her Max, was dead.

"This is flat country," Caitrin said.

"That's Lincolnshire for you," Bethany said. "Nothing taller than a short tree for miles and miles." The road, flanked by budding hedgerows, ran pencil-straight through endless fields. A pair of Hurricane fighters roared low overhead and scattered a flock of gulls.

Caitrin gazed through the windscreen and said, "All of the light is in the sky, nothing on the land. Living here would make me feel very small. I'm small anyway."

Bethany gave an encouraging smile and patted her knee. Caitrin had aged in just a few weeks; she had lessened. "It's not far now. Kirton-in-Lindsey is just a few miles ahead."

They reached the village, turned off Church Street, and parked under a yew tree at St. Andrew's Church. Bethany saw Caitrin stiffen and asked her, "Are you all right?"

Caitrin nodded, opened the car door, and got out. The church, with its square limestone tower, glowed golden in the sunlight, and Bethany took her hand as they walked toward the graveyard. The green spears of early crocuses showed between moss-covered, tilted headstones, and snowdrops and daffodils splashed brave colors. Caitrin saw the grave first. "There it is," she said, her voice tight.

They stopped at the foot of the grave, a fresh mound of earth in an ancient graveyard. The headstone, white and unweathered, said: MAXWELL EVARTS, BORN SONORA, CALIFORNIA, NOVEMBER 29, 1914. DIED LONDON, MARCH 8, 1941. AGED 27. 71

EAGLE SQUADRON. FOLDED WINGS. Above his name was carved the Royal Air Force crest and motto, *Per Ardua Ad Astra*.

"Through struggle to the stars," Caitrin said, reading the motto and shaking her head. "Have we gotten used to all this, all these bombings and deaths? If this is the new normal, why aren't we going mad? Or are we already mad?"

Bethany tightened the grip on her hand. Caitrin glanced at the other headstones and read the names. "Marris, Hill, Parry, Travis, Walker. Generations of local families. The squadron is leaving here next month, going closer to London, closer to me." She edged away a tear. "Max will be left here alone with other peoples' families. I saw his face, I held up the wedding ring to show him, and . . . nothing."

A Hurricane flew overhead, flaps and wheels lowering, engine throttling back to make an approach to the airfield. Caitrin watched until it disappeared from view.

Unchained, link by link, from trauma, Caitrin's memory reassembled: an emotion, a sound, a sight, an image. They were mental jigsaw pieces fitting together, but out of sequence and incomplete. She lay in bed, the room dark and quiet, her eyes closed. A white flash—Max's face—blue, vivid, painful—a pressure on her chest, like a boa constrictor, tightening every time she breathed out—a singing hiss—numbness—a voice as someone took her hand, "I'll be having this, missy. Won't do you any good where you're going." Another voice, "Come on, Badger, coppers."—silence—moans—a scream—blackness.

She got out of bed, switched on a light, went to her desk, and brought out a sheet of notepaper. The letter wrote itself.

> *Dear Hywel,*
> *I am Caitrin, and I was going to marry your son Max. We hadn't known each other very long, but it was time enough to be sure we wanted to be together. My parents*

*had a wonderful loving marriage, and I thought, no, not
thought, knew, I knew, ours would be too.*

*Max was always talking about you and his family and
the farm. He was so proud of you, and we intended to
come to Sonora after the war.*

*We were in the Café de Paris, having a rare evening
together, and he, in his usual charming Max way, had just
proposed to me. I showed him my mother's wedding ring.
She gave it to me so their love would become our love,
and perhaps one day in the future, if Max and I had a
daughter, she would wear it too.*

*The ring had an inscription: Dwy galon, un daith. Two
hearts, one journey. Max and I never got to take our journey together, and the ring was stolen by looters. You and
I have both lost who we loved most, and I only wish we
lived closer, so we might comfort each other. Perhaps once
this awful war is over, I will meet you. I would like that.
Max told me there was someone you always wanted in
your family: here I am,*

Your daughter,
Caitrin

She put down the pen and settled back in the chair as a cold
rage rose in her. She was left alone and had nothing. Not quite;
her memory had retrieved the name of the man who stole her
ring. Badger. She was going to hunt down Badger, no matter
how long it took. Because the ring belonged to her, and to Max.

11

The flower beds along the Broad Walk in Regent's Park were badly neglected, but the cherry blossoms were appearing. Spring was here, despite the ruined city's continued devastation. *I suppose nature is indifferent to our stupidities*, Bethany thought as she sat on a bench across from the Griffin Tazza, with her eyes closed, face tilted toward the sun. Winter had been endless, a time of great losses, and she was glad it was over. The Blitz wasn't over, though, and the last few nights had been particularly heavy. She opened her eyes and glanced at her watch. Caitrin should be here soon.

Sometimes, in the midst of all the strife, she forgot how young her operatives were, and no matter how well 512 trained them, they were still women. They did not start from the same place as men and did not have centuries of acceptance as warriors. Instead, they were considered by many in power as lacking in intelligence and mental stamina. Obviously, they said, women were physically much weaker than men and prone to capricious and overly emotional behavior at inopportune moments every month. And, as was pointed out by many men of authority, women traditionally, not to say biblically, were meant to be helpers for their husbands, not equal competitors, and this partnership had been and still was the bedrock of society.

Perhaps there was a certain comfort in being the submissive partner; it relieved you of responsibility, Bethany thought, but dismissed the idea. *Although a chained dog might be warm and well fed, it never runs free to see the horizon.*

Bethany saw Caitrin approaching. She looked small, fragile, and had endured so much for someone so young. Perhaps 512 was a failure after all, albeit an honest one. She closed her eyes again and faced the sun. There had been early successes, but none recently, and Churchill may have been right and it was time to shut the unit down and scatter the operatives to the other agencies. It would be a terrible loss of talent, though, and most of all, a tragic betrayal of women's hopes and dreams.

"I just discovered something," Caitrin's voice broke her train of thought, and she opened her eyes.

"Tell me," Bethany patted the bench, and Caitrin sat next to her. Most of the injuries had healed, but there were still deep scratches on her forehead.

"My new digs at 37 Fitzroy Street. George Bernard Shaw lived there when he first came to London."

"Good for George, and you."

Caitrin's expression clouded. "I want to resign from 512."

"That's disappointing. Why?"

"Because in the Café de Paris someone stole my mother's wedding ring, and I want it back."

"It could be anywhere by now."

"It's somewhere, I know it is, and I'm going to find it."

Bethany sighed and glanced at the balloons floating over the garden. There was a brown smudge of smoke smeared across the clouds in the distance. Something was always burning in the city nowadays. It seemed bizarre that this fresh spring day would fade into a night darkness of bombs and destruction, and that, in turn, it would fade up on another bright day. "I know you well enough not attempt to change your mind, but I don't want to lose you. Do not resign. Why not train our new recruits, even part-time?"

"Thank you," Caitrin said.

"Use our resources, and be aware, London's criminal underworld is a violent one."

Caitrin laughed. "Unlike the one we live in?"

"Touché. Just be careful."

"I will do that."

"How are you going to start your search?"

"I'm no longer on the force and may not get access to police records, so first methinks a wee chat with a certain teddy bear."

The milk float was gone, and the bomb crater had been clumsily filled in, but the Blind Stag looked no more inviting in daylight than it had at night. Apart from a broken wall to her left, the pub was the only vertical object in a rubble-strewn landscape. There was no traffic and no people on the streets because no one lived there any longer. The Blind Stag stood alone. *Monarch of all you survey.* Closer, Caitrin saw that most of the boarded-up windows had red crosses painted on them, while signs pasted on the walls said the building was unsafe and condemned. A stubby man wearing a flat cap sat on a beer crate outside the front door and stood as she approached.

"Would you be Miss Colins?"

"Colline. Where's Large Eric?"

"Drowned."

"Sorry to hear that."

"In an Anderson shelter."

"They do fill up a bit with water. But not usually enough to drown."

"He was drunk."

"Oh, that will do it, and at least the Jerries didn't get him. You are?"

"Ernie."

"Eric, Ernie. Teddy's working his way through the E's. Learn to swim and stay sober, Ernie, or he'll be into the F's before you know what hit you. Sit down, I'll show myself in." Caitrin swept past him and entered the pub.

Daniel Teddy Baer, blond hair Brylcreemed and face freshly shaved, was there to greet her. In his blazer, blade-creased slacks, and Guards cravat, Teddy would have looked at home at the Henley Regatta, although the provenance of the cravat was dubious. Teddy had never been within a million miles of a Guards regiment, and the moment he spoke, the gentleman illusion vanished. Try as he might, well-dressed Teddy would never be anything but a Whitechapel barrow boy.

The empty pub interior was spotless: black-and-white tiled floor, polished wood gleaming, and brass fittings shining. The northern-exposure windows had not been boarded up; instead, an amber theatrical lighting gel covered the frosted panes, and a warm light flooded the interior.

"That's a lovely dress you're wearing," he said, admiring Caitrin. "Smashing bit of stuff."

Caitrin knew he wasn't inspecting the dress. "And look at you, every inch the pukka sahib," she lied.

"Now we've lied so elegantly to each other, I thought we would have lunch here," he said and led her to a table in the back of the pub, directly beneath the window. He had gone to great lengths to impress her. The tablecloth was Irish linen, with a floral centerpiece, and the settings were of fine silver and crystal. Caitrin was about to sit when she noticed her chair faced the window, which meant she would be in an interrogatory full light, while he would be a detail-less silhouette. Perhaps it was happenstance, but she was quite sure it was not and slid her chair around ninety degrees. Teddy relaxed a few muscles into the slightest of smiles and moved his chair to face her.

"A soft sidelight, especially an amber one, is so flattering for both of us, don't you think?" she said.

"It certainly suits you," he answered.

"Where is Florence?"

"Gone home to her mum," he said, rotating the place settings to face them.

"Who is stone dead."

"Did Florence tell you that?"

"Yes."

"She's a devil for the porkies, that one."

His glib answer bothered her. From their time working together as policewomen, Caitrin knew Florence was not a strong woman, but she never struck her as a liar. She asked, "Aren't you concerned about being in a condemned building?"

Teddy laughed. "There is no gas or electricity, but the building is solid. I put the postings up outside to keep people away."

A man in a white apron appeared and showed Teddy a wine bottle. "This is Charles Beauchamp. He was at the Arlington in Chelsea until it was bombed. Now he's here with me. And glad we are to have him."

"Thank you, sir," Charles said as he waited for Teddy's approval of the wine before pouring glasses and leaving.

Teddy raised his glass. "A toast to friendship, peace, and honesty."

Honesty. Caitrin kept a straight face as she lifted her glass. Teddy had obviously used this routine with women before.

"Now, tell me, what happened to you?" Teddy asked and gestured to the scratches on her face. "Go a few rounds with Freddie Mills?"

"I was at the Café de Paris."

"Oh."

They fell silent as Charles appeared with plates of salmon and fresh vegetables.

"I haven't seen food like this in a long time," Caitrin said, knowing it would please Teddy's ego. Teddy had a naughty-boy charisma, he was a *puer aeternus* many women would find intriguing, but she had no interest in lovable rogues. They were far too calculating, too self-absorbed, and beneath that beguiling exterior was a flint-hard man chiseled out of the granite of the unforgiving Whitechapel slums.

"Fresh pineapple and bananas in an orange sauce with vanilla ice cream for dessert. Thank you, Charles."

Charles left, and Teddy, sensing he had misjudged Caitrin's reason for meeting and she was not there to be seduced, waited until the kitchen door closed and asked, "Down to business. Why are you here?"

"After the bomb went off, I don't remember much, but looters moved in, and one of them stole my wedding ring."

"You're married?"

"No. It was my mother's ring, but would be mine when I did get married."

"You were marrying the Yank you met here at my New Year's Eve party?"

"Yes."

"That was fast."

"There's a war on."

"I heard about it."

"Max was killed in the blast."

"I'm sorry to hear that. He seemed like a good enough bloke."

"Thank you, yes, he was. Now I want the ring back."

"And you think I can help you?"

"Yes, I do."

"Why should I?"

"Because I can help you in return."

"I rarely need outside help."

"Rarely doesn't mean never."

"You're doing what nowadays?"

"Trying to survive and thrive in difficult times," she said and paused for a moment. "Just like you."

"Quite the Lady Mysterious," Teddy said, enjoying the duel. "If I was to help you, where do I start? Do you have a description or the name of the man?"

"I was only half-conscious and never saw his face when he stripped the ring away, but heard someone say to him, "Come on, Badger, coppers.""

"Badger. *Hmm*, I wonder where I would find a bloke named Badger?" Teddy sat back, sipped at his wine, and gazed at her. He put down the glass and locked his hands behind his head. "A bit of history for you. The Elephant and Castle gang goes back to the 1700s, and they run South London. The Clerkenwell Boys arrived a bit later. Then you have Alfie Solomons with his Yiddishers; the Hoxton boys; the Bessas in Whitechapel—always fighting the Odessas, both bloody thirsty East Europeans—"

"And the Sabinis—now interned on the Isle of Man—and the Black brothers moving into their patch, what jolly fun," Caitrin interrupted. "The Messinas and their prostitutes; the Titanics—who sank with all hands a while ago; nasty man Jack Spot; blade-happy Billy Hill from Camden Town; and, of course, the inevitable drunken Irish gangs fighting everyone, but mostly each other. All of them work on their home turf with little idea of the big world outside. I was a copper working the East End, remember?"

"How could I ever forget?"

"And you, Mr. Baer, are a police enigma. Where do you work? What's your gang?" Caitrin asked. Teddy was used to getting his own way, and she guessed he normally steamrollered women. Not this time, not this woman.

"I don't like being dependent, and there's always a weak link. I hire men only when I need them. Pay well and send them away." Teddy's expression hardened, but he softened it with his little-boy smile. "There's so much more to my world than the slums of Whitechapel."

Caitrin let him continue.

"Now, the Café de Paris is in the West End, and that's a foreign planet for some of the mobs, so I'd say your Badger could be King's Cross, the Finsbury mob, or the Hackney boys. Maybe the Elephants. That's a lot of men to investigate who don't like being asked questions." He unlocked his fingers, placed his hands, palm down, on the table and leaned forward. "It could also be some humble tea leaf who was wandering by and just happened to get lucky."

"So you can't help?"

"Didn't say that," Teddy said, took a notebook from his pocket, and slid it across the table toward her. "Give me a description of the ring."

He watched her as she wrote in the notebook. "I don't want to upset you, but the odds are it's already been fenced, and if it's gold—"

"It is."

"Then it's probably been melted down." He sipped at his wine. "Unless our Badger took a liking to it as a present for the old trouble and strife."

Caitrin nodded as she handed back the notebook.

He read the description. "You're Welsh."

"Yes. Coal-mining town."

"Row house, cold water, no bathroom, outside toilet with the *Daily Mirror* ripped up into squares for toilet paper."

"Yes."

"Just like Whitechapel. Subhuman housing conditions for the workers, and no one gave a damn about us. It took Jack the Ripper slashing his merry way through the women of Whitechapel in the late 1800s to bring attention to the slums. They cleared some away, but not all, and now the Luftwaffe is demolishing the rest. Maybe Adolf's doing us a favor."

"Some favor."

"You have to look after yourself out here. Nothing is ever free; there's always a price tag for everything, and when it comes due, one way or another, you have to pay up, or else. Understand?"

"I understand."

"Leave it with me."

Caitrin nodded in agreement, but Teddy wasn't convinced and said, "One more thing, don't get in my way by running around playing Sherlock Holmes."

"I don't play," Caitrin said. "Let's just find Badger."

Charles arrived with dessert.

"Would you like some coffee, Caitrin?" Teddy asked, adding, with a roguish grin, "Freshly stolen, and freshly ground, of course. American coffee."

Coffee. Maxwell. Max. "No," Caitrin said, knowing she now owed Teddy a favor, and he would not be shy about collecting. Whatever the price might be.

12

Winston Churchill was hidden somewhere behind that dense cloud of cigar smoke; Bethany could just make out his outline and hear him muttering. She pushed her chair back to avoid the smoke. The prime minister's office, with its cigar smoke and ever-present whisky tumbler, smelled like one of the Pall Mall clubs. At least Bethany imagined that is how they would smell because, being a woman, she had never been allowed inside one. Not that she would accept an invitation.

"Rommel," he growled.

"Rommel," she repeated.

"El Agheila," he said, and that she did not repeat, but sat quiet and let him continue. "Rommel, with his Afrika Corps, has taken El Agheila in Libya and is driving our forces back. Italian MTMs, which are one-man boats filled with explosives, sank the heavy cruiser HMS *York*. Bristol has suffered another heavy bombing, and the Atlantic convoy losses are appalling. The latest one lost half of their vessels. There is no good news to be had anywhere, Mrs. Goodman. We are surrounded by three hundred and sixty degrees of enemy."

"It appears so."

"Which means this is a time to concentrate our forces, lest we be overwhelmed. What do you have to offer me regarding your organization?"

"Nothing concrete, other than I believe it would be a mistake to shutter 512 before we have been given the chance to prove our worth."

"We are beyond hopes, wishes, and theories. And most certainly chances. The war is costing us ten million pounds a day. 512 must be ended and all of its operatives dispersed to the other organizations."

"We have just begun the training program for a new batch of operatives. May we at least finish that so they will be of some use?"

"How long?"

"Training lasts twelve weeks, and they are two weeks into the basic part of the course."

"Then you have ten weeks."

"Respectfully, Prime Minister, I consider this a grave error."

"That is mine to make, and the responsibility to accept it, but it is a decision that stands. The very existence of our empire is in peril, unless Roosevelt commits soon to entering the war. So far, he is reluctant, yet somewhat receptive. Good day, Mrs. Goodman. Pray for the Americans."

"Good day, Prime Minister. I will pray for the Americans, and for us too."

A few minutes after Bethany had left, Caitrin arrived. Churchill stood, took her hand, and patted it. "I will not offer you false sentiment. This is not the time or place for hollow paeans of praise. Please, sit down."

They sat facing each other at the fireplace, and he was struck yet again by her bravery. She wanted to cry, but was refusing to do so. To him, she looked delicate, so fragile and feminine, yet he knew she was so strong.

"I know the pain of personal loss. My daughter Marigold died just before her third birthday and four days after my mother's death. It is a profound heartache. What was your fiancé's name?"

"Max."

"That is a good American name," Churchill said. "One that befits a good American, and a man who came voluntarily to fight for us. You obviously loved each other."

"Yes. I was going to the States with him once the war was over."

"That would have been a grand adventure for you. But a grievous loss for us."

"A sunny farm in Sonora, California, up in the Sierra Nevada mountains, with a donkey, ducks, and a dog. And a set of drums to bang on."

"I have ducks at Chartwell, and tremendous fishes. They swim up to me when I go to feed them. You must come see them once we are allowed to reopen the house. I insist."

"Thank you, sir."

"Promise you won't bring your drums, though?"

She laughed and bit her lips to hold back the tears. "I won't, promise."

"If you like, we can have you relieved of duty for a week or so."

She shook her head. "No, that would be unfair to the others, and it is better if my mind is occupied."

"I had my doubts about putting women into the battle. I was certain they were not strong enough physically, or emotionally." He sat back and gazed at her, this small female warrior. "You have made an old fool out of me, Caitrin Colline. Not many people can do that."

"Some fool."

"I notice you didn't say old."

She blushed, and said, "Old? I feel ancient."

He patted her hand again. "It might seem like that now, but there is a grand life ahead of you, young lady. It will be filled with heartbreaks and triumphs, large and small. You must accept them all, because they are what will make you strong. If you do that, in years to come, you will look back over your life and be grateful for those who were part of it, even if they were with you for only a short time. We will endure."

She trapped an errant tear with her handkerchief.

"Up the hill-side; and now 'tis buried deep, In the next valley-glades: Was it a vision, or a waking dream?" His voice was low, yet resonant, thrilling. "Fled is that music: Do I wake or sleep?"

"Keats. 'Ode to a Nightingale.' "

"What's far worse than a bright, strong Welsh woman? An educated and poetic one."

"With you leading us, we shall indeed endure. Thank you, sir."

"Thank you, young lady," He grinned his baby's grin as they both stood and he put out his hand. "Knowing there are women like you at my side makes it easier. Good day, Caitrin Colline."

"Good day, Prime Minister."

13

Billy "The Brick" Donnelly stood squarely in the center of Langland Priory's great hall, beneath the hammer-beam ceiling and surrounded on all sides by portraits of long-dead disapproving Langlands. Liverpool-Irish Billy, with a compact body and low center of gravity, was 512's weapons instructor and got his nickname from the way he shot. Regardless of weapon calibre, recoil, or blast, when Billy pulled the trigger only his finger moved. He didn't even blink. Billy was a stone-cold marksman.

Furniture had been cleared from the hall and replaced by exercise equipment. Sitting on two benches facing him were 512's latest recruits: ten young women of whom only a few, if any, would succeed. Bethany Goodman had told no one they were probably the last recruits. Caitrin stood at Billy's right. They had never worked together as instructors, but in Caitrin's training as a recruit, Billy had admired her shooting and combat skills. She seemed to be unafraid of anyone. Or hid it well.

Caitrin stepped forward, her feet grazing a mound of boxing gloves. "This edifice before you, ladies," she said and put out her hand as she half-turned to Billy, "is a man."

She got giggles in response, although Billy, used to working in an all-female organization, was impassive.

"Tell me, what does a man have that you do not?"

"The vote!" one of the women said.

"True until recently. Anything else?"

"Better pay."

"True, for now. What else—no, stop, I'll tell you," Caitrin said and bit back a grin. "Testicles."

She did grin at the collective gasp, while Billy remained a statue. His mind had flown elsewhere.

"They have other names: balls, bollocks . . ." She opened her arms to the women.

"Nadgers," someone said.

"Cobblers."

"Cwd," a third said, and Caitrin pointed at her. "Good girl. North Wales."

The young woman beamed with pride.

"The family jewels," Billy said, but no one saw his lips move.

"Whatever we call them, next to his brain—they are directly connected—testicles are the weakest part of a man's body," she said and faced Billy. "Don't worry, Billy; we won't make you show us yours."

"I grew up with six sisters," Billy said.

Caitrin turned back to the women. "Some of you will be familiar with testicles and their sturdy little chum, but that is a personal story. You must remember one thing: supposedly, the way to man's heart is through his stomach, but killing him often begins with his testicles."

There were no happy faces now, and Billy winced.

"Yes, kill. You work alone, and the enemy will invariably be a man, who is probably going to be bigger and stronger. Forget all the death and glory nonsense, it's unnatural to hurt someone, let alone kill them. But you might have to prevent them from killing you. That means using everything and anything you can. Gouge out an eye, bite through an artery, kick, knee, or punch your assailant in the balls. Never stop until he's dead—or you will be."

The recruits were transfixed, holding their breath. A few looked terrified.

"I need a volunteer." Caitrin picked up a boxing glove and slipped it onto her right hand. She pointed to a young woman at the end of a bench, who rose and stepped in front of her. "Put on some gloves."

The woman managed to find a left and right pair and slipped them on. "What's your name, and where are you from?" Caitrin asked.

"It's Grace Baker and—" Caitrin hit her before she could finish answering. It was not a hard blow, but unexpected, and, in reflex, Grace turned away. Catrin clamped her left hand deep into Grace's hair. "You're dead."

She let go, and Grace sat, rubbing her cheek.

"The first blow invariably controls the fight; the second one will end it, unless you are trained. My punch was not hard, but it surprised Grace, and to defend herself, her instinct was to turn her back to me." Caitrin pulled off the glove, dropped it, and brought a knife from her pocket. "That gave me ample time to kill her anyway I wished. Are you all right, Grace?"

Grace nodded and gave a brave smile as she held back tears.

"Everyone—stand up, pair off, and put on gloves. Boxers are used to getting hit. They do not turn their backs after the first blow. That one has already landed, and they know another is coming. They take it, absorb the pain, and fight back. I want you to do the same thing. Go to it, with gusto."

She watched with Billy as the women lined up, at first swinging hesitant punches and then growing bolder. A door opened, a secretary leaned into the room, waved at Caitrin, and made a telephone gesture.

"Don't let them kill each other," Caitrin said and hurried out. "At least not until I get back."

"It's a police sergeant Goodwillie for you," the secretary said as she handed the telephone to Caitrin and left the office.

"Angus, how are you?"

"Caitrin, you're in a home for unwed mothers?" Angus Goodwillie's Scottish-accented voice boomed in her ear. "Have you been a naughty lass?"

"No more than usual. I'm working here, saving broken hearts and souls as best I can. What news?"

"You do know that me sharing police records with you, now a civilian, is highly irregular. Illegal too."

"I could listen to a Scot saying highly irregular all day long. So musical those rolling Rs. If you get nabbed, I promise I'll visit you in prison."

"Your compassion is humbling. What do you want first?"

"Badger."

"No luck there. There are a half-dozen Butchers, two of them in the Hackney mob, a Weasel, and a Rat, but no Badgers."

"Sounds more like a chapter from *Wind in the Willows* than members of a London gang."

"If you're more inclined to the pantomime, there's also a Horrible Harry, Slippery Willy, Dodger Dunham, and Mutton Malcolm."

"They're an inventive lot."

"Not what I'd call them. I'll keep looking."

"Thanks. And what about Teddy Baer?"

"He is an oddity, a real loner. We've brought Teddy in a dozen times over the years, but can never pin anything on him."

"How does he make his money?"

"No idea, but he's not poor. Or legitimate."

"His girlfriend Florence Simmonds might know something."

"Nothing about her either. I've got her mother's address, if you want it."

"I do. You're a savior," Caitrin said as she scribbled down the address.

"Warning. While you're trying to find out what Teddy's up to, a dickie-bird told me he's been asking around about you. Be very careful."

"I will. Perhaps you could spread an enticing rumor his way that I'm not exactly kosher."

"Burglary? Blagging? Smash and grab?"

"Make it serious but mysterious, out of town so he can't check on me. One more thing. Could you put together a list of small-time fences in London? The kind who deal with stolen watches, jewelry, that kind of thing."

"Yes."

"Thanks, Angus, 'bye." Caitrin hung up and looked at the address she had written down. 45 Lancaster Avenue, Peckham.

She returned to the great hall, where the women had punched themselves out, with red faces, a few nosebleeds, and a reckless air of accomplishment.

"How did they do, Billy?"

"Some I wouldn't want to meet in a Glasgow pub at closing time."

"Good." She faced the women. "In almost every fight, the person being attacked lets the attacker land the first punch. But our training will teach you to strike first, and last. You can apologize if you were mistaken, but not if you're dead. Before we go on to the various holds, kicks, and weapons usage, pair up with a new partner."

She watched the women choose new partners, except for Grace, who held back. "You don't want to do it, Grace?"

Grace wiped a drop of blood from her nose, grinned, put up her gloved hands, and said, "Oh, yes I do. With you."

* * *

While 41 and 47 Lancaster Avenue in Peckham existed, 43 and 45 no longer did. The previous night, a stick of bombs had straddled the street, and one landing in the front garden of number 43 destroyed both houses. Firemen were dousing embers as Caitrin arrived.

"Any survivors?" Caitrin asked a weary air-raid warden. "Mrs. Simmonds in 45?"

"Over there," the warden pointed to a church hall at the end of the street.

Caitrin entered the hall and stopped. Rows of bodies, covered with blood-stained sheets, lay on the floor. She choked back the smell.

"Are you looking for someone, dearie?" a tiny woman in a grubby uniform asked.

"Mrs. Simmonds in 45."

"She's at the end, but I don't think you'll want to look at her, poor thing. She was standing at the window when the bomb exploded and is in such a terrible state. Shattering glass is so unkind."

"Is her daughter here?" *No, please say no.*

"We haven't seen Florence in ever so long. Her mum was upset she didn't write or come to visit anymore since she met that bloke."

"Thank you," Caitrin left. She needed to breathe and see the sky. At the new year's party, Florence said her mum had died in a bombing raid, which was not true, until last night when she did, and at lunch, Teddy told Caitrin she had gone home. But she had not, so, as Teddy would say, porky pies were being told. And the only way for her to learn the truth would be to find Florence.

14

This visit there was no Irish linen tablecloth, no floral center-piece, no silver or crystal settings. The amber northern-light windows were covered by blackout curtains, and when Ernie showed Caitrin into the pub, Teddy was alone behind the bar, pulling a pint of beer.

"Bitter?" he said.

"About what?"

"Beer."

"Oh, sorry. Half pint."

Teddy pulled a half pint for her and came around to a table. He put down the glasses as they sat, stretched out his legs, and, with a self-satisfied air, said, "It's a fortunate man who owns his own pub."

"An empty pub. Where are the regulars?"

"Dead or disappeared to Dorking to stay with mum for the duration. You've seen the neighborhood."

"Pity."

"I like it this way," he said. "If I want company, I call for it."

"Why, when I telephone, do I not get you answering, but instead a little boy, and usually a different one calling me back with a message?"

"That would be because I have no telephone here. And I don't want one," Teddy said. "There's a box about a quarter-mile away. That's the number you're calling. I pay a florin to anyone who answers, which means there's always a gang of kids hanging around the box waiting for the telephone to ring. I hear there's a regular donnybrook to get to the phone first. I taught them to use the A and B buttons, and how to be polite. At least as polite as Whitechapel kids can be."

"So you decide who to talk to?"

"That's about it." He pointed at her slacks. "I notice you're back to wearing bowsers."

"And with that cardigan and those corduroys, you're quite the English gentleman in his country home library. All you need is a cocker spaniel, a pipe, and a suit of armor in the background."

"One day soon," he said, with a vehemence that surprised her.

"Yes?"

"Yes, just a minute," Teddy said, left, and returned moments later with a folder. He placed it in front of her. She opened it and leafed through the pages. They included a detailed description, with photographs, of Ramilton Woods, a Surrey country estate.

"You're buying this?"

He made to answer, but paused for a moment before saying, "Row houses, outside toilets, no bathrooms, Wales and Whitechapel. That's where we came from, you and me, but it's not where we intend to end up, right?"

"Right."

"I can't stay here, you can't go back to Wales; so where do you want to go to?"

A sunny farm in Sonora, with a donkey, ducks, and a dog, a

*set of drums to bang on, and my Max. Once, not now, gone for-
ever.* "A green place, not a city."

Teddy rapped hard on the folder. "This is what I want and
intend to get. Six thousand acres of farmland, eight hundred
acres of woods, and a fourteenth-century manor. Six duck ponds
and two stables. And three other houses on the land, any one of
which is ten times bigger than anywhere I've lived. It will be
mine soon."

The intensity of his expression startled her. This was not
some half-baked dream. Teddy had real plans.

"Scratch the surface of our landed gentry and you'll find
crooks and thieves. They chatter about family and honor and
heritage, but they killed and stole what they own. I'm going to
be the first honest one to buy my estate."

Caitrin held back an answer. *Honest with stolen money.*

"In a few generations, the Baer name will be as honorable as
the rest," he relaxed a little and laughed. "Might even change
the name to something like Debarr, so it doesn't sound so Yiddish."

"Or you could aim even higher and become Lord Whitechapel."

"Why not? Disraeli did it."

"Big plans cost big money."

"Do you know how many of our *best* families died out or
are bankrupt because their only sons went off to die gloriously
in France in the last war? No, not die, they fell heroically in the
field, as if it was some silly public school game. Only you don't
get to stand up and toddle off for tea and cucumber sandwiches
with the crust cut off. It's old, weak blood and ready for some
fresh strong Teddy Baer infusion."

He was a little boy at Christmas, open with excitement, and
for the first time, Caitrin saw past the Cockney chappie façade
and liked Teddy Baer. They were alike in many ways, both trying to rise from their backgrounds.

"Where does a Whitechapel immigrant Jew, even a very bright one, expect to find the money?"

"Not by smash and grab or extorting the bookies," he said. "Certainly not by belonging to some gang of morons fighting over the same little piece of turf." He stopped abruptly, cautious he might be revealing too much, and said, "I hear you've been asking around about me."

"I hear you've been asking around about me."

"Who told you?"

"Who told you?"

"Fair enough." He sat back, folded his arms, and gave her an admiring grin. "You haven't asked why a fine young fellow like me isn't in the army."

"I would assume it is because you have some rare ailment that tragically denies you the honor of dying for your country?"

"Right you are. My allegiance is to me, not to a country owned by old families who want us to die to keep them alive," he said, the smile gone. "Are you still an ex-copper?"

"What do you mean?"

"Ex, as in no longer connected with the force."

"I'm definitely ex-copper. That doesn't mean I don't think like one, but instead I now do it for my own benefit."

"The hardest part of making money is getting the first one hundred pounds. With that, you can buy services or influence for leverage to the next one hundred. Without it, you're just a bloke on the street with a daft dream."

"What would you suggest a daft bloke do with his first one hundred?"

"No petty crime, no violence, and nothing you'd have to fence. Cash, hard cash, or gold is even better. I'd hire the best safe crackers, who come out of Glasgow and bring their own gelignite. No names, no details. Wait until the middle of a Blitz, when everyone's in a shelter and the bombs are falling so no one cares about the noise. Blow open a bank safe, maybe two if the banks are close together, and take only cash. Pay the Jocks their money and send them home. They'd be drunk and spent out before reaching Carlisle and would forget what happened. This is all hypothetical, naturally."

"Naturally," she heard herself say, although it was not at all hypothetical. Teddy had just described a double bank theft from last year that had baffled the authorities. The operation was fast, nonviolent, and bore none of the marks of any London gang. There were no witnesses, and not one penny of the stolen money had surfaced since, which was unusual because the average impulsive gangster liked to splash his loot around. That was usually how the police caught them. It was a brazen, confident admission.

"You know mine. Now, what's your hypothetical?"

Caitrin's mind was still swirling with his calm confession, and the question surprised her. She recovered, remembering a half-developed plot the police had uncovered. "Before the war, savings and insurance stamps were printed in Poland. Don't ask me why. His Majesty's Stationery Office in Harrow is where they're printed now. Postal stamps are printed in High Wycombe. Every day, at the same time, a van picks up the stamps and takes them to the railway station. From there they go nationwide."

"How much?"

"A minimum of three million."

"Too complicated, and the government would never give up chasing you. It would take weeks of planning; you'd have to fence the stamps, get pennies on the true value, and need far too many men," he shrugged. "After the caper, I'd have to shoot them all to guarantee silence."

The excited little boy had vanished, and Caitrin knew he was not joking about shooting the men.

"Give me another one, a better one," he said, his voice fast, hard. She had misjudged him. This was the real Teddy Baer, shorn of his protective charm. This was a dangerous and driven man.

"June 1 clothes rationing comes into effect. Stolen ration books could be resold at three, four times—"

"We take the risk, and the fences make the money—again."

"Cash, hard cash. I get it," Caitrin said, putting up her hands to end the conversation. She changed the subject. "Have you spoken to Florence recently?"

"No, why would I?" he answered and also changed the subject. "I heard nothing from anyone about your ring. No Badger."

"That's disappointing."

"It needs sugar to get Mr. Badger out of his hidey-hole. Offering nothing gets you nothing. How much can you afford as a reward?"

"I hadn't thought of it."

"Think of it. No one does charity work."

"What about a hundred pounds?"

"It's not your first hundred?"

"That's a secret," Caitrin said and glanced at her watch. "I should leave before the bombing starts."

"They won't bomb here."

"They've done it before."

"They won't."

"How do you know?"

"Because they'll bomb more to the west. Ernie will drive you home."

"I don't live in the Elephant and Castle anymore. It was bombed out. I'm farther away."

"He'll take you to the station, then, unless you'd like to stay the night." His demeanor softened, the charming smile reassembled. "I have two bedrooms."

"You're very kind." Caitrin stood and put out her hand. "Thank you, for your gracious offer, my Lord Whitechapel."

They shook hands.

"I will offer the sugar around and hope there's one badger with a sweet tooth. Good night."

Ernie was waiting for her in a Chorlton's Bread & Cakes van with ARP painted in clumsy letters over the sign on the side. He was wearing an ARP armband and a tin helmet. She waited until they were some distance away before asking, "You're not really an ARP warden, are you?"

Ernie had the good grace to look embarrassed. "No, but it gets us around the city without fuss."

"I thought so."

The rest of the journey was silent, until he pulled up outside the station and said, "Safe journey, miss."

"Thank you, Ernie. You too."

She had taken a step away from the bread van when he hissed, "Florence needs you."

Before she could react, Ernie put the van in gear and drove away. In the far distance, off to the west, air-raid sirens moaned.

15

Bethany poured tea from her ancient brown teapot with the chipped spout and turned the teacup so the handle faced her. It was a familiar, comforting routine that brought Caitrin unexpected tears.

Bethany saw them. "What's wrong?"

Caitrin slumped into the sofa and released a great sigh. "I don't know where that came from, sorry."

"Is it Max?"

"Yes."

"It's hard, I know."

"I'm doing fine until I remember he's gone, ripped out of my life. It hurts, and I have no defense."

"It will hurt for a while," Bethany said, remembering her dead husband. *For a long while.*

"And the others. My brother Dafydd is flying secret operations, which means it's dangerous, and Gareth is somewhere in the Atlantic, where the U-boats are sinking hundreds of ships. I could lose my family as easily as I lost Max."

"This war is a monstrous evil," Bethany said. "You're one of the strongest women I know, but you're still just a human being, Caitrin. Remember that."

"Thank you."

"Have you had any luck finding the ring?"

"No. Some of the usual fences have disappeared, and the rest are pure angels who would never dream of accepting stolen goods. I have another problem. A friend of mine, Florence Simmonds, is missing, and I think she's in trouble. I have to find her."

"I'll help if I can."

"Thank you," Caitrin said, sniffed away her tears and sat up. "Enough of me. What is happening here?"

"The Palace of Westminster was bombed last night. The House of Commons Chamber was destroyed and the Clock Tower damaged."

"It must have been a heavy raid."

"Nearly fifteen hundred deaths in London. Still no sugar, sorry," Bethany said as she poured fresh tea. "The Luftwaffe were surprisingly accurate."

They'll bomb more to the west. Catrin remembered Teddy's remark.

"And it is now official. 512 has only weeks left before it is disbanded. I tried my best, but Churchill is insistent."

"What will you do?"

"I shall put on my mother superior habit and send up a few prayers." Bethany put her hands together in prayer, adopted what she hoped was an angelic expression, and gazed hopefully to the ceiling.

"I hope your prayers are answered."

Bethany dropped her hands. "Meanwhile, you could help me by running the shooting lesson today."

"What happened to Billy? He never misses a lesson."

Bethany paused and struggled for an answer. "We're down to six recruits, and one of the most promising is that elfin-faced Grace Baker. Do you remember her?"

"I do. She can punch."

"Our Miss Grace Baker can do a lot more than that." Bethany was enigmatic. "You can ask her what happened to Billy."

When 512 moved into Langland Priory, Billy discovered a basement beneath the great hall. Next to it was a series of disused pantries and maids' rooms, ready to be transformed into an underground shooting range of Billy's creation. Working alone, and with great determination, he knocked down walls, put up baffles, sealed off doors, and made what he considered the perfect soundproof shooting range. It was his inner sanctum. But today there was no Billy the Brick, just Bethany, Caitrin, and the remaining six recruits, one of them Grace Baker.

"Grace," Bethany said. "Please tell Caitrin what happened to Billy." It was a command, not a request.

Grace hesitated for the briefest moment, inhaled a deep breath and began. "We recruits were practicing hand-to-hand fighting, and Billy got very frustrated because no one was really going all out. He grabbed me in a bear hug and told me to get out of it. It was a shock, and my training took over a bit faster than either one of us expected."

"Go on."

"I kneed him hard in the testicles, scraped the edge of my boot down his shin, and stamped on his instep."

Every face showed horror, and Caitrin shivered.

But Grace was not done. "I started by biting his ear. It's Figs. 27 and 28 in the manual."

"Ouch," Caitrin said, wincing at the thought.

"He did tell me to get out of the bear hug," Grace said in defense, and there was just a hint of wickedness in her expression.

"And so you did," Caitrin said. "Let us move on to weapons training."

She watched as the recruits loaded and fired their weapons. Of all of them, Grace was the most relaxed, using a Walther P38 semi-automatic 9mm pistol, and Caitrin noticed there was little movement when she fired.

"The other girls call her Little Brick after Billy, because she's so still," Bethany said. "It might be a good idea to take her along as support in your exploration of London's underworld and give her some field experience while we still can."

"How old is she?"

"Just turned twenty-one."

Twenty-one, and I'm twenty-seven. Caitrin watched Grace as she fired. *But I feel thirty long years older.*

The day was almost over, the sun diminishing to a fading orange band behind the trees as Grace hurried through the woods. Caitrin was sitting on a bench, waiting for her at the edge of a pond. A bat flickered through the gathering darkness, and a few ducks muttered to each other as they paddled home.

"Bethany said you wanted to see me," Grace said.

"I do," Caitrin said. "Sit down. I wanted to meet here at this time so we could skip the nun and unwed mother dress-up routines."

Grace sat on the bench, the dying sun picking out her black hair.

"I had a meeting with Bethany, and she suggested you might come work with me."

"I'd love to."

"It's not the usual 512 operation. It's a more personal matter."

"That's all right. I'll still learn things from you."

"I haven't read your file, so why don't you tell me a little about yourself?"

"I'm from Dunster; it's a small village in Somerset. My parents have a dairy farm. Not very big."

"But owning a farm is still hard work."

"We don't own it; we're tenant farmers, because the Luttrell family owns everything."

"What a big surprise."

"There's a castle overlooking the village, and the Luttrells have been there forever." She giggled, which surprised Caitrin.

"Ages ago, centuries, Sir Geoffrey Luttrell married a wealthy heiress named Frethesant Paynell. What a silly name."

"I wonder what Geoffrey called her when they were in bed? Frethers, darling?"

"Paysnie, old chum?"

Caitrin sat back and let the humor fade. "You understand, Grace, this could be dangerous, and I'm not a nursemaid."

Grace nodded in agreement.

"I want you to tell me about Billy the Brick."

Grace was puzzled. "I did tell you, at the range."

"No, you told me what happened. Now tell me, in your mind, who was Billy the Brick when he hugged you?"

There was a slight gasp and silence for a long moment.

"I, um . . . he was, James was . . ."

"I thought so." Caitrin saw the tears forming, leaned forward and held her hand. "You can stop if you want to."

But now she had started, Grace needed to finish. "We grew up together. James was my friend, and one day he became so violent—and he broke me. I'm not whole anymore."

Caitrin wiped away the girl's tears with a handkerchief and asked, "Did you tell anyone?"

Grace shook her head. "I was so ashamed, and my parents are very strict. I never told anyone, until today, with you."

Caitrin wanted to scream in outrage at the pain. *There are so many broken young women all alone with their tragic secrets.* "You're not alone. I know what it's like."

"The instant Billy the Brick grabbed me, he was James, only now I fought back because of what I've learned. I'm sorry I hurt him, I didn't mean to."

"Billy Donnelly has balls of steel. He'll survive. Might have a squeak in his voice for a bit."

"Hope so, the steel balls, I mean, not the squeak bit."

"And at least you know the training works."

"Now Billy knows too," Grace said and laughed a nervous, tension-lifting laugh.

Caitrin saw a hurt little girl, and saw herself. "When I was fifteen, I went away to service as a lowly scullery maid in a place in Somerset. The youngest son of the family was spoiled beyond belief and believed everything belonged to him, including the maids. Before I arrived there, he had already hurt a couple of them and gotten away with it."

"He hurt you too?"

"Me too."

"Oh, Caitrin, it's so unfair."

"I found an axe handle that made it a little more fair."

Grace's hand flew to her mouth. "You didn't?"

"I waited until dark, so there was no one around to be a witness, and I did. With all my might."

"Didn't you break his skull?"

"That's not where I hit him."

Grace's laugh was full-throated, her eyes wide. "What happened?"

"Let's just say that unlike Billy the Brick, he did not have balls of steel."

Grace clapped her hands in glee. "Yes!"

"You're wrong about one thing. You are whole; you are Grace Baker."

"Thank you," Grace said.

"I know about you, and now you know everything about me, so we can work together as equal partners. And you need to buy a pair of slacks before rationing starts."

16

Somewhere close, a bird sang its morning song, and Caitrin guessed it was a thrush. She lay still in her bed, listening, eyes closed, mostly asleep and reluctant to surface. *Hail to thee, blithe spirit!* Then she remembered Shelley had written about a lark, not a thrush. Perhaps it was a skylark she heard. *Thrush thou never wert.*

Max's face was fading away, no matter how hard she concentrated on keeping him after the explosion intruded. White haze and dread silence, the moans and cries of pain coming later. Fingers fumbling on her to remove the wedding ring, and a voice close. "I'll be having this, missy. Won't do you any good where you're going." Another voice from memory, rinsed clean of trauma, "Come on, Thatcher, coppers."

Her eyes flew open. She was awake. "It wasn't Badger! Thatcher! It was Thatcher!"

Police sergeant Angus Goodwillie agreed to meet Caitrin and Grace at the priory. A tall, well-built man, Angus was eggshell-bald, which was somewhat compensated by a prodigious orange mustache. He loved the police force and, although he had his personal doubts about women police constables, hoped one day Caitrin would return to the fold. Good female coppers were hard to find.

Caitrin and Grace led him past several instructors dressed as nuns shepherding unwed mothers and entered the chapel, where they could speak privately.

"We know of two Thatchers," he said. "Harvey and Donnie. Both are tea leafs. Donnie has aspirations to a higher calling, but doesn't have the necessary brains. Unfortunately for him, he's too stupid to know he's stupid."

"Can we find them?" Caitrin asked.

"Harvey's been in the clink for the last six months, so he's not your man. Donnie is mobbed up, or thinks he is, with the Finsbury Boys."

"How do we get to him?"

Angus exhaled a deep breath and looked copper-serious. "Caitrin, you were one of us. You know exactly what these people are like."

"I do. Violent, impulsive, and not very smart."

Angus glanced at Grace. He had a daughter her age. "In their world, women are either wives who stay at home to take care of them, or pushovers and prostitutes."

"We'll be all right," Caitrin said.

"You might be," Billy said and half-turned to Grace. "But this lass—"

"Gave Billy the Brick bruised balls and shoots better than I can."

Angus stiffened behind his mustache. An Outer Hebrides lad who had grown up in the Free Church, he still had difficulty with these modern young women being so blunt. "Have it your way, but don't say you weren't warned. You could try Soho. The Palm Beach Club, or maybe the Bridge and Billiards Club, but women aren't welcome there. There's Kid Lewis's

Fox's Club on Dean Street, but it's an ugly dive. On Saturday nights some of the Finsbury boys like going to the Phoenix Club on Little Denmark Street off Charing Cross Road."

"What does Donnie Thatcher look like?"

Angus took an envelope from his pocket, opened it, and slid a photograph across the table to Caitrin. "Not a good picture. Handsome chap, isn't he?"

Caitrin glanced at the poor-quality photograph of a middle-aged man with a comb-over and a straggly mustache. She handed it to Grace as Angus gave her Donnie's record. "I didn't see his face, but would recognize the voice."

"Two women going alone to a nightclub can be asking for trouble. If you're really determined, I can go with you."

"And have the club empty out?" Caitrin said. "Thanks, Angus, but you look like a copper from head to toe. We can take care ourselves."

"Are you quite sure? You could run into Albert Dimes, who doesn't give a damn who he cuts. Jack Spot or Billy Hill aren't any better, especially if they're boozing, and if it's not razors or knives, it's guns. They don't have rules, not even for women."

Caitrin patted his knee and grinned. "If I get into trouble, I'll blow my police whistle."

Angus shook his head. "The odds are your wedding ring is long gone."

"I know, but I have to find out." Caitrin said. "And Florence Simmonds?"

"I have heard nothing about her."

"Missing persons?"

"Every night there's a bombing and people die. Some we don't find for days. Thousands leave the city to escape the attacks, and London is nothing but missing persons."

"Teddy Baer's driver said Florence needed me."

"What else did he say?"

"Nothing. He drove off before I could reply."

"Name?"

"Ernie is all I've got."

"Can't help you there, unless you get me his surname." Angus stood and spread his hands. "Caitrin, these men are brutal. Ask the wrong questions of the wrong man and they won't worry if you're a woman."

"I know." Caitrin stood and embraced him, to his embarrassment. "Thank you, Angus."

"Teddy is the worst because he's intelligent."

"He confessed to me he did the double bank job on Carter Street last year."

"He did?"

"Theoretically, he said, but he did it."

"That's what I mean, intelligent. The others are obvious, and you'll see trouble coming. Not with him. I have to go. Nuns give me nightmares."

Grace was nervous, but tried not to show it as she walked with Caitrin down Little Denmark Street toward the Phoenix Club. At Caitrin's suggestion, she wore no perfume, was modestly dressed in slacks, and had an FN .25 Baby Browning semi-automatic pistol tucked away in her pocket. She glanced up at the night sky. "It's quiet. Maybe no Blitz tonight."

"At least not from the Luftwaffe," Caitrin said. "Let no one buy you a drink. We'll get our own, but don't touch it. Nervous?"

"I don't like these kind of places."

"Neither do I. If we get separated, keep an eye on me. I'll do the same with you. It's going to be a Saturday night grope and grind in there, and every man will have a half-dozen hands. Avoid what you can and keep moving. Don't hold eye contact or smile."

Grace shivered at the thought of being pawed. "How do we find Donnie Thatcher? The photograph didn't help."

"We'll let him find us. Do you want to be Pamela or Polly?"

"Pamela."

"You're now Pamela Partridge. I'm Polly Parker. Two Puh-Ps in a pod."

Inside, the club was what Caitrin expected. It was crowded, dark, with a rotating mirror ball shooting out short-lived light rays over a small dance floor, and it smelled of years of tobacco smoke, cheap perfume, and spilled drinks. In one corner, a three-piece band was insulting a piece of music; it might have been "Baby, It's Cold Outside," but only they knew, and everyone was talking at the same time. They found a tiny table in a corner away from the band, and a waitress with an un-blinking stare appeared as soon as they sat down.

"Yeah?"

"Whisky," Caitrin said. "With a dash of water. Two."

The waitress vanished before she finished ordering.

"I feel as though I'm being scoured by a hundred eyes," Grace said.

"Men hoping to get lucky are not subtle, especially in a dive like this," Caitrin said as she scanned the club. This was the first time she had been out since Max died, and it was all so medi-ocre, so damn dreary: the talent-deficient band, the sweaty-faced men with Brylcreemed hair, the women with too much paint on bad complexions, and their cheap, badly fitting clothes. There was so much posturing, and she knew it was the women who carried guns for the men, tucked away in their plastic handbags, just in case their heroes were stopped by the cop-pers. For all the tough gangster preening, these men still needed to be looked after by mummy. Across from them was a table of Americans officers, and Caitrin was struck again by how differ-ent they were from the English. They were bigger, had more teeth, white precise teeth, and certainly more money. They also had a bemused air, as though England was a dotty old aunt they were visiting.

The waitress returned and put down the drinks.

"I see the Finsbury boys are having a good time, as usual," Caitrin said to the waitress and watched her reaction as she snatched up the money and left. "They're at those tables near the band," Caitrin said. "The waitress glanced at them, but then stopped herself from replying."

"What do we do? We can't just go over there and ask if one of them is Donnie Thatcher."

"He's not there, and they'll come to us," Caitrin said, sat back, sipped her whisky, and sent a broad smile harpooning across the room.

A man in a suit with lapels the width of Spitfire wings got up from one of the Finsbury mob tables and approached them. He tilted forward as he walked, his hands, blunt and square, hanging loosely at his side. He stopped at their table, opened his arms wide, grinned to reveal a few gaps and a gold filling, and boomed, "Well, well, well, there you are, my lovely."

"Are you talking to me?" Caitrin said.

"No, I'm talking to my gorgeous wife here," the man said, leaning in toward Grace.

"I'm not your wife," Grace said.

"The night is still young, and many wonders await. I'm Big Ben, like the clock," he said, stretching out his arms like clock hands and jerking them to point out the hours. "And you are?"

"Pamela Partridge," Grace said.

Big Ben put out a hand and bowed. "May I have the honor of a dance, Pamela Partridge?"

Caitrin fought back a laugh at this ludicrous man. Grace glanced at her, and she nodded.

"Just one," Grace said.

He tugged her away from the table before she could react and plowed onto the dance floor. Caitrin watched them, Grace tiny in Big Ben's arms. They were talking to each other as they danced. Perhaps it wasn't such an ordeal for her and she could coax information out of him.

"Howdy, sweetheart," one of the American officers said as

he sat opposite her and blocked the view of the dance floor. He smiled his perfect American smile, and a sadness stabbed her heart at hearing his accent. *Max, oh my lovely Max.*

"Nice try, general, but you're not Clark Gable," she said, but not unkindly, and put a hand over her right eye. "And I'm no Veronica Lake."

"That would be Joel McCrea, not Gable."

"What?"

"*Sullivan's Travels.* Joel McCrea and Veronica Lake. Did you know Clark Gable wears dentures? That ladykiller grin of his is plastic and—"

He was talking to an empty chair. Big Ben and Grace had vanished from the dance floor. They had not gone through the front door, or Caitrin would have seen them leave. She raced across the club, through the kitchen, and out into an alley. In the shadows of a doorway Big Ben had Grace pressed face-first against a wall, right arm twisted behind her back as he growled, "Who did it, tell me!"

Caitrin pushed the muzzle of her Baby Browning pistol into the back of his neck. "Let her go, Big Ben, or you've chimed your last hour."

Big Ben released Grace, and she slipped away from him.

Caitrin pushed the muzzle harder to force him against the wall. "This is a small pistol, but it fires a bullet at nine hundred feet a second. That means it will be through your empty skull and halfway to Buckingham Palace before you hit the ground. Now, who did what?"

"She said she was a close friend of Donnie's. Lost touch with him, she said."

"What's wrong with her being Donnie's friend?"

"I never heard him mention a Pamela Partridge, and we've been close mates since we were kids. I know all his friends."

"Not all. Why don't we go talk to Donnie and sort it all out?"

"That would be difficult."

"Nothing's difficult when you're a finger tightening on the trigger away from the Pearly Gates."

"It's difficult because Donnie's dead. Somebody went and shot him."

"Who?"

"Don't know."

"How do you know he was shot?"

"It's what I heard, and that's all I'm saying."

"You can do better."

"Then it won't be you putting a bullet through my brain."

17

Caitrin listened, said yes, and hung up the telephone. To protect her anonymity, 512 had provided a room with a line that bypassed the priory switchboard. She sat across from Grace and poured them both tea.

"Everything, good or bad, begins and ends with tea," Grace said.

"No tea would mean no British Empire," Caitrin said. "Still no sugar, though."

"I'll survive."

Caitrin watched as she stirred her tea. *Survive, yes, but not without damage.*

Grace was small, nervous, her right wrist red with bruises and her cheek scratched. "It all happened so quickly. We were dancing, I asked about Donnie, said we were good friends, and the next thing I know I'm against a wall outside and he's shouting at me. What should I have done?"

"You were a little hasty asking for information. Then, as soon as he became aggressive, it should have been teeth and claws. Scream, gouge out an eye, fight with everything, every part of your body. If you had done that, I could have stopped him."

"I'm sorry."

"You did your best."

Grace gave her a brave smile. "We did discover Donnie Thatcher is dead."

"Supposedly."

"You think he's alive?"

"Big Ben was probably telling the truth."

"But we're no closer to finding your ring."

The telephone rang, Caitrin answered, listened and said, "I'll be there." She hung up and turned to Grace. "You should rest."

"No, I'm all right."

Caitrin sat beside her. "Your training here is not at all finished."

"I can learn from you."

"Not tonight.

Throughout London, the night streets were mostly deserted, apart from air-raid wardens, volunteers, and policemen, but this part of Whitechapel around the Blind Stag was devoid of all life. A cigarette glowed in the shadows near the front door of the pub as Caitrin approached. "Evening, Ernie," she called out.

The man who moved away from the shadows was not Ernie. He was taller, but much wider, with hair brushed back hard, thin lips, and a blank face. "I'm not Ernie."

"No, you are not. Which E would you be? Eric, Edmund—"

"Samuel."

"Teddy skipped down the alphabet."

"What?"

"What happened to Ernie?"

"Who's he?" Samuel stepped in front of her as she moved toward the front door and asked, "And who are you?"

She fought back a sarcastic reply. Samuel did not look like a man who would understand if she confessed to being Queen Victoria. "I am Caitrin Colline, here to see Teddy."

He edged aside, and she entered the pub, to find Teddy was being his most melodramatic self. It was dark inside except for a half-dozen candelabras. She could only imagine where he found so many candles. A gramophone somewhere was playing a barely audible record, something choral.

"Good evening, Caitrin," Teddy said, appearing from the dark background. He wore an ornate smoking jacket in which anyone else would have looked ridiculous, but not Teddy.

"Teddy, or is it Basil Rathbone?"

"Come sit down," he gestured to a table on which sat a bottle of whisky, a carafe of water, and two glasses. "Bell's whisky. I'm told it's what the Scots prefer to drink while they ship the fancy rubbish to us."

He poured the whisky and slid the carafe toward her. She added a dash of water.

"To peace and honesty," Teddy raised his glass in a toast.

Caitrin lifted her glass. "To peace and honesty. Whatever they might be."

Teddy sat back with a satisfied expression, and she wondered if he practiced smiling in a mirror as he went about constructing the future landed gentry Teddy Baer. "Thank you for coming," he said.

"Your telephone message, delivered by a little boy who was probably missing his front teeth, was enigmatic, so how could I possibly refuse?"

"You look to me like a woman with a lot of questions."

"I have a few. Where's Ernie, for one?"

"Gone his own way," he said and waited.

"And—"

"And I have a surprise for you," he interrupted. "Put your hand, your left hand, on the table and close your eyes."

She hesitated.

"I won't hurt you. Promise."

Caitrin closed her eyes and stretched out her left hand. Before she could touch the table top, Teddy slid his left hand under hers and sandwiched it with his right. He pressed his hands together for a moment and pulled them apart. Caitrin opened her eyes. The wedding ring was on her finger.

"Two hearts, one journey," Teddy said. "I won't attempt the Welsh version."

Caitrin stared at the ring, then slipped it off her finger to read the inscription. "How did . . . ?"

He put a finger to his lips.

"Did you kill Donnie Thatcher?"

"Who's he?"

"The man who stole the ring."

"I thought someone called Badger stole it."

"I got the name wrong."

"I never heard of him."

"So, how did — ?"

"Caitrin, there is no honor among thieves, but there is an excellent communications network. I asked around, made a serious offer, and there you are, I found the ring."

"Thank you. What do I owe you?"

"Nothing."

"Nothing is ever free; there's always a price tag, and when it comes due, one way or another, you have to pay up. Remember saying that?"

He laughed. "I do, but you don't have to pay anything right now. No, I tell a lie; there is something. We're alike, both in background and ambition. But there's one problem."

"What's that?"

"I asked around and found the ring; that was easy enough.

But when I asked about you, I got nothing. Not a single dickie bird, apart from a few vague remarks. Which is very strange. Why is that?"

"I didn't work in London."

"Where?"

"Cardiff, Swansea, Bristol," she said, annoyed with herself at not giving Angus Goodwillie an acceptable background story to disseminate. She should never have left him to do the work.

"That's small stuff."

"We all start small, and I have ambitions. That's why I'm here now, and women tend to be invisible to most men."

"Not to me."

"You're different," she said, well aware it would please his ego.

"What's your interest in me?"

"An ambitious girl needs a friend in the big city."

"I'm not the friend kind, and you're not a girl."

"A partner, then."

Teddy shrugged and said nothing.

"What's your interest in me?"

He stared at her over the rim of his glass. There was an immense, seductive strength behind those eyes. She had once read that when an animal is caught by a predator, after the initial pain, there is a brief moment of ecstasy as it surrenders its life. She forced herself not to look away, not to surrender. The gramophone record ended, and the needle skipped and crackled. He rose, lifted the needle from its groove, and returned. They faced each other through a marble-dense silence.

"You found the ring," she said to break the moment.

"I did."

"Could you find Florence?"

"That's different." His voice hardened as he vanished inside himself. He swallowed his whisky and poured another one without refilling hers. The meeting was over. "Maybe I'll ask around."

Caitrin stood, thanked him again, and left. Teddy was lying. She was certain he had killed Donnie Thatcher or had someone do it, but why? And the chances of finding Florence now seemed slim. But as far as she was concerned, Florence Simmonds was alive, until proved otherwise.

18

Bethany Goodman hurried into the office, slid behind her desk, and waved an apologetic hand to a waiting Caitrin. "So sorry I'm late."

"Hardly late. A few minutes."

"Do you mind waiting for tea until the others arrive?"

"Others?"

In answer, Bethany allowed herself a satisfied smile.

"Is that a beatific mother superior smile I see, or just a smug one?"

"A bit of both," Bethany said, her smile flourishing into a grin as she leaned forward and stage-whispered, "We're saved."

"As in, hallelujah, we're all going to heaven, or . . . ?"

"As in 512 is saved, almost."

"I would say beatifically smug, then."

"Yes, but before I divulge more, I want to hear about your private odyssey."

Caitrin held up her hand to show the wedding ring.

"Congratulations and well done. That didn't take long. I was worried it might have disappeared forever. How did you find it?"

"Would you mind if we talk about it later?" Caitrin said, without knowing quite why, but for some reason not yet clear, she wanted to keep her dealings with Teddy Baer secret. There was so much unanswered, and she sensed so much more to come.

"As you wish," Bethany said. "I know better than to force you." Which was true. She had long since learned that Caitrin, while never insubordinate, had little regard for rank or position. She spoke if she wanted to, stayed quiet if she didn't, and, in doing so, had frequently bewildered Winston Churchill. Since the Café de Paris bombing and Max's death, Caitrin had become even more blunt.

"Thank you."

"I assume this success means you have now returned to us."

"Yes."

"Good to have you back on board. How did our Grace Baker fare?"

"She tried hard."

"Should that be considered as faint praise?"

"No, she will be a good one."

"In time?"

"She's young."

"Only five years younger than you."

"Young in time, not years."

That was true enough. Max's death had aged Caitrin. This damn war was aging everyone—those it didn't kill.

"Who are the others we're waiting for?" Caitrin asked.

Bethany put up a hand to pause the conversation, opened a desk drawer, took out a cigar box, and placed it in front of Caitrin. "Winston gave me this, La Aroma de Cuba, although I'm told he prefers Romeo y Julieta. Imagine, our romantic little PM."

"He gave you cigars?"

"No." As she reached to open the lid, the telephone rang.

She answered and said, "Send them in, please. And some tea, for four."

She hung up the phone. "Our visitors are here."

Caitrin gestured to the mother superior habit hanging up behind the office door. "Shouldn't you be in costume?"

"And you with a cushion shoved up your jumper? No, not for these visitors."

Bethany came from behind the desk as the door opened and Brigadier Sir Alasdair Gryffe-Reynolds entered. With him was Lord Hector. Hecky.

"Brigadier, Lord Hector, good morning," Bethany said.

"Mrs. Goodman," Gryffe-Reynolds replied.

"Hector, please," Hector said and winked at Caitrin. "Or Hecky."

"Hecky, what a lovely surprise. How are you?" Caitrin said.

"Well, Cat, and you?"

She saw the sympathy in his eyes and didn't want it. There was no place or time for pity in her life. No time to slow down for reflection or remembrances; that would come later, if ever. They could all be dead tomorrow, and nothing would matter. "I am all right."

"Sit, please, everyone, sit down," Bethany said as a secretary arrived with the tea tray.

They sat around the desk and performed the inevitable tea ritual, with Bethany playing mum. Once spoons finished rattling on china and exploratory sips were taken, she began a curated speech, while Caitrin wondered what was in the cigar box.

"Winston wants to shutter 512 or merge us with a larger organization. After our success at rounding up Nazi spies and saboteurs, he insisted we had worked ourselves out of a job," she said, paused, and nudged the cigar box. "Or so he believed."

"Oh, please," Caitrin could control her curiosity no longer. "What the hell's in the box?"

Bethany flipped open the cigar box and emptied its contents onto the desk. There were a dozen small pieces of metal, most of which appeared to be twisted or broken, and all were burnt.

Caitrin inspected them. "I thought La Aroma de Cuba would be more exotic. What are they?"

"We don't know exactly, but we do know by the stampings that they are German, although more intriguing is where they were all found." She opened a folder and read aloud: "They were discovered when several Wren churches were bombed, including St. Andrew-by-the-Wardrobe, St. Bride's, St. Lawrence Jewry, Christ Church Greyfriars, St. Dunstan-in-the-East, then the London Guildhall, Buckingham Palace, St. Paul's, and finally and somewhat incongruously, the Café de Paris."

Café de Paris. Caitrin heard Max's voice. *This is a very exclusive place. It's a replica of the Palm Court on the* Lusitania.

"I heard it was the *Titanic,*" Caitrin said.

"What?" Bethany said.

"Sorry, I lost my train of thought." And Max was gone.

Hector touched her arm. "Are you all right?"

"Yes, yes."

Bethany continued. "We investigated the air-raid logs on the nights these places were struck, and one remark kept turning up. Reports said there was an air raid, and then a single aircraft flew directly over the location and bombed with great accuracy."

Caitrin poked the metal pieces with a pencil. "What's the connection?"

Gryffe-Reynolds pulled a folder from his briefcase. "The Germans have X-Gerät, a radio navigation beam system that guides them over a city. That is all it can do. It is not precise enough to identify individual targets."

"But something did identify them, and those bits of metal were part of it," Bethany said. "We believe someone is planting homing beacons on chosen targets as a terror weapon."

"I understand targeting Buckingham Palace, but why the churches?"

"I am guessing it's an attempt to damage morale by attacking our heritage," Gryffe-Reynolds said.

"And why the Café de Paris?"

Her question triggered an awkward silence.

Bethany broke it. "You were there that night; perhaps you might remember things, or people. I'm shortly to get a guest list. I'd like you to go through it and see what you can unearth."

No, I don't want to do that. I don't ever want to go back in there. "If it will help. You were there too, Hecky."

"Yes, but I was a little tipsy, and I don't have your keen memory."

"Are you quite sure there were homing beacons?" Caitrin picked up one of the pieces. "A single aircraft could just be a lost pilot, and this might belong to anything."

"But it doesn't; it belongs with these," Hector said, opened his case, brought out an envelope and spread its contents on the table. They were clean, undamaged copies of the broken pieces.

"Where did you get them?"

A look passed between Hector and Gryffe-Reynolds, and both women caught it.

"Instead of closing us down, Churchill wants 512 to work with SOE because you have expertise in sabotage in enemy country. He wants it; I don't, not for a minute," Bethany said, her irritation growing. "Are you going to keep secrets tucked inside your old-boy organization, again, or are we going to be truly equal partners?"

"My apologies," Gryffe-Reynolds said, surprised at her candor. "Old habits die hard."

"Those habits almost killed Caitrin. Old boys, old habits, old dogs, and new tricks. How do we know it will be different this time?"

"You have my word—"

"As a gentleman?" Caitrin said.

"Yes, naturally, and I have strict orders."

"I don't believe you. You'll have to show me."

"We found out about them by accident," Hector said to deflect attention away from a ruffled Gryffe-Reynolds. "I was training a new group of scallywags."

"Scallywags are small groups of men who will form a resistance if the Germans invade. There are hidden bases and arms caches all over the southern counties," Gryffe-Reynolds explained, and Bethany was polite enough to look as though she didn't know.

"It was a night exercise," Hector continued. "We were on the Sennen Cove beach in Cornwall, at the far end, away from the lifeboat slip. It was pitch-black, no moon, and one of my men spotted a shape in the water. It was a body. We found two more and a capsized boat. They must have landed from a submarine. Next to the boat were several waterproof boxes, and inside were devices to which those parts belong."

"Homing beacons?" Caitrin said.

"We think so."

"Think?"

"They are not complete, so we don't know exactly how they work. Perhaps there were other boxes that got washed away," Hector said.

"There was one other thing," Gryffe-Reynolds said. "The men wore money belts, which is probably why they drowned. The belts were loaded with British gold sovereigns. Rather heavy for a swim."

"What concerns us is that there might well have been other, successful landings we don't know about," Hector said, "and the saboteurs who placed the beacons in London are still unknown and at large."

"Which means 512 has work to do," Bethany said and turned

to Caitrin. "And so, Caitrin, it appears that you and Lord Hector temporarily will be back in harness again."

"We'll see about that."

Hector diplomatically said nothing. In the previous year, together they had saved the Crown Jewels from the Nazis, but he and Churchill withheld vital information because Caitrin was a woman and thought not capable of doing a man's job. Their deceit had only made the task harder and more dangerous for her.

"Would you take Lord Hector for a stroll around our splendid grounds," Bethany said, "while the brigadier and I define a few rules for future cooperation?"

They slipped out of a servants' entrance at the back of the building so no one needed to hurriedly become a nun or an unwed mum. Caitrin led Hector to a pond in the middle of a woods. Spring had freshened the landscape, foxgloves stood sentinel in a mist of bluebells, and birds were practicing for the warm months ahead. She came here often after Max's death, always alone, until today.

They sat on a bench and gazed out over the water. A heron, offended by their presence, unfolded its articulated length, stretched, and shifted to the other side of the pond. Ducks bickered near them, and at their feet something, probably a frog, plopped beneath the surface for safety.

"Ducks," Caitrin said, staring at the pond.

"Ducks?"

"Ducks. I used to think there had to be a god because who would ever knowingly design a duck?"

"He makes wondrous things. All things bright and beautiful, all creatures great and small."

"I don't think there is a god anymore. Ducks just are. We just are."

Silence settled between them.

"I'm sorry, Cat. I can't imagine the hurt." He reached for her hand, but she pulled away.

She nodded, her jaw tightening.

"I was away on some silly training exercise for weeks in the wilds of Scotland before I heard about the bombing. I would have been there for you, you do know that."

She avoided answering. "How is your mother?"

"She is well, and asks about you constantly."

Caitrin had met Hector's mother while on their mission to save the Crown Jewels; they liked each other, and she had promised to return once the war was over. It seemed unlikely now, and so long ago.

"Do you know what bothers me?" he said.

"I know it's not duck design," she said, and her mouth softened.

"No," he said. "The Blitz is lessening, and how we endured months of bombing is beyond me. I suppose you just have to carry on, don't you?"

"Or go mad. Keep buggering on, Winston says."

"I got used to the nightly raids, assuming the odds were they would hit the other chap, not me. And I can accept some Nazi idiot pulling a lever and haphazardly spilling bombs across London. But it's chilling to imagine a Luftwaffe bomb-aimer deliberately chalking my name on a bomb the way our men do when they write 'Cheerio, Adolf' on theirs."

"It would have to be a bloody big bomb for him to write Lord Marlton Hector Neville-Percy, also referred to in certain quarters as Bobby."

"Jest away you may, young lady, but it's an uncomfortable feeling to think someone over there might be waking up this morning with bad intentions aimed at me."

"You're not important enough to warrant your own bomb, Hecky, but just in case Göring's upset at you, we'll have to stop him, won't we?"

"How?"

"I'm going to start with the casualty list from the Café de Paris and see if there's something to learn. You?"

"As Bethany said, you and I are in harness again, which means we should do it as a team."

"Which means you don't have a clue what to do next."

"You could say that. For the time being. But together—"

Caitrin took his hand. "It's good to see you again, Hecky."

"It's good to see you, Cat. All things wise and wonderful, the Lord God made them all."

"All except the ducks."

19

Bethany gave them a room high in a tower at one end of the priory to use as an operations center. There they would be isolated from 512's daily routine, although Caitrin insisted that, to fit in, Hector should wear a cassock and have his splendid blond hair shaved into a monk's tonsure. Bethany listened to his horrified protests, pretended to give the matter serious thought, and decided a clerical collar would suffice, to be worn only if he were out in public with any of 512's operatives. His scalp could remain unshorn, for now. However, to maintain the subterfuge of a church-run home for unwed mothers, she did ban all military uniforms, which Brigadier Gryffe-Reynolds was relieved to hear. He had no intention of wearing civilian clothes, which meant he would not have to visit a place infested with brash, intelligent women who had not the slightest respect for his rank or upbringing. He secretly believed they were all mad suffragette socialists.

Grace Baker came to work for them, after her training exercises were done, and proved to be a terrier at unearthing information.

Caitrin and Grace sat at a long table in the middle of the room, while Hector, adjudged to have the best handwriting, was given command of a blackboard set up against a wall. He began with a simple heading: WHAT DO WE KNOW?

"First," he said, "the Blitz reached its peak in the middle of April and, apart from a day or two this month, has been steadily decreasing since. At least in London." He wrote: BLITZ DECREASING.

"That's good for London, but poor old Liverpool's getting walloped."

"Second, solo German bombers are now being directed to particular targets by homing beacons. He wrote: SOLO BOMBERS/HOMING BEACONS.

"Supposedly, likely," Caitrin said. "We don't have definite, concrete proof."

"Let's say the preponderance of evidence points that way."

"Agreed. And you think this targeted bombing will replace the Blitz?" Caitrin asked.

"Probably. Indiscriminate bombing can seem anonymous to the country at large, but striking well-known and well-loved targets is a different matter. It becomes more personal."

"It's also a more effective use of their aircraft because they don't have to mindlessly scatter bombs all over the place," Grace said. "It's a fright weapon."

"Exactly. Third, German saboteurs are working in this country to set beacons, and more will be coming. That's what we do know," Hector said and with a flourish wrote: WHAT DO WE DO?

"What do we do?" Grace read aloud each word as he wrote.

"Two things," Caitrin said. "Work out why they chose their original targets and try to guess their future ones."

"I have no idea why they bombed the first ones, but for the future targets I'm guessing the Tate Gallery, Westminster Abbey, and the Tower of London," Grace said, and Hector scribbled them on the board.

"The Bank of England is also a tempting target, but if I were a Nazi and wanted to make a statement, I'd strike the Houses of Parliament," Caitrin said, and Hector added that to the list. "We should have them post sentries and sweep the buildings daily for devices. Now, why did they choose their first targets?"

"Gryffe-Reynolds was right when he said they were attacking our heritage. Hitting Buckingham Palace could have been a disaster if they had killed the Royal Family."

"And the Café de Paris?" Grace said. "Why did they decide to bomb that? Was it a mistake?"

"We found part of a beacon there," Hector said. "It was no mistake."

Silence thickened in the room. A woman laughed some distance away, and a crow rattled by a window.

Hector put down the chalk, sat opposite Caitrin, and murmured, "This is the moment where you have to go back, Cat. You have to go back into your memory and try to find the reason."

"Not into my memory," Caitrin stared past him. "I have to go back to the Café de Paris."

"When?"

"Now."

Harvey Coggins, a fussy man clutching a clipboard and oblivious of the irritating effect he had on people, pushed the key into the lock of the Café de Paris front door. Caitrin heard only the sound of metal on metal as he turned the key. There was no other sound like it in the world. Hector folded his hand around hers as Harvey opened the door.

"Watch your step. There's no lighting, and it hasn't been cleaned up at all," Harvey said and led them to the stairs. "Just the personal things, and the victims, of course. The incident hasn't been mentioned officially yet, to prevent the Germans from learning about the effect of their bombs."

The grand staircase, covered in gray dust, split and curved left and right past one floor, then dropped through the darkness to the bandstand and the oval dance floor. The bomb blast had demolished the left staircase from the balcony to the floor, shattered mirrors, and stripped away all ceiling decorations. Daylight seeped in from a hole in the roof, and to Caitrin, the air smelled of a cold silence. Lives had ended violently here. Things had stopped. They reached the dance floor, a confused mass of broken furniture in the gloom. Sheet music lay scattered in a corner, and next to a comically bent trombone, glass shards caught edges of light.

"Thirty-four killed, including the owner, Mr. Poulsen, Snake Hips Johnson, decapitated, and Dave Williams, a Trinidadian saxophonist, who was cut clean in half," Harvey said, reading from his clipboard. Caitrin tightened her grip on Hector's hand, and Grace moved closer. "But the Café cabaret dancers, all ten of them, survived because they were waiting behind the stage to go on."

"This is a very exclusive place," Max said.

"It was, until the war," Caitrin said, and added, "Now they let anyone in. The hoi polloi, the low polloi—and, horrors, even Americans."

Max ignored her teasing. "It's a replica of the Palm Court on the Lusitania. *"*

"I heard it was the Titanic, *" Caitrin said, with an arched, disbelieving eyebrow. "Let's hope the Café de Paris is more unsinkable."*

Harvey Coggins waved vaguely across the room and said, "Albert Weaver, he's the manager of the Mapleton Hotel across the street, came right over to the café as soon as he heard the bomb blast. He and his staff helped the injured. It was terrible;

all those poor people dressed up for a night on the town. Some didn't have a mark on them and were still sitting at the tables as though nothing was wrong. The blast done them in."

"*I was hoping for a different table, quieter, because I wanted to talk to you,*" Max said.

"*You are handsome, and I love you, Max.*"

Max deflated in relief. "*Thank God. I love you, Caitrin.*"

"*If you hadn't proposed, I was going to,*" Caitrin leaned forward and kissed him. "*I even come with a wedding ring, see?*" She held up her hand to show him her mother's ring. "*Made of Welsh gold from the Gwynfynydd mine, near Dolgellau, your grandad's birthplace. Dwy galon, un daith. Two hearts, one journey.*"

And at her feet was the table, what remained of it, where Max had died and her wedding ring was stolen.

"Some had their fancy clothes stripped off them by the blast. Completely naked, they were," Harvey coughed and said, "Others were slashed to pieces by flying glass. The firemen and the police came as soon as they—"

"Please stop talking," Caitrin said, silencing him as she ripped the clipboard from his hands.

"Cat," Hector whispered. "Are you all right?"

She turned to face him. Hector was there; they were both there at that table with Max. *My Max, lying in a distant graveyard.* "No."

She lay in bed, the room dark and quiet, her eyes closed. A white flash—Max's face—blue, vivid, painful—a pressure on her chest, like a boa constrictor, tightening every time she breathed out—a singing hiss—numbness—a voice as someone took her hand, "I'll be having this, missy. Won't do you any good where you're going." Another voice, "Come on, Thatcher, coppers."—silence—moans—a scream—blackness.

A ringing telephone pulled Caitrin from her nightmares. Asleep more than awake, she stumbled across her darkened bedroom to answer.

"Cat, it's Hector."

"What time is it?"

"Five. I'm sorry to call you so early. Last night was the biggest air raid of the war on London. You and Grace guessed correctly. Westminster Abbey and the Houses of Parliament were struck. The Commons Chamber was destroyed, just walls left standing. We have to find the men planting the homing beacons, Cat. And soon."

20

Grace was clutching a thick folder as she rushed into the tower room, the impetus of her entrance settling around her as she sat and said, "Sorry, I'm late. I just put this together."

She flicked open the folder and slid documents across the table to Caitrin and Hector. "The top page is a list of people who made definite bookings that evening at the Café de Paris. Oh."

"Oh, what?" Caitrin said, looking up, "And why do you look so horrified?"

"That was unthinking of me. I should have left that bit for later. I don't want to upset you, after our visit there."

"It's all right."

Hector rested his hand on Caitrin's. "Is it? Are you really all right?"

"Right enough." Caitrin nodded and fought back a tear. Max Evarts, third name on the list. "I am fine, and thank you both for being so caring. Go on, Grace."

"The list is of people who booked a table, but it does not include anyone who just dropped in for a drink."

"Like me," Hector said.

"Yes, and that night there were a lot of people like you."

"There's no one like Hecky," Caitrin said.

"Should I consider myself complimented or insulted?"

"I don't know, what do you think?" Caitrin flashed him an impudent look.

"Good to have you back, Cat."

"Thank you." She scanned the names on the first page. "I see no one here who might warrant their own bomb." She turned the page and read the next heading. "The London Season?"

Grace failed to hide a proud grin. "I have learned so much. The London Season began in 1780 when the upper classes returned to London from the country at the end of the hunting season."

"To the great relief of the deer and bunny rabbits. Did you do that sort of thing, Hecky?"

"No."

"In 1788, King George III held a grand ball to raise money for a new maternity hospital and named it after his wife, Queen Charlotte. Now it's become the highlight of the Season."

"How frightfully smashing. Absolutely ripping," Caitrin said to Hector, eyebrows arched and fingertips tapping together in faint applause.

"Your Karl Marx memorial flat cap is on too tight," he replied.

"Debutantes were launched into society," Grace continued bravely on. "And after the event at the Grosvenor House Hotel, they and their delights, as the accompanying gentlemen are called, intended to go to the Café de Paris, but they obviously did not."

Caitrin read the list of debutantes and their escorts. "Hector, is there anyone on this list worth bombing? As far as I'm concerned, they all are, but is there anyone worthy of a custom Nazi attack?"

Hector ran a finger down the list of names. "I see no one of any great value to the Germans."

"For once we're on the same side as Adolf."

"Cat, stop it. It's not my fault you spent the first ten years of your life chained to your pick, digging coal underground."

Grace was shocked. "You did?"

"No, but Lord Hecky and his debs wouldn't mind if I had. Someone has to work to pay for Hecky's fancy balls."

"Do you two always do this?"

"Do what?"

"Constantly bicker like a long-married couple."

There was silence, as Caitrin and Hector waited for the other to speak first.

"Do you?" Grace said.

Caitrin shrugged. "I don't, he does."

"Cat."

"Hecky."

"You do." Grace moved the conversation on to safer ground. "So, it seems we have no idea why a homing beacon was placed in the Café de Paris?"

"None," Hector said.

"How do we know there actually was a beacon?" Caitrin asked.

"Air-raid wardens mentioned a single bomber overhead, and"—Hector took a piece of metal from his pocket and sent it rattling across the table—"one of them found this on the pavement outside the café. It matches with photographs of the other pieces we sent to the emergency services."

Caitrin picked up the piece and rotated it for close inspection. "It's different from the other pieces. A bit bigger."

"But it's not big enough to tell us how the beacon works."

"The guards and security we suggested placing at the Houses of Parliament might have seen something."

"Um, it was in the works."

"As in, there were no guards?"

"None."

Caitrin sighed with frustration.

Grace said, "Perhaps, instead of one important person, they intended to obliterate all the debs and their escorts. To curdle the cream of society and demonstrate that no one is safe. That would be a shocker."

"Which would assume the Germans had good enough intelligence to know the debs were going to the café after Queen Charlotte's Ball. In that case, their aim was perfect; just the timing was off."

"I don't think that was the reason, and no, I don't have a better answer," Caitrin said. "But I do know Winston was wrong. The saboteurs have not all been captured, which means that, far from closing down, 512 has a monumental task ahead to find them."

The telephone was ringing when Caitrin entered her room, and it would not be ignored. She kicked off her shoes, sank into a sofa, and picked up the receiver to hear an unexpected voice: Teddy Baer.

"Caitrin."

"Hello, Teddy. What a surprise."

"Can you drive?"

"This is new—personally calling me instead of using one of your street urchin messengers."

"Can you drive?"

"Yes, can you?"

"No, and that's why I'm calling. I need a favor."

"Teddy, I am so busy, and so very tired."

"It's important. I wouldn't ask you otherwise."

"What's important?" Caitrin asked. He was a smart one, was

Teddy Baer, not asking for a specific reward after finding her wedding ring. She wondered how many more favors would be called in before he considered her debt was paid.

"I have to meet the Right Honorable Rupert Horatio Ramilton at his country estate, Ramilton Woods. It's two hours south of London, and I need a driver."

"What's wrong with Large Eric driving you, or whatever troglodyte is currently guarding the Blind Stag front door?"

"They'd get lost six feet outside Whitechapel, and having a geezer like that drive me would send the wrong message."

"And what exactly would that message be?"

"The right message is about being taken seriously."

"You, or me?"

"Me, because of you."

"I'm lost."

"I need someone as smart as me and a bit more polished. Good to look at don't hurt neither. That would be you."

"Is that a compliment? I'm not quite sure."

"Will you come? It's—"

"Important."

"Very. He's a toff, and his wife spends her life running around to hospitals showering her grace and charity on everyone. How else can she find virtue? We drive down Saturday afternoon and return Sunday evening."

Caitrin sighed and closed her eyes. Men, so predictable. There was a dread fascination to Teddy Baer. He was a singular character who, like her, had risen from his background, although by taking a different path. She was disappointed in him being so obvious. "Stay the night? I thought we agreed a while ago I wasn't the fur coat and no knickers type?"

"This is all strictly business. I'm not going to get clever with you. Honest."

"Honest, Teddy? Can we not use that word anymore. Coming from either one of us it seems—dishonest."

Teddy laughed, and he sounded like a little boy: such a complex yet often curiously open man. He said, "I heard about you flattening a copper in Bristol."

"What about it?" Teddy was suspicious of the "criminal" record she and Sergeant Goodwillie had created for her, so they had added more fictitious details. It was a surprise Teddy had learned about it so quickly, though, which meant Goodwillie would need to tighten his security.

"Not something you hear about everyday."

"Not something I do everyday."

"Why'd you do it?"

"Let's just say the long arm of the law was a bit too long and adventurous, and as we just discussed, I'm not that kind of girl."

He laughed again. "Bring something posh to wear for dinner and sensible schmatte for Sunday morning, so we can walk the estate."

"Don't say schmatte there, Teddy, it makes you sound like a Whitechapel Jew."

"As if it ain't apparent. Be at my place about one. Better yet, give me your address, and I'll have the car delivered there."

"It's—" Caitrin caught herself. What a crafty man. He had no idea where she lived, and it was going to stay that way. "No need. I'll be at the Blind Stag at one."

"A question before I ring off. Do you know how to use all them knives and forks and glasses at dinner? In the right order, I mean?"

There was his appealing vulnerability, exposed: Daniel Teddy Baer, working-class Whitechapel Jew, trudging his way through life by making it all up as he went along. He was a crook, but she could not help but respect him, and also wonder a little about herself and why she was interacting with him. Perhaps she enjoyed dancing on the razor's edge more than was wise.

"Yes, I do. I'll place my index finger on the appropriate one so it doesn't look as though you're copying me. See you at one."

"Yes, cheerio."

"Cheerio."

21

Teddy's car was parked outside the Blind Stag: a gleaming, two-tone green Daimler DB18 with a sweeping, Hooper-designed Empress body. It was an alien spaceship in a demolished landscape. There were two small flags fixed above the windscreen: one was Swedish; the other, with an elaborate coat of arms, Caitrin did not recognize.

Teddy, hair Brylcreemed into submission, and neatly dressed in a dark gray lounge suit and a white shirt with an unfortunate tie, stood next to the car, waiting for her as she stepped out of a taxi.

"Hello, Teddy. Imagine seeing you outside in daylight."

"Think I'm a Jewish Dracula, sucking the blood out of defenseless Christian babies?" Teddy said. "That's what we Jews were supposed to do."

"I wouldn't know, and there's not much blood in a baby, so it seems like a lot of hard work for such little return," she said and pointed to the car. "What are the flags for?"

"The blue and yellow one is Swedish."

"And the other?"

"Transylvania."

Caitrin laughed.

"Toffs had to hand their cars in because civilians ain't supposed to be driving, and they're all garaged or commandeered for the duration. This one belongs to the Swedish embassy."

"I won't ask how you got it."

"Innocence is bliss."

"Ignorance is better."

"Shall we go?"

Caitrin moved toward the back of the Daimler. Teddy stopped her. "Not in the boot. Put your bag in the back seat."

They put their bags in the back seat, Caitrin slid behind the wheel as Teddy sat next to her, she started the engine and pulled away.

Teddy unfolded a map. "Go across the Southwark Bridge, through the Elephant and Castle, Lambeth, Vauxhall, and Clapham. Take the Brighton Road south past a lot of places I've never heard of until you get to Chipstead Lane. Turn left, go past Mugswell, what a stupid name, and the estate is on the right. They said it takes about two hours." He folded the map. "You're a good driver."

"You're a good passenger, perhaps a bit nervous."

"I've never been driven by a woman before. Where'd you learn?"

With a gaggle of other women training to be secret operatives. Learned to kill too. "Helped the local doctor on his rounds," she lied. "He was old and a bit of a boozer."

The Daimler sped through the city streets and was soon into the countryside. Teddy was still nervous, and Caitrin guessed why. "Is this your first time out of London?"

"Second." He rattled his knuckles against the window and chuckled. "Didn't go very well the first time."

"Pray do tell."

"This stays between us?"

"Yes."

"It was years ago. The toffs have a thing called the Season."

"I know all about it. It's a load of balls," Caitrin said, and paused. "Dancing balls, in ballrooms."

"Right, and while they were all away swanning about in London, me and Billy Tricks and Eddie Long decided to burgle their fancy country houses."

"Good idea. Houses would be empty and all that lovely loot unguarded."

"The idea was all right; putting it into action was another thing all together. Instead of a car, Billy Tricks stole a BSA motorbike with a Colonial sidecar. It all started well enough, but soon went haywire. He didn't know how to drive it properly, and it broke down. We got lost and almost run over by a herd of cows. We finally broke into a fancy house and were chased out by the biggest butler I've ever seen in my life. He had a double-barreled shotgun in each hand."

Caitrin put a hand to her mouth to hold back laughter.

"It was like being in a foreign country out there. Nothing but trees and hedges and cows. We split up, and I got a lift back to London in a lorry taking pigs to Smithfield. I smelled terrible for weeks."

"Oh, Teddy." Caitrin burst into laughter. "That is so funny. You poor, city-dwelling man."

"Fields and fields and more bloody fields. I was as happy as a horse on a church roof. What the hell do people do out here?"

"Perhaps enjoy not being in the city?"

"That makes no damn sense. Hello, what's this then?"

Caitrin slowed as a policeman stepped into the road ahead and held up his hand.

Teddy sighed. "Coppers. I'll take care of this; you can chip in and translate."

Caitrin stopped and wound down her window as the policeman approached. "Good afternoon, Sergeant."

"Constable, madam. You do know that civilian cars are supposed to be off the road?"

"Yes, I do—"

Teddy interrupted with a torrent of some strange foreign language as he pointed ahead through the windscreen, up at the flags, and then at his watch. The policeman wilted under the onslaught.

"The Swedish ambassador, Jens Jensen, is explaining we have a very important meeting with the Right Honorable Rupert Horatio Ramilton on matters of state security," Caitrin said, and in a more serious tone added, "Our empire is in grave peril. There's not a moment to be lost. You do understand?"

The policeman straightened, took a step back, saluted, and said, "Yes, madam, I understand."

Caitrin waved, rolled up the window, and drove off. She turned a corner, and the policeman was gone.

"I had no idea you spoke Swedish," she said to a smug Teddy.

"Me neither. It was Yiddish with a funny accent. I guessed a country bumpkin copper wouldn't know the difference. You could have spoken Welsh. It's all about doing what's needed to survive."

"About now you should tell me why we're driving into deepest, darkest Surrey." She sensed Teddy withdrawing. "I'm as smart as you, remember? But I can't help if I don't know what's going on."

"I know," Teddy said. "I'm used to doing everything myself. Always have. Simple answer is, as you know, I want Ramilton Woods. I intend to have Ramilton Woods."

"And what does the Right Honorable Rupert Horatio Ramilton, current owner of said Ramilton Woods, have to say about that?"

Teddy had been staring through the windscreen. Now he turned to face her, and in his expression, she saw he was very driven. Shrewd and calculating Daniel Teddy Baer would never be at rest until he owned a place to be admired, a place in which he would be admired because he owned it. Until then he would never be more than a pushy Whitechapel slums Jew.

"The Right Honorable Rupert Horatio Ramilton is heavily in debt and doesn't know he's selling, yet."

"The toffs always are in debt," she said. "Avoiding paying the butcher and baker is part of who they are. We peasants should consider ourselves honored to be owed never-to-be-collected money by such gods."

"It's not just money."

"What?"

"I'll tell you later. You don't like the toffs any more than I do."

"Their time is over; the people deserve better."

Teddy shrugged. "When I take over Ramilton Woods, I'll be a different kind of toff."

"In your fevered dreams. So what are we going to do there? What's my job?"

"Keep the old mince pies open, search for weaknesses, and try not to look too intelligent."

"Rupert Horatio Ramilton wouldn't notice if I were a blazing genius because we are of different classes. In his world, I barely exist. But I'll watch, observe, and report."

"Good girl." Teddy's expression changed, the determination fading. "What do I call him? Lord?"

"What's his title?"

"He's a baron."

"A baron is the bottom rank of the peerage, life peerage, not hereditary, so call him Sir Rupert, not Lord. His wife is Lady Ramilton."

"How do you know all this?"

"Know thine enemy, Teddy, and I do know mine," Caitrin said as she slowed and turned left onto Chipstead Lane. They passed Mugswell village and a few miles farther on drove through the gates of the Ramilton Woods estate. The house, surrounded by beech trees, sat at the end of a long gravel drive. It was a seventeenth-century Jacobean, Dutch-gabled building with checkered brick walls and a Welsh slate roof. Standing at the front door waiting for them were Rupert Horatio Ramilton and his wife, Emma. Both were tall, slender, and elegant. They belonged there.

"Don't call me Teddy here. Daniel, please," Teddy said.

"Here we go, Daniel," Caitrin said as she stopped the car and switched off the engine. "Fix bayonets, over the top, and into battle."

22

All country homes smelled the same to Caitrin. With subtle permutations, they were infused with the scents of wood-smoke, damp, wet dogs, oil lamps, candles, cigars, and yesterday's spilled brandy. Ramilton Woods was no different. She had recently read that much of household dust was made from the shedding of human skin cells, which meant she was probably breathing in the residue of Rupert's great-grandmother. To Caitrin, no matter how large the rooms were, with their dark wood paneling, shabby furniture, and ancient oil paintings, they always felt claustrophobic. She wanted to fling open every door and window wide enough to banish the air of dead generations and let in the astringent present.

The dining room was darkened by blackout drapes covering the windows, and what light there was came from oil lamps in the corners, a wood fire, and a candelabra centered on the table. Rupert and Emma sat at either end of the table, and both had dressed for dinner. It was their unspoken way of pointing out that Teddy and Caitrin, sitting across from each other in the middle, did not belong there. If they had belonged, they too would have known to dress appropriately.

"That's a rather fetching frock you're wearing," Emma said to Caitrin. "Are you one of those clever young things that can whip up a dress from scraps of nothing?"

Clever young things. Only the English could call someone clever and have it be a withering insult. Caitrin held back an angry reply and wondered how Emma Ramilton, with her sharp features and letterbox-shaped mouth, would react if she said the dress came from Rupert's mistress. Or, better yet, from Rupert's secret wardrobe. Instead, she thought of Teddy and his business with Rupert and sat behind a defensive smile. But she could not guarantee staying quiet all night.

"I do envy you so. I can't sew a stitch," Emma said. "I have no choice but to use a dressmaker."

"Pity that, you miss so much," Caitrin said. *And I doubt you ever pay them, you desiccated witch.*

"The war," Rupert said. "How is this silly war treating you?"

Caitrin rarely disliked someone on first sight, but she did Rupert. He was in his fifties, with the clean edges of a man who stayed in physical shape. She detested his aristocratic languor, the tilted chin and precise, clipped diction.

"I manage to survive," Teddy said.

"And you, Catherine?"

"Caitrin," she corrected his deliberate mistake. "The Germans haven't got me yet. I notice you're quite safe down here, though, aren't you? Well out of the firing line."

"It can be exciting at times. We get the occasional lost Heinkel jettisoning its load to terrify a cow or obliterate a rhubarb patch before racing off home." He picked up a bell and rang it.

A man in his sixties, who leaned a little to one side, appeared. "Sir."

"Rogers, tell Cook we're ready."

"Yes, sir."

"Rogers was my batman in the war, the last war. Got himself wounded on the Somme," Rupert said as Rogers trudged away. He was still in the room when Rupert added, "Not the brightest to be found, but a fine chap." He raised his voice. "I said you are a jolly fine chap, Rogers."

"Thank you, sir," Rogers said and left.

"He's a rather incompetent butler, but after he served his country so heroically, I couldn't very well let him starve, could I?"

"That's so very noble of you," Caitrin said.

"Nonsense," Rupert said, oblivious of Caitrin's sarcasm. "One has to be charitable to the less fortunate. His son Kevin works for me too after Rogers's wife ran away with a merchant seaman."

"In the trenches, Rupert was so beloved by his men," Emma said.

"Daniel, do you know Oswald?" Rupert asked. "I suppose not. Different circles, really."

"Oswald?"

"Mosley, Oswald Mosley. He and I were at West Downs and Winchester together. He was an expert foil and saber fencer. I did my best, naturally. Do you fence?"

"I do," Teddy said and laughed. "But not that kind of fencing. Why do you ask if I know him?"

"I asked because I thought you might have been at the Battle of Cable Street."

"I was not."

"The Jew," Rupert said. "Oswald challenged the Jewish interests of this country, and charging into the heart of the Jewish community with his Black Shirts was, to say the least, ill-advised. He was concerned about the Jew commanding commerce, commanding the press, commanding the cinema, and dominating the City of London."

Caitrin saw Teddy's jaw tighten, and for the first time, she wondered if he was carrying a gun. She hoped not. The door opened, and Rogers appeared with dinner on a tray. A young man Caitrin assumed was his son Kevin followed him with several bottles of champagne.

Rupert continued as they were served. "Oswald was, and still is, a mesmerizing orator, and will be again once he gets out of prison. They put him and Diana, his wife, in Holloway. While he was right to mention the Jews, he was wrong to castigate them so publicly."

"But he was not the first," Caitrin said, feeling her temper rise. This pompous, parasitic man was irritating her.

"True," Rupert said, surprised at being interrupted. "Edward the First kicked them out in 1290—"

"Not before making them wear badges to be identified as Jews."

Rupert ignored her interruption. "And it took four hundred years before Oliver Cromwell brought them back."

"Only because he needed their money, not them."

Rupert shook his head as though to rid himself of this quarrelsome woman. "What Oswald got wrong and what needs to be said is the Hebrew race has always been inventive and entrepreneurial. Instead of turfing them out of England, it would behoove we white men to learn from them. What say you, Daniel?"

"I'd say," Teddy picked up his champagne glass, tasted it, and said, "It ain't a pint of wallop, but it'll do for now."

"I'm glad it meets your approval," Rupert said and raised his glass. "A toast to our ingenious Jews."

Caitrin noticed Teddy put the glass to his lips, but he did not drink as Rupert continued. "And also a toast to our resourceful white men, our Englishmen."

Senses dulled by too much champagne, and weary of Rupert's prating arrogance, Caitrin was relieved to get to her room. She undressed, put on a nightgown, and slipped into bed. The room was a black, featureless void. She got up, drew the black-out drapes, and opened the window, and a full moon printed crisp rectangles on the floor. She had just reached for the bed-clothes when a knock came at the door.

"Who is it?"

"It's Emma," Emma said from the hallway. "May we talk?"

"I'm really tired."

"Just for a moment, please."

"All right, come in."

The door opened, and Emma entered. She was wearing a floor-length, silk dressing gown and produced two glasses of champagne from behind her back. She offered one to Caitrin and shook her head. "Men, talking business. It's always so important to them and so frightfully dull to me."

Caitrin refused the champagne. Emma put down the glasses and pirouetted. "Do you like my gown? It's Japanese silk and hand-embroidered. Must have taken ages."

"Lovely, it suits you."

"I think it would look so much better on you." Emma un-tied the belt and, in a matador's sweep, took it from her shoul-ders and draped it around Caitrin. She stood naked, facing her. "It does look so much better on you."

"I—"

Emma held the belt and pulled Caitrin closer. "This won't be frightfully dull."

She released the belt, put a hand under Caitrin's chin, and tilted her head. Caitrin felt the close heat of Emma's naked body pressing against hers. There was a movement in the door-way as Rupert appeared. He too was wearing a dressing gown that was unbelted and open. He too was naked. Emma moved closer, her lips an inch from Caitrin's.

Caitrin raised her right hand and pressed it between Emma's breasts. She felt the woman's heart pulsing in her palm. "The only woman I would ever kiss would be my mam. Mum, mummy, mater."

She straightened her arm and drove Emma backwards to the door. Rupert watched, amused.

"Rupert, not fair. She doesn't want to play," Emma said, pouting.

"Then we will have to teach her," Rupert said, and grinned. "We haven't had a droit du seigneur for so long, an ius primae noctis."

He reached for Caitrin and winced in pain as she clamped onto his hand and bent it in. The pain drove him to his knees, and for an instant, a 512 unarmed combat rule flashed through Caitrin's mind: Never fight a big man in a small room. You might win, but he will do damage. It didn't matter to her, and she would gladly fight this awful man in a phone box. A kick to his ribs sent him tumbling back into the hallway, his dressing gown flying open. She pushed Emma out of the room and threw the dressing gown after her. "The little girl in the cheap frock's too rich for you."

Rupert's protective aristocratic façade reassembled as Emma helped him to his feet.

"Manners, Sir Rupert, do cover up your peanut," Caitrin said. She slammed the door shut, locked it, and moments later heard a tapping on a door farther down the hallway, and Emma whispering, "Daniel, may I come in?"

There was another sound, this coming from outside the building. She went to the window. Below her in the courtyard, Rogers and Kevin were removing boxes from the Daimler boot and carrying them into the house. Once the boot was empty, Rogers gently closed the lid and went away.

Caitrin slipped into bed, closed her eyes, and wished for sleep. But too much had happened, and it did not come right away.

23

They left early next morning, Caitrin glancing in the rearview mirror to see the Ramiltons standing in the exact spot where they had greeted them the previous day. They gave her a final desultory wave and turned toward the house. Teddy settled lower in the seat and closed his eyes.

"Are we done with Daniel, and can we go back to calling you Teddy now?"

He grunted.

"I don't know you well enough to interpret that sound," Caitrin said.

"Yes, I'm Teddy again, and I didn't sleep much last night."

"I wonder why?"

"Did they come to your room?"

"Yes, before they came to yours."

Teddy opened an eye and squinted at her. "And?"

"I threw them out."

"Both of them? Rupert's a big man."

"I was an angry woman." She felt no need to elaborate about

Rupert's rape attempt, nor to mention it had happened to her once before when she was a housemaid. That time she had not been successful in resisting. It was long ago, but always near.

"What happened?"

"Doesn't matter."

Teddy sat upright, his eyes blinking open. "It was a different story in my room. I discovered what people do in the country. Each other."

"I don't need the details."

"Why not? We've got two hours of nothing but fields and cows ahead."

"An abridged version, then."

"What does abridged mean?"

"It means short and devoid of lurid details."

"Lurid?"

"Lurid means: I did this and she did that until our eyes were watering, and so on and so on." A belated thought struck her. "Is that why you wanted me to come? To be a sacrificial popsy for the Ramiltons?"

"No. I had no idea what they would get up to."

"I should have known. Rupert's chum Oswald Mosley, the expert swordsman, married Lady Curzon and promptly embarked on an affair with her sister and then her mother."

"That's what I call marrying into the family."

"They're cut from the same cloth, both ignorant, self-entitled men who are a cancer on the country."

"I will admit that I, an East End barrer boy, thoroughly enjoyed ploughing into Lady Ramilton while her husband sat watching, hand wrapped around his nudger and giving it the old pedal and crank. Judging by her noise and thrashing about, she enjoyed it too."

"That was far too much detail."

"Fair enough."

"You handled Rupert's insulting behavior at dinner well."

"I don't mind him thinking he's smarter than me. Under-estimating is a weakness, and he's a weak man. I had his wife, and I'll have his home. There's more to life than knowing which fork to use."

"Which you also did well."

"Thanks to your help."

"Were your business dealings successful?"

"Yes."

"Yes?"

"Yes."

Teddy was obviously not about to volunteer any further in-formation. Caitrin turned right off Chipstead Lane and onto the main road to London. She shifted focus and asked, "What was in the boxes Rogers and son took out of the Daimler boot last night while you were laying waste to the English aristoc-racy?"

Teddy hid his surprise well. "General Civilian Anti-Gas Respirators. Mark 1."

She glanced at him. "Why?"

"It seems the villagers of Mugswell, Bagsby, and Ruthon are annoyed at the government for not looking after them as well as they do Londoners."

"They sound like a Dickensian firm of solicitors."

"They ignore the fact they're not getting bombed every night. Rupert heard their complaint and decided to play lord and master to the serfs. No doubt they'll be thankful for the masks and in gratitude give him a half-dozen virgins and their first rhubarb harvest."

He sank lower in the seat and closed his eyes again. "If you won't let me describe how I galloped a squealing Lady Ramil-ton over the jumps and around the bedroom, I'm going to catch up on my sleep. Wake me when we reach Clapham."

Caitrin was glad of the silence. Teddy was amusing to be with, but exhausting too.

"I have a question," he said.

"I thought you were sleeping."

"Just one before I go. Have you spoken to Florence?"

"No, have you?"

"No."

"She was living with you."

"She was, and then she was gone. Clapham, remember? Wake me up then."

The miles sped by in blessed silence until they reached the city. She nudged Teddy awake. "Clapham."

He yawned, sat upright, opened his map, and with relish read, "Clapham, Vauxhall, Lambeth, Elephant and Castle, and across the Southwark Bridge to home sweet home, and no more bloody fields and cows. Thank you, Caitrin."

"It has been an adventure."

"Where can I drop you off?"

"Drop me off? I'm driving."

Teddy bestowed upon her his best Sunday grin.

She stared at him in amazement. "You can drive?"

"Yes."

"Then why—?"

"You wouldn't have come with me otherwise, would you?"

Caitrin shook her head. "I'm speechless."

"Knowing you like I do, that won't last long." He patted her hand. "It's been an adventure."

24

Bethany Goodman arrived early in the tower room and had brought breakfast with her. The table was cleared of documents and replaced with chafing dishes, plates, glasses, cutlery, two sturdy teapots, and tea things. She did not have to wait long for the others.

"Do I really smell bacon? I do. Oh, I do, heaven," Grace said as she entered the room, followed by Caitrin and Hector. They sat at the table, wondering.

"We have a lot to talk about, so I thought starting the day with a good breakfast would help. Some of what I will tell you must remain secret, actually all of it, so it was best to avoid the canteen," Bethany said as she tapped a chafing dish and looked conspiratorially around. "I also broke a rationing law or two. Eat, before the coppers come and take us away."

They needed no further encouragement as plates were filled with bacon, eggs, mushrooms, and toast.

"I even managed to get butter and Keiller's marmalade for the toast. Do not ask me how, or I will be forced to lie, or shoot you, and I never lie."

They ate without talking, and Caitrin glanced at Hector. With her subtle guidance, Teddy had navigated the cutlery maze at dinner with the Ramiltons, but he did not have Hector's innate manners. They were men from different ways of life, and intriguing characters in their own right. She had once told Hector he had dangerous eyes, which he did, although he himself was not. Teddy, however, *was* dangerous. She was attracted to both men, but not to a degree where she would make some fateful decision. Not yet.

"I spent some considerable time with Winston," Bethany said as she poured tea. "It felt like forever, but he has decreed that, because of this new threat, 512 should not be shut down or absorbed by another agency. At least, not yet."

"Cheers to that," Caitrin raised her teacup, and the rest followed suit.

"And Gryffe-Reynolds has reluctantly agreed to Hector being officially transferred from SOE to 512 until we solve the mystery of the German homing beacons."

Caitrin poked Hector. "No more scallywagging for you, young Hecky."

"Is that all right, Hector?" Bethany asked.

"Yes. Hiding under hedges being a scallywag quickly loses its charm."

"Welcome to the staff of Langland Priory. I look forward to seeing you in a clerical collar," Bethany said, which startled him.

"And at least you'll never have to stuff a pillow up your jumper to look like an unwed mum," Grace said.

"Before we terrify poor Hector into flight, I want to give you the latest war news. The Atlantic convoys are being badly mauled by U-boats and HMS *Hood* was sunk by the German battleship *Bismarck* with almost a complete loss of life. Our ships are hunting her as I speak."

The room was silent.

"My brother Gareth's in the navy," Caitrin said. "On convoy protection. I'm surprised he's still alive."

Hector put his hand on hers.

"We'll keep Gareth in our prayers," Bethany said. "The Blitz appears to be lessening, at least in London, but we expect the lone raids using homing beacons to increase."

"What do we do about it?" Grace asked.

Bethany picked up a briefcase at her feet, pushed aside her plate, and opened it on the table. "We do know their intended targets," she said, sliding a document in front of each of them. "This came to us from the British embassy in Lisbon. They were given it by the Germans."

Caitrin scanned the pages. She looked up. "What a list. While I can suggest a few stately homes I would love to see as targets, there are at least eight hundred castles and goodness knows how many cathedrals. How on earth are we supposed to guard them all?"

"I agree. It might have been better to make a list of places they wouldn't bomb. In his latest broadcast, Lord Haw-Haw offered a suggestion. He says the Germans will start obliterating the great estates owned by the upper classes, whom he insists oppress the English people."

"Bringing out the socialist in National Socialist?" Caitrin shrugged. "And who am I to disagree with Lord Haw-Haw?"

Hector raised a hand.

"You can speak, Hector," Bethany said. "This is not school."

"No, it's not, but as the only man here, I am heavily outnumbered. If they intend to bomb the country estates, we'll find out which ones are pro-German and belong to Die Brücke. They would be left unharmed."

"The Bridge?" Grace translated.

"Die Brücke is an organization that connects some of the English upper-class families with Germany. There are quite a few with pro-Nazi feelings."

"Sir Oswald Mosley, a man who haunts my dreams, married his mistress Diana Guinness at Joseph Goebbels's Berlin home," Caitrin said. "Hitler was a guest. That kind of pro-Nazi feeling."

"We can ask the families to be aware of strangers," Bethany said, "while we concentrate on catching the men planting the beacons."

"We know nothing about the men, not much about the beacons, and no idea how they plant them," Hector said.

"We have a little more information," Bethany said and brought photographs out of her briefcase. It showed a rectangular piece of wood, about a foot long and six inches wide. Attached to it was a battery with wires and some mangled, burnt metal. "St. Paul's was bombed in October last year. One of the workmen cleaning up thought this was part of the cathedral organ, until he noticed the German markings. He remembered the photographs we distributed of the pieces we found and took it to the police. MI5 has it, and we're having a turf war."

"Next step?" Caitrin asked.

"We go over everything, again and again. We write down every thought, every idea, no matter how tenuous. Hector, you have the most legible writing. To the blackboard, if you will."

"It's not my writing you like. None of you want to get dust on your clothes." Hector said as he picked up a piece of chalk, stood at the blackboard, and marveled again at the command structure of 512. There appeared not to be one, at least nothing comparable to the military's rigidly stratified system, and anyone could raise a question or propose an argument. It worked well, though, that he would admit. Perhaps women were less afflicted by ego and position. Or perhaps they were more trusting of each other.

"We'll start with you, Caitrin. You were at the Café de Paris when the bomb exploded. Do you remember anything?"

"I have a question first. I still don't understand, if they were intent on destroying historical buildings, why did they bomb the café?"

Hector wrote Caitrin's question, put a question mark next to it, and said, "So far, we cannot find an answer. There were no public figures there that night."

"What do you remember, Caitrin?" Bethany asked.

"Very little. After the blast, a man whose name I thought was Badger took my ring. Later I recalled it was Thatcher."

"How did you get it back from him?"

"First, I went to police sergeant Goodwillie. I served in the force with him. He found two possible men, Harvey and Donnie Thatcher, but Harvey was in prison. Grace and I had an adventure when we went looking for Donnie, only to discover he was dead."

"Just a minute," Bethany said. "Let Hector catch up."

Hector scribbled the salient points of Caitrin's information.

"All right. Donnie Thatcher was dead, so how did you get your ring?"

Caitrin hesitated. She was reluctant to mention Teddy Baer, but did not know why.

"Caitrin?"

"I was invited to a New Year's Eve party in Whitechapel and met a man there who is a . . . a . . . who lives on the other side of the law. I thought he might be able to help me find it."

"Did he?" Bethany's question was blunt.

"Yes."

"His name?"

The room was quiet, and Caitrin felt everyone staring at her. *Why am I so reluctant?*

"Caitrin, you know the system. Everything goes up on the board. Everything. His name, please."

"Daniel Teddy Baer."

"Address?"

"The Blind Stag pub, Whitechapel. I don't remember the street because every building around it was flattened."

"We can find it. Why were you so reticent?"

"I don't know." *And I truly do not know, but revealing Teddy's name was a mistake.*

"Before I forget." Grace snatched the last piece of bacon and said, "I don't think you should write this down, Hector, but next Wednesday, the first of June, clothes rationing goes into effect. So now's the time to buy yards of knicker elastic."

"Hector doesn't wear knickers," Caitrin said, relieved the interruption had stopped further questions. She looked sideways at him. "Or am I making an incorrect assumption. You don't, do you, Hecky?"

"How will you ever find out, Cat?" Hector fired back, which caught her off guard. He might be outnumbered and a little embarrassed, but was not going to be outsmarted. At least, not all the time.

Bethany approached the blackboard and scanned Hector's writing before turning to face them. "Breakfast was good, but nothing on this board helps us find the men or the beacons. We have not moved forward an inch."

Hector said, "We could—"

Bethany interrupted him and barked, "You didn't raise your hand to speak, Hector."

He stared at her in utter bewilderment. "But—"

"I'm teasing you. Just lightening the moment. Go ahead."

"I've forgotten what I was going to say."

25

Luftwaffe Hauptmann Karl Trautloft's aircraft was flying alone at night on what he considered a gift operation. The Heinkel 111, named *Lotta* after his mother, always got through to the target, and this target, a remote English estate, could not have been easier. London, with its myriad defense systems of guns, balloons, searchlights, and night fighters, had become hazardous, but this estate had no defenses at all. Karl loved his Heinkel almost as much as he loved his mother. The nose was made almost entirely of perspex and there was no floor, so the crew could look directly down at the land below. Many aircrew disliked the cockpit because they felt exposed and vulnerable. But not Karl.

The X-Gerät radio navigation beams had guided the aircraft from France to a darkened area of Essex. The Toppesfield Hall estate was marked with an X on the navigator's map, near a town called Steeple Bumpstead, although, from the air, all Karl could see was a featureless landscape. He continued flying a straight line until he heard the first beacon tones in his headset. It was a faint warbling sound that grew stronger until it became a single-pitched tone. Ernst, the bomb-aimer lying prone at his feet, heard the steady tone too and triggered the bomb release. Incendiaries struck the eleventh-century building below and straddled the roof. In moments, Toppesfield Hall was burning. Karl banked hard for home, his work done. X-Gerät had brought them close to the target, but it was the Lighthouse homing beacon, placed earlier on the roof of the building, that guided his bombs with lethal accuracy, while *Lotta* carried him safely through another successful flight.

Caitrin was driving again, but this time not a Daimler. Instead, she was behind the wheel of a more modest motorcar, a Wolseley Hornet saloon with suspect steering and a gallantly optimistic thirteen hundred cc engine. The man sitting next to her, navigating with a map spread across his lap, was Hector, not Teddy, and they were traveling north from London, not south. Grace was tucked into the rear seat.

"You drive well," Hector said.

For a woman you mean? Stop it, Madam Sensitive. "Thank you."

"Try as hard as I might, I can never get in or out of second gear without teeth grinding."

"Which must upset your dentist no end."

He shot her a sharp look.

"I'm sorry, Hecky, but at times, most times, you are so teasable. I'd promise not to do it, but we both know that would be a gigantic fib. How long to—where is it we're going?"

Hector smoothed out the map. "Steeple Bumpstead."

"Bless you."

"Who invented these names?" Grace asked from the rear seat.

"One Christmas, they let a drunken Charles Dickens loose with a map. How long to Beeple Stumpstead?"

"Two, perhaps two and a half hours. The estate is just out-side—"

"Bumple Sheepshead."

Grace joined in. "Stumble Bleedhead."

"Grace, do you have a notebook?" Hector asked.

"Yes, sir."

"Don't call him sir," Caitrin said. "It will give him danger-ous ideas. He'll think he's nobility."

"I am."

"Not here. To us you are, and always will be, Hecky. Father Hecky of Langland Priory on sacred occasions."

Hector waved a hand in surrender. "Open your notebook, Grace. We're going to continue our blackboard session. First, Toppesfield Hall was burnt to the ground last night."

"Tell me about the Toppesfields," Caitrin asked as Grace scribbled notes.

"Colonel Basil Toppesfield was badly wounded in the last war. Paralyzed from the waist down. His wife, Emily, is shoul-dering the load of running the estate, although they sold off much of the land. Their son Jeremy is a lieutenant with the 42nd Royal Tank Regiment in North Africa. If he is killed, the family line dies out. Not exactly a thriving estate."

"There are lots of much larger and well-known targets, so why would the Luftwaffe bomb them?"

"Perhaps as a warm-up, or a warning."

"The battery."

"What?"

"Sorry, I changed subjects," Caitrin said. "Grace, did you find out how long the German battery we found in the St. Paul's beacon remains would last?"

Grace shuffled through her notebook. "Hard to be exact, but our technical boffins estimate fully charged between one and three hours, depending on the load."

"That's not much time to place and activate the beacon," Hector said.

"They said if it were connected to a VSRT—"

"What's that?"

"A Very Short Range Transmitter; it would probably supply power for about an hour."

"Which means someone had to visit the estate and place the beacon, probably on the roof, an hour before the bombs fell," Hector said. "I'm sure the Toppesfields get few visitors, so they'll surely remember who called on them yesterday."

"Maybe it was Beadle Pumplead," Caitrin said, feeling pleased at her wit.

"It was a police inspector Langton, who came down from London," Emily, Lady Toppesfield, said. "He was a polite man who appeared concerned about our well-being. He and a constable were so careful inspecting the property."

The ruins of the house still smoldered, and little remained standing. Caitrin and Hector walked the outside of the building, searching for clues, while Grace stayed with Emily and Sir Basil, her wheelchair-bound husband. They returned, and Hector asked, "What time did they arrive?"

"I don't know exactly," Emily said. "Just after lunch."

Basil nodded in agreement and said, "No later than two."

"What did they say? What was their reason for coming here?" Caitrin asked.

"Inspector Langton said there was intelligence suggesting German paratroopers had recently landed, intending to attack local RAF airfields. They were supposedly in hiding, and the inspection was to make sure none of them were on the estate."

"What did Langton look like?"

"Nothing unusual. Tall, broad-shouldered. Well spoken. I hardly noticed the constable. He said little, but had a London, Cockney accent."

"Were they carrying anything unusual? A box, or a case?"

"No. They spent about an hour searching the house, outside only, and the immediate grounds, thanked us and left."

"The bombs struck at what time?"

"Just after midnight—"

"It was so frightful," Emily interrupted, and her words became a torrent as she relived the night's horror. "It was quiet, and I heard an aeroplane, just one, and I thought it was one of ours. Then bombs exploded, and the building shook. The windows were glowing orange, and there was a rushing, groaning sound. I got Basil into his wheelchair and pushed him down the driveway to the gatehouse. That's where we're staying now."

"Remarkable." Caitrin glanced back at the grooves the wheelchair had left in the gravel. "I cannot believe you had such strength."

"Things were banging and crackling behind us. I suppose fear gave me wings."

"You are an astonishing woman."

"Not at the time, I wasn't. I was so scared." Emily quivered, and Caitrin saw she was close to both mental and physical collapse.

"Why don't you, Grace, and I go back to the gatehouse, and I'll make a nice cup of tea?" Caitrin said and led her away without resistance.

"I see you're not in uniform, young man," Basil said.

"No sir, I am not," Hector answered, expecting an indignant remark about his duty and loyalty to king and country.

"Mind you keep it that way." Basil stared at his burnt home. "Military service was once about devotion to one's country, with glory and honor and all that nonsense. It never really was, though, and certainly is not that now. War has become solely about killing people, killing civilians. It seems that's what we like to do, kill each other and as many as possible. Men, women, and children. Stay well away from the uniform."

"Thank you, sir."

"Once you've made the mistake, like I did, you can never get your life back. Not the life you wanted, not the one you expected."

"Is there anything I might do for you?"

"No, everything is gone." Basil's mouth tightened as he fought back a tear. "Bring back my son alive and unhurt. Can you do that?"

"No, sir. I only wish I could."

They sat at a round table in the Fox and Hounds, a half-timbered building on Church Street in Steeple Bumpstead, and drank beer. Grace opened her notebook and made a note while she said, "There is no steeple in Steeple Bumpstead."

"Are there any bumps?" Caitrin asked.

Hector groaned and said, "Can we please leave this poor village's name alone? You are both absolutely incorrigible."

"I have a question," Caitrin said. "The so-called Police Inspector Langton visited the Toppesfields at two in the afternoon, and the bombing took place after midnight. But the beacon's battery lasts only an hour."

"Is there a question in there somewhere?"

"It's implied, Hecky. There was a ten-hour gap between the visit and the bombing. The battery would have been dead when the plane flew over. Question is, how was the beacon activated?"

"I have no answer."

"I do," Caitrin said.

"I knew you would." Hector released a great sigh. "Cat, you can be so irritating at times."

"Took years of practice, usually with you. I was thinking about Germany and their leather shorts, sausages, and clocks."

"It's Switzerland that has—"

"A clockwork timer!" Grace interrupted Hector.

"I'd bet Hitler's bad breath the beacon had a clockwork timer," Caitrin said. "Which would give the saboteurs plenty of time to plant it and get away."

Hector glanced at his watch and rose to his feet. "I should call Bethany and tell her what we've found."

Grace waited until he had left before saying, "He likes you, Cat."

"He's a kind man."

"There's nothing in the rules or regulations about, you know, being very good friends."

"The rules are not a problem. I can just imagine taking Hector back to Wales and introducing him to my socialist family. Hello everyone, this is my beau, Lord Hector Neville-Percy, otherwise known as a member of the class that oppresses us, the working people."

"Stranger things have happened."

Caitrin shook her head. This war had warped time and place. Sometimes it seemed as though Max had died years ago, and sometimes it was just yesterday. *Did he and their plans to move to California ever really exist?*

Hector returned. "It seems we have a break. Another estate was bombed last night, but, fortunately, the house is surrounded by trees that deflected most of the incendiaries. The rest were extinguished, and they found a beacon on the roof. Intact."

"Where?"

"The Stone-Ellington Estate near Owmby-by-Spital."

"Where on earth is that?"

"Lincolnshire, and we have to go now and get the beacon before MI5 gets there and swipes it," Hector said and downed his beer. "It's a good long drive. Hope your knicker elastic holds up."

26

With a folder tucked under her arm, Bethany Goodman rolled a blackboard into the tower room and placed it next to the first one. She joined the others sitting at the table, in the center of which was the captured German homing beacon.

"After all the fuss, it's not much, is it? A bit of a disappointment, really," Grace said as she poked it with her finger. "It looks to me like an oversized wooden pencil box. Harmless."

"More like a brick," Caitrin said as she picked the box up and tilted it in her hands for closer inspection. As a devout socialist, she would be delighted to one day soon see all country estates and ancestral homes demolished or turned into refuges for retired miners and their wives. That being said, her heart went out to frail Emily Toppesfield and her crippled husband. They had lost everything because of a device like this one. "A swastika's printed on the bottom."

"It's damn silly to do that; it gives the game away," Hector said.

"The Germans have a long history of confusing thoroughness with efficiency."

"I can only imagine they assumed, correctly until this one, that the beacons would be destroyed in the bombing," Bethany said and opened her folder. "This is the boffin's report. I'll spare the technical details because they're Greek to me. In plain English, it is a battery-powered homing beacon, the power being activated at the right time by a simple clockwork mechanism."

Caitrin looked smug, Grace grinned, and Hector ignored them both.

Bethany continued. "It is a VSRT, a Very Short Range Transmitter, which is also directional."

"Which means what, exactly?" Grace asked.

"The boffin spent a long time and spoke slowly, using short words to ensure I, being a simple woman, would understand some of what he said. It was explained to me as a kind of radio water hose. Instead of spraying everywhere, the water, or signal, goes in a narrow-focused direction. It also does not spread wide, or very far; a mile or two at the most is the effective range."

Hector asked, "Is there no way of jamming or bending it?"

"I asked that question too and the answer is no, not unless you happen to be within a half mile of the transmitter, perhaps even closer. And, don't forget, it is aimed vertically and transmits for only an hour. We would have to know where it was to find it."

Hector sat back and sighed. "What's our next step?"

"We now know what the beacons look like and how they are made and activated. The next step is to find the men who are placing them, and how they could do it undetected. This is too big to hide up your sleeve. Did anyone report anything suspicious at the Stone-Ellington estate?"

"There was only the caretaker and a few servants there," Hector said. "The house is closed up, and the family is in Switzerland."

"How splendidly brave and patriotic of them."

"The caretaker said a police inspector and constable . . . you know the rest of the story."

"Any descriptions of the men?"

"Matched the men at Toppesfield. One spoke well, the other was a Cockney."

"We have to find them."

"How?"

"Get their descriptions out to the police, and it's back to the blackboard," Bethany said. "Hector, pick up thy chalk and write."

Hector did as he was told. "Write what?"

"You found several men and parts of some homing beacons."

"Yes, on the beach in Sennen Cove in Cornwall."

"Write that down."

While Hector was writing, Bethany asked, "How many men?"

"Three, though actually a fourth body washed up later."

"Were they wearing civilian or military uniforms?"

"Civilian."

"German or British clothing?"

"British labels."

"Why does that make a difference?" Grace asked.

"If they wore British clothing, they are British or could be Germans intending to stay and perhaps be the saboteurs. If it was German, they were probably just messengers delivering beacons to someone waiting for them. They would hand over the beacons and paddle back to the submarine."

"Hand over to whom?"

"That's the bit we don't know."

"What about the money? That has always puzzled me." Caitrin said. "It was gold sovereigns in money belts, right?"

"Right."

"Don't you think that's a trifle odd? The Germans must have plenty of British paper currency, real and counterfeit, which would be much easier to carry. So why lug around heavy gold sovereigns? Paper money is so much simpler to spend, and without raising suspicion, but buying a pint with a gold sovereign down at the old Cock and Bull would raise an eyebrow or two."

"Good question. Are there any answers?"

There was silence, broken only by the squeak of chalk as Hector wrote on the board.

"What if the saboteurs are not a German fifth column, and they're not doing it for a political cause? What if they are not German at all and only doing it for the money?" Caitrin said.

"I still don't understand why they would want gold sovereigns," Grace said.

Hector raised his hand, remembered he didn't have to, and quickly dropped it. "I do. If the Germans invade Britain and win the war, British currency will be worthless. If the British win, then no one would want German marks."

"Gold," Caitrin said. "Gold supports no sides and keeps its value, no matter the victor or loser."

That remark brought silence again. Until Caitrin scanned the first blackboard and a name caught her eye: Daniel Teddy Baer.

She heard herself say, "I believe the saboteurs are mercenaries, which means they are crooks and thieves." In one of her early meetings with Teddy Baer, when he was talking about becoming wealthy, he said: "No petty crime, no violence, and nothing you'd have to fence. Cash, hard cash, or gold is even better." *Gold is even better.*

"Caitrin, a question for you." Bethany had taken the chalk from Hector to underline Teddy's name. "This man found your wedding ring, and you say he works on the other side of the law. Might he be of help?"

It was a question Caitrin knew would eventually surface and one she did not want to answer. Teddy was an intriguing character, but so far, she had kept him at arm's length. If she were to ask him for further help, the price to be paid might be far more than she could afford. *Dance on the razor's edge for too long and you were bound to slip. No, say no. No, no, no.*

"Yes, I suppose I could." *Did I just say yes? Oh, God, I did. This war, this bloody war will kill us all. And if not the war, Teddy Baer might. One false dance step.*

Grace hurried after Caitrin and caught up with her on the path as it wound away into the woods.

"Mind a bit of company?"

"Only if there's no talking until we're at the pond. I need the fresh air and quiet."

Grace pressed a fingertip to her lips, and they walked in silence through the woods to the pond and sat together on a bench near the water's edge.

"Well done," Caitrin said.

"What did I do?"

"You didn't talk. Most people get uncomfortable and dislike silence."

"I don't. May I ask you a question?"

"Stop asking if you can ask a question, because that gives the person you're questioning a moment to assess their answer. Ask the question and you take command of the conversation. As an agent, you might not have much time to gather information, so be direct and get the answer right away."

"All right, thank you. I watched your expression change when Bethany asked for that man's name."

"Teddy Baer."

"That's a funny name."

"He's not a funny man. What's your question?"

"She thinks he might be able to help us. Do you?"

"A two-word question, that's better. Answer is, I don't know, mostly because I have no idea how to mention our problem to him," Caitrin said, stooped to pick up a stone, and sent it skittering across the pond surface. "I can hardly say, hello, Teddy, you might not know this, but I work for 512, which is a government secret agency, and we need your help to root out Nazis who are bombing the ancestral homes of England."

"Why not?"

"Another two-word question. Good. Teddy believes I'm a crook, a smaller female version of him. If I were to tell him the truth, it would reveal my identity, and that ends the relationship. If he refuses, we've lost a good contact for nothing."

"But wouldn't he want to help his country?"

"Teddy Baer is the son of immigrant Polish Jews, and he grew up in the slums of Whitechapel. The moment Teddy opens his mouth, he reveals his background. If he helped us, do you think the grateful landed gentry would invite him into their homes or clubs? This country has given him nothing, except the opportunity to die for it. Whatever Teddy has, he got for himself."

"It sounds like you admire him."

"I respect Teddy. I do not admire him, but that doesn't make him any less dangerous."

"I have an idea."

"Questions and ideas. You are a treasure trove."

"And you are a socialist."

"A proud socialist, that's one word, and a permanent member of the Keir Hardie Appreciation Club. That's also one word."

"You dislike the landed gentry."

"I don't care about them, but I do care about the strangle-hold they have on this country. They are parasites whose time has come and gone."

"Perhaps that's how you approach Teddy. Tell him you read about ancestral homes being bombed, want to join up with whomever is doing it, and does he have any ideas who they are."

"Would that work?"

"It might."

"I was asking me, not you."

"He comes from the slums, so he probably feels the same way you do about England's landed gentry."

Caitrin laughed. "The difference between us is, I want to eliminate them while he wants to become one."

"Oh." Grace looked away for a moment, before saying, "Last question."

"It will be. Go ahead."

"Would you mind if Hecky and I went out for a drink?"

"There's a war going on, young lady, and—" As her voice rose in pitch, Caitrin checked herself. "And listen to me being a vinegary old spinster, sorry. Of course it's fine, and none of my business. Has he asked you?"

"I was going to ask him."

"Oh, that's very modern of you. When?"

Grace stood and brushed at her skirt. "This instant, now that I've spoken to you. Thank you. 'Bye."

Caitrin watched her skip away like a happy little girl, was envious and wondered how she had gotten so old so soon. A chill shot through her at the thought of asking Teddy for help again. This time it wouldn't be about just a wedding ring; lying would be harder, and getting it wrong might be a death sentence.

Caitrin went to bed early, exhausted, and was asleep in minutes. The ringing telephone intruded; she woke and glanced at the clock. Midnight. Blinking to clear her head, she picked up the receiver to hear a boy's voice and recognized it; he was one of Teddy's couriers, a boy missing his front teeth, which gave him a whistling lisp. "Message from Teddy," the boy said. "He says he knows what you're up to, what you're doing. Noon tomorrow at the Blind Stag. Don't be late."

27

The same few thoughts roiled Caitrin's mind as the taxi carried her to the Blind Stag: *Do not speak first—What does Teddy know?—How does he know?—Do not guess—Do not defend—What the hell am I doing?—Should I ask the driver to turn around and take me home?*

Teddy was waiting for her outside the pub and made the last thought moot. He wore a well-tailored lounge suit, a white, soft-collared shirt, and expensive, polished shoes. *Always check the shoes; it's the last thing they think of*, Caitrin thought as she stepped out of the cab. *But not Teddy, he thinks of everything.* He opened the taxi door for her, and she noticed his new haircut and pink cheeks.

"Hello, Teddy," she said and tapped her cheek. "You're glowing. Been out in the sun?"

"Sun, what's that? Never seen one in Whitechapel. Maybe it got nicked and melted down." He took her up the steps and into the pub. "I see you're wearing trousers again."

"Slacks."

"There's a difference?"

"Men wear trousers; women wear slacks."

"Is that really the difference?"

"I have no idea, but it'll do for now."

"Fair enough. Our table awaits."

The table, with linen tablecloth, fine china and silver, sat in the center of the pub, colored golden by light from the amber-gelled window. The gramophone was playing a piano piece, but with the volume low, and Caitrin did not recognize the music.

"Luncheon, m'lady," Teddy said and pulled out a chair for her.

"Thank you, sir."

"The pleasure is all mine." He sat across from her and waved at the rows of cutlery. "I am now an expert in using these, thanks to you."

"Then shall we consider my wedding ring retrieval debt erased by the Ramilton adventure?"

"Done," he said and grinned. His teeth were whiter, his accent had faded, and she wondered if he were taking elocution lessons. Teddy Baer was reconstructing himself, a chrysalis waiting to become a butterfly. No, the thought of Teddy as a butterfly was absurd. He was building himself, one piece at a time, until he became fit for his own ancestral home. It was hard not to accept his insatiable drive, but she still had no intention of speaking first.

Charles, his chef, appeared and gave her a professional nod. "Ma'am."

"It's Caitrin, Charles."

"Caitrin. Thank you."

"What are we having for lunch, Charles?" Teddy said.

"I have a delicious piece of fresh halibut."

"Fish?" Teddy wrinkled his nose.

"The English don't like to eat fish, unless it's fish and chips," Charles said. "They don't consider it a proper meal, like roast beef, but I promise this halibut will change your mind."

"Mind-changing halibut it is, then," Teddy said.

"And I also have this," Charles said, producing and opening a bottle of wine. "A Viognier to accompany the fish. From the Rhône Valley. It has a hint of peach, tangerine, and honeysuckle."

Teddy squinted, uncertain whether Charles might not be making a fool of him. "Not like a pint of Truman's pale ale, then?"

"No, sir, but that's a good taste too," Charles, sensing he had made Teddy uncomfortable, put down the bottle, backed away from the table, and left.

And still there was no mention of what Teddy knew and why he had called her.

"Do you know what's funny about Disraeli?" he said.

That opening she had not expected. "He bought the Suez Canal for Queen Victoria?"

"He did?"

"He did. Quite the charmer was Benjamin, unlike Gladstone, who detested him. Victoria loved Disraeli because he flattered her shamelessly."

"No, not the canal. Disraeli was an ambitious Sephardic Jew, who claimed his father was from Venice because he thought it would be considered a background of some distinction. He ignored his mother, but she actually had the more impressive lineage. Funny, that."

"He so wanted to be accepted by the right people. By English society."

"He did become the Earl of Beaconsfield."

"Did that unlock all the sacred gates, though?"

Teddy's expression saddened. "No, not really. But still, not bad for a Jew."

And you, Teddy Baer, are following Disraeli's footsteps, although with a different set of skills. Don't be disappointed,

when you finally get there, if they don't fling open the gates for
you, and I'm still not asking you why I'm here.

Teddy poured them each a glass of wine and raised his. "A
toast to the *Bismarck*."

Another surprise. "It's German, and it sank."

"Yes, taking two thousand men with it."

"I don't want to toast all those deaths. Fifteen hundred men
were killed when the *Bismarck* sank the *Hood*. Thousands of
ordinary working men on both sides dead for no reason."

"Whose side are you on?"

"Me, I'm on my side," she said and was weary of the game.
"Your boy with no front teeth called me with an enigmatic
message. You knew what I was up to, and what I was doing. I
have no idea what he was talking about, so why don't you en-
lighten me?"

Teddy seemed embarrassed. "I sometimes make things too
complicated when they should be easy. I thought we hadn't
spoken recently because you were sulking. That's what I thought
you were up to."

"I don't sulk, and what would I sulk about?"

"About me not telling you I could drive."

"What?"

"If I'd said I could drive, you might not have come with me
to the Ramiltons."

"I might not have; then again, I might have said yes. That
would have been my decision to make. An honest one."

"I understand, and I'm sorry," Teddy said, and he was a little boy caught being bad. He was vulnerable. "So you're not
sulking?"

"No." Caitrin was aware of something else. In his remorse-
less drive to better himself, Teddy took no one along with him
because he trusted no one. That meant he had only his own
counsel, but to an extent, he trusted her. It was a delicate trust,
though, and she would need to tread carefully. She raised her

glass. "A toast to the memory of those poor British and German sailors, and their families."

He raised his glass and toasted in silence.

"I am on my own side, Teddy," she said. "I hate this war, and do not want Germans in this country. But this is the time and opportunity to rid ourselves of the entitled classes. To unseat the people sitting safe in their estates while ordinary men go off to die and their women and children are bombed in their slum houses."

"They have been tucked safely away there for a long time."

"All things, good, bad, and aristocratic, come to an end."

"What do you have in mind?"

Now was the moment. If she were not careful and made him suspicious, this would be the last time they would ever meet. White teeth, expensive suit and shoes did not diminish his slums-honed character. Teddy Baer had few enemies because they did not live long.

"I have heard, but I cannot say right now who gave me the information, that the Germans have a new target-homing device more accurate than anything in our arsenal," she said. *No backing out now.* "They recently bombed an estate in Essex, and my source says they intend to bomb others. And more historic sites too, like castles and cathedrals."

"They have radio direction, that's not new. So do we."

"True, but those radio waves are beamed from France or Belgium, and will only get them to a city. But if someone plants this new device on the target, it will lead a bomber directly there."

She paused to assess his reaction. He was impassive, impossible to read as he asked, "What do you want to do, and what makes you think I can help you?"

Caitrin saw Charles coming out of the kitchen with their meals. *Do I answer before or after he serves? Before.*

"I want to help the men planting the devices. I want to

plant them and demolish the landed gentry. You know people I do not."

Charles arrived, put down their plates, and waited for them to taste the food.

"*Hmm*, good, very good," Teddy said, putting down his fork. "Yet another invaluable lesson from you, Charles. Halibut has changed my mind about eating fish."

"Thank you, sir. Caitrin?"

"Delicious, thank you."

"Enjoy." Charles removed himself.

Teddy leaned forward to whisper. "It is good, isn't it?"

"Yes."

He sat back, wiped his lips, sipped his wine, and said, "What you're asking for is not a swipe some apples off a barrow and run like hell thing now, is it?"

"No."

The air between them was still. She sensed she had gone too far, and there was no going back.

"What makes you think I would know these people?"

"I don't, but there isn't much that happens in this city you don't know about. I had to start somewhere."

He let the silence thicken again, and she was tempted to get up and leave. But knew he would never let her.

"I'll sniff around, but it will call for a bigger *favor* than I got for finding Donnie Thatcher and your wedding ring. You understand that?"

"What do you have in mind?" she said with relief. She had not gone too far.

Teddy laughed, raised his glass, and tapped the rim against his newly whitened teeth, so it made the faintest of chimes. "You've spent some time thinking about this, haven't you? I should too."

28

Hector was driving the Wolseley Hornet north to Lincoln, and Grace was his navigator, sitting next to him with a road map spread across her lap. Caitrin had been demoted to the back seat because supposedly Grace had been to Lincoln before and knew the way. But Caitrin was not fooled. Grace was chimpanzee-smiling at Hector as though he were her dentist, while he roared with laughter at everything she said. They had obviously progressed past having a drink. Caitrin did not mind, or at least she told herself that.

Grace handed her a folder and said, "Here's all the information about the bombing."

She opened it and sat back to read. "A single aircraft unloaded bombs directly on the cathedral."

"They dropped high explosives to tear the roof open," Hector said. "Followed by incendiaries to burn the place down. But this time—"

"The high explosives were a dud."

"Right. And the roof has a steep pitch, so the incendiaries bounced off. The UXB squad is defusing them as we speak."

"Rather them than me."

"The bombs also fell across the cathedral and not down its length. That made the target area much narrower."

"Read Lord Haw-Haw's list of targets," Grace said. "He broadcast it last night."

Caitrin read the list. "Lincoln Cathedral's not on here."

"He's usually accurate with his information, which means we were sent off on a wild-goose chase to protect the others on the list while the Luftwaffe was free to flatten the cathedral."

"Who are we meeting there?"

"The chief ARP warden is a Mr. Bernard Talle, that's tall with an E," Hector said.

"I bet they called him Shorty when he was a kid," Grace said, and Hector laughed at her scintillating wit.

They met him outside the cathedral, and Bernard Talle, a middle-aged man with white, close-cropped hair, was aptly named and broad-shouldered too. He was not the kind of man you would call Shorty, at least not to his face.

Caitrin was accustomed to seeing impressive buildings in London, but Lincoln Cathedral overshadowed them all. With its triple towers and Early Gothic architecture, it dwarfed the town.

"God was on our side," Bernard said in his flat Lincolnshire accent. "The bombs skelled off the roof. If they had punched through, the cathedral would have gone up in seconds. The timbers up there are over nine hundred years old and bone-dry. Come on, I'll show you."

They followed him like dutiful baby ducks, up endless steps through one of the towers and into the steep roof of the nave. A narrow wooden catwalk ran into the dark distance and creaked underfoot.

"Building started in 1072, not long after William the Conqueror. It was consecrated in 1092, and it's survived a lot worse things than Nazis." They were all out of breath when Bernard stopped in the middle of the catwalk. He seemed unaffected by the exertion. "I showed this to the men from MI5," he said.

"What men?" Caitrin asked.

"Yesterday morning, two men came down from London. They showed me their MI5 identification, I made sure of that, and said they had to inspect the cathedral because there were fifth columnists lurking about in the area."

"Did you go with them?"

"Yes, I showed them through the cathedral."

"What did they look like?" Hector asked.

"The one in charge was well-dressed and spoke well, the other was a bit of a Cockney."

"Did they come up here?"

"The tall one did. The short one couldn't manage it."

"Were they carrying anything out of the ordinary?" Caitrin said.

"Not that I remember. I would have noticed."

"Was he ever alone here?"

"No. Yes, but just for a minute," Bernard said and pointed down the catwalk. "He asked if he could go down to the end. I said it was narrow, and I'd wait for him. He went off and came back a bit later dusting himself down. There's nine hundred years of dust up here."

"Do you mind if I go look?" Caitrin said.

"Better take this with you," Bernard said, giving her a penlight. "Be careful."

Caitrin walked away from the group and went farther down the catwalk until she was lost in the darkness. The penlight beam danced as she explored the end of the catwalk, and she returned a few moments later. "At the end of his footprints," she said, holding up the homing beacon to show Bernard. "You never saw the man with this?"

"No, what is it?"

"It's what brought the German bomber here," she said and sneezed. "The dust is getting to me. Let's go down."

Outside the cathedral, they blinked in the bright June sunlight and brushed the dust off their clothes.

"What do you say to an early lunch?" Hector said. "We could talk a little more about these mysterious MI5 chaps over a pint and a pickled egg."

"The Adam and Eve pub on Lindum Road is my local," Bernard said. "It's a good one too."

"You go ahead. I'll catch up," Caitrin said. "I want to spend a few more minutes here."

She waited until they had left and entered the cathedral. The nave was empty as she sat at the end of a row, settled, hands in lap, and closed her eyes. The air was cool and still. The moment silent.

"I beg your pardon and do hope I'm not being inconsiderate," a man's voice said, and Caitrin opened her eyes. He was slim, about her age, with otter-bright eyes, and wore a dark suit, also about her age. "I don't usually bother congregants when they're praying, but you looked sad."

"I wasn't praying, I was hiding," Caitrin said. "Are you the vicar?"

"Goodness no, not yet. I'm an aspirant, soon to become, if ever the bishop gets around to signing the papers, a postulant."

"Apprentice vicar, then."

"You could say that." He put out his hand. "Peter Derwent."

She shook his hand. "Peter, good name for a vicar. Caitrin Colline."

"You're Welsh."

"And you're not."

"Lincolnshire lad, from Boothby Graffoe, just up the road. May I sit?"

"It's your house, at least your Dad's house."

He sat sideways on the chair in front of her and leaned on its back. "What brings you to Lincoln?"

"Chasing Nazis."

"Because of last night's bombing?"

"Yes."

"We have not been blitzed like London. Too far out of the way, I suppose. Mrs. Rogers in Prial Close was killed by a bomb a few weeks ago, as were Andrew Tollerton and his baby girl in Westwick Gardens. Tragic, but I think the Germans were actually aiming at the RAF station just down the road. You said you were hiding, not praying?"

The question caught her off guard. "I don't pray."

"No?"

"As a little girl I went to Sunday School at King Street Baptist Chapel with my brothers, but that was just to give my parents a morning to themselves. There I learned Jesus wanted me for a sunbeam, which is not one of my better attributes, and watched Moses and his animals go sailing across the flannel board. That's the extent of my religion."

"It's a start."

"It's an end. I don't believe in God. My big brother died in the last war. My fiancé was killed by a German bomb, and I've seen enough little old ladies and babies pulled in pieces out of blitzed buildings to know we just like to kill each other, always have, always will. And while we're doing that, God's away on holiday in Blackpool, moving in mysterious ways."

Peter began to speak, but she put out a hand to stop him. "I'm sure there are the usual answers tucked away in your apprentice vicar's bag, but I've heard them all, so you can leave them there."

"I don't have any answers," Peter said, "and the mistake the church so often makes is in assuming it does. Or offering some pointless platitude. That's a disservice."

"You might not get your vicar's badge with that heresy."

Her heart softened. "I'm sorry, Peter. I'm being a bit nasty while you're just trying to be kind."

"You're not nasty; it's the way you see the world. It's the way much of the world is. But not in here. That's why you're sitting there, isn't it?"

"Yes."

"The church has been a refuge for hundred of years."

"When it's not burning witches and heretics."

"Have to keep the buildings heated somehow."

Her eyes widened in surprise at his answer, and she laughed. "With you on the inside, perhaps there's hope for the church yet."

"Or its complete collapse. You said you were hiding, not praying. From what?"

His question triggered a release in her. She could talk to this man, she *had* to talk to someone.

"Caitrin?"

"Fear." Caitrin felt the warmth of tears and held them back. She settled in her seat and exhaled a long sigh. "In the last war, we accepted the daily killings of thousands of young men and went about our day. When it ended, we were like drunks waking up from a night of destruction. We couldn't believe what we had done, taken mass slaughter and made it normal. Now we're doing it again."

"And the fear?"

"I'm twenty-seven, Peter, and old. I work mostly alone, dealing with squalid, dangerous people doing ugly things that make me ugly too. My normal is not normal, and that frightens me."

"You're fighting to save our country."

"Saving this country is not worth it if it doesn't change."

"That might be your next task, after the war. To change it for the better."

"I'm not God."

"Sometimes God isn't God either," Peter said. He took a small notebook from his pocket, scribbled down a number, tore out the page, and gave it to her. "Ring me up, or send a letter, whenever you need to. Have faith. I know Caitrin will carry Caitrin through. Don't give up the fight."

"I will ring," Caitrin said as she stood and put out her hand. "Thank you."

He stood, and they shook hands. "Thank you."

She left and was a few feet away when he called out, "You are no longer alone. You are in my prayers now, Caitrin Colline."

Tears came; she could not hold them back, had no wish to, and turned to face him. "And you are in my thoughts now, Peter Derwent."

On the return drive to London, Grace still beamed at Hector, who still laughed at whatever she said. They were an endless, exclusive source of fascination for each other, while Caitrin sat cloaked in her own silence in the rear seat. Until Grace sat up with a jolt and passed a note back to her.

"Sorry, I completely forgot about this. I called Bethany from the pub to report in, and she said Teddy Baer left a message for you."

Caitrin unfolded the note. It was cryptic: *Have something. Teddy.* "This came from Bethany?"

"Yes."

"She would never answer the telephone in my room, which means he called the office."

"Yes."

"How would he have that number?"

"What's wrong?"

"What's wrong is he now knows where Caitrin works," an irritated Hector said.

Caitrin's expression tightened. "And he might also have found out about our organization."

29

Bethany sat at the tower room table across from Caitrin, Grace, and Hector. The room was quiet, and everyone was motionless because it was early and there was no tea. On the blackboard behind and to Bethany's left, the letters of Daniel Teddy Baer's name had been thickened with yellow chalk and double underlined.

"First order of business," she said and opened a folder. "Last night, two more country estates were bombed. In Cambridgeshire, Broadstowe Hall, a fifteenth-century house, was hit, and at Forncett St. Mary, just outside Norwich in Norfolkshire, the Blake House, which was first built in the twelfth century."

"Broadstowe Hall is nearer," Hector said. "And we could go on to the Blake House after."

"You're not going to either. Both were burnt to the ground, so there's nothing to see. We have details from the owners of one and the land agent of the other. At Broadstowe, they were visited by two army officers, who supposedly inspected the building, and at Blake House, it was the same routine with our MI5 chums again," Bethany said and sent a sheet of paper skimming across the table. "You'll notice that, in last night's broadcast, Lord Haw-Haw did not have either one of these places on his list of targets."

"He's trying to confuse us again."

"I don't understand why are they not attacking the bigger targets?" Grace asked. "The castles and cathedrals they mentioned?"

"They still might. With the exception of Lincoln Cathedral, most of them are in cities, which means they have ground security and antiaircraft defenses. And there are several busy airfields around Lincoln, so a lone aircraft flying overhead would not have been unusual."

Caitrin held up the sheet of paper. "Lord Haw-Haw also offers a reason. According to him, the Luftwaffe is bombing the country estates to rid the working poor of their parasitic oppressors. I suppose he's hoping to start a revolution. Being English, you think he'd know getting the British to do anything but complain about the weather—it's raining, what a surprise—is impossible."

"I thought we asked for all the likely targets to be forewarned?" Grace said.

"We have tried our best; unfortunately, some of the estates are remote and do not have telephones, or the families have left. At the beginning of the war, the Remington-Blythe family of Broadstowe moved to their estate in Ireland," Bethany said and shot a look at Caitrin. "Don't roll your eyes, young lady. Your personal revolution will have to wait until after we've won this war."

"There's another reason," Caitrin said, returning the look. "The government won't listen to a protest from some housewife in Cheam getting bombed out every night, but they will pay attention to Lord and Lady Fancy Knickers tucked away in the country. Bomb enough of them and Winston will get an aristocratic earful."

There was a knock on the door; it opened, and a young

woman entered with a tea tray. She put it on the table and left. All discussion stopped until everyone had made a cup of tea to their liking.

"We now have two intact homing beacons, but no clues about who planted them, or their organization, or where they will strike next. We are completely in the dark." Bethany gestured to the blackboard. "Which brings us to him, our only and very long shot, Mr. Daniel Teddy Baer. Caitrin, no one here knows much about him, so what can you tell us?"

"He got into trouble as a boy, but has never been convicted of anything since. Teddy's a successful crook, because he is ambitious, shrewd, smart, and suspicious."

"What makes you think he could possibly help us?" Hector said.

"His information network is immense; that's what interests us. Teddy works alone and has no close friends or acquaintances. He also has no enemies."

"No enemies?" a doubting Hector said.

"Correction, no living enemies." Caitrin did not tell them about Teddy's intention to become landed gentry and was not sure why she omitted it.

"How did he get the office telephone number?"

"I didn't give it to him," Caitrin said.

"Then who did?" Grace asked.

"Stable door and all that," Hector said. "What are we going to do about it?"

"Caitrin, have you replied to his message?" Bethany asked.

"Not yet."

"His network managed to find the priory telephone number. Do you think they learned it's actually a cover for 512?"

"I have no idea. If I tell him the priory is just a home for unwed mothers but he knows the truth, I will have lied, been caught in my own trap, and that will be the end of any contact with him. It could be the end of me too. On the other hand, how will I know if he is being honest with me?"

"He doesn't want to help his country?" Grace asked, and Caitrin's look of scorn silenced her.

"How do we find out how much he knows?" Bethany asked.

"I can't tell until we're sitting opposite each other, eyeball-to-eyeball," Caitrin said. *And that's the last thing I want to do.* "And perhaps not even then."

There was silence.

"Have you told us everything you know about him?" Bethany asked, and to Caitrin the question felt like a blow.

"Of course I have," she said. *But that is a lie, isn't it?*

"I'll go with you," Hector said.

"No."

"I'll go. I look harmless," Grace said.

"No. Teddy went to the trouble of finding the priory telephone number to show me what he can do and who's in charge. I go alone."

Caitrin studied Bethany's expression and saw she did not trust her.

"But you will not go to his place," Bethany said. "You will not meet there, not this time."

Caitrin wondered if Bethany was sending her a loyalty message by suggesting she meet Teddy at the ABC Tea Shop on Rathbone Place. It was there she had been recruited into 512 less than two years and a lifetime ago. Only now it was Teddy Baer sitting opposite her in the crowded teashop, and not Bethany Goodman. It was a warm day, and Teddy wore slacks, a Fair Isle pullover, an ice-blue shirt, and an immaculate cravat.

"I have questions," Caitrin said.

"I'm sure you do, but it's me first," Teddy said. "Why did you not want to come to the Blind Stag?"

"Within, the Blind Stag is pleasant; without, it's a blasted landscape, and I am so weary of seeing destruction. So much destruction."

"Eloquently said."

"And I like this teashop. Shaw came here frequently."

"Who?"

"George Bernard Shaw."

"That's jolly good for George."

"How and why did you get the priory telephone number?" she said, not interested in long, jockeying-for-position silences.

"How is my business, trade secret, and why is because you're still a bit of a mystery and never told me where you lived or worked. Mysteries bother me because they can be dangerous, so I found out."

The erratic bursts of the East End barrow boy's speech were fading away, and Teddy now enunciated each word. He had indeed been going to elocution lessons. She imagined him practicing how now, brown cow in front of a mirror, and there was something touching about that thought. "Now you know where I work."

"Do I?"

"What does that mean?"

"Just that a home for unwed mothers seems a strange place for you."

"I need to work to stay alive," Caitrin said and watched his expression, but he gave no sign of disbelieving her, which meant 512's cover was probably still intact.

"Doing what?"

"My mother was a nurse before she got married, and I used to go along on her rounds. I teach feminine hygiene to the young women who come to the priory. Some are just girls, and they know so little about their own bodies. The stories I could tell you," she said and watched him squirm. Men were always so uncomfortable when the inner workings of women's bodies were discussed. Such fragile creatures. It was the perfect answer to prevent too many further questions.

"Do you live there too?"

"Where I live will remain a mystery for now. Your message said you had something."

"Might have."

"Being coy doesn't suit you, Teddy."

"Careful, not coy."

"Careful's just a longer word."

"Caitrin," he tilted closer, his voice lower, "what I do is illegal; what you want to do, planting devices to demolish the landed gentry, is treason."

"Revolution, not treason."

"Revolution's just a longer word."

"Nothing ever changes without being pushed, hard." She leaned toward him. "Do you have something for me, or not?"

He sat back and sipped at his tea. "There is still time for you to withdraw that question and join me in an adventurous life of filling the family coffers. Thrills, spills, lots of loot, and no fear of spending the rest of your life shackled to the rack in the Tower of London."

"Do you have something for me, or not?"

He put down his cup and looked past her, staring into the distance for a long moment before their eyes met again. "Yes, I do."

"I suppose I'll owe you a big favor?"

"No, I'll need much more than that," he said, waving a cautionary finger. "And you might wish you never asked me for help."

30

It was late morning, and Caitrin, Hector, and Grace had been waiting with impatience for some time in the tower room. There was, however, a compensatory fresh pot of tea, and some considerate soul had scrounged up a few biscuits. Hector looked at his watch, again. "Late. Where the dickens is she?"

As though his question were a cue for some theatrical farce, the door swung open, Bethany swept in, planted herself in front of the blackboards at a jaunty angle, hands on hips, and said, "Have any of you ever seen Winston Churchill dance?"

Three piously blank faces answered her.

"I thought not," she said. "Well, I just have, and it was a sight not to be missed, or ever repeated." She buried her chin into her chest to create Churchillian jowls, inhaled a deep breath, and performed an odd shimmer with a few spasmodic gestures, as though she were being periodically electrocuted. The dance came to a vertiginous end with three eccentric rotations. She stopped to a profound silence, bowed, looked up, and said, "I wasn't expecting flowers, or thunderous waves of applause, but not even a bravo?"

"Bravo." Hector complied.

"Brava," Grace said.

"Winston got dizzy, poor thing, and only managed two and a half turns before he had to sit down and pour a stabilizing brandy down his throat." Bethany touched her fingertips to the teapot, found it was still hot, made herself a cup of tea, and sat. "Now, you may very well ask, *why* did he dance?"

"Why *did* he dance?" Hector asked.

"I'll answer with a question. Who knows who Frederick the First was?"

Hector raised a hesitant hand, which Grace promptly tugged down as she hissed, "You don't have to raise your hand. It's not school."

Caitrin watched them, her face impassive. *There's a romantic affair torpedoed and sinking beneath the waves. Wonder which one is the U-boat?*

"Go ahead, Hector."

"Frederick the First was the Holy Roman Emperor, I think in the twelfth century, who reunited and expanded Germany. He was known as Barbarossa because he had red—"

"Hair," Grace interrupted.

"Beard, a red beard."

"If he had a red beard, then he had red hair too," an irritated Grace said.

"He could have been bald."

The good ship HMS Love Affair *was definitely going down with all hands*, Caitrin thought, but said nothing. *Nearer my God to Thee.*

"Children, children," Bethany admonished them. "The connection between a dancing prime minister and a red-hirsute Emperor Barbarossa is a simple one. Mr. Hitler has just declared war on Russia in an operation he called Barbarossa."

"I don't understand," Grace said.

"Our intelligence reports that the Germans are moving their

military east to fight the Russians. It means the fear of the Wehrmacht invading England is gone."

"Hitler is going to fight the war on two fronts? Has he never heard of Napoleon?" Hector said. "That's sheer madness."

"True, but it's rather sporting of us to let him do it. Hence, Winston's joyous sarabande."

"How does this affect us?" Caitrin asked.

"Winston believes Operation Lighthouse, that's its official name now, will probably intensify. Using only a few bombers instead of hundreds, but with greater accuracy, the Germans will keep us at bay, while letting the bulk of their army march off east. May I have that biscuit?"

Bethany took the remaining biscuit, dipped it in her tea, ate it, and said, "There were two more estates hit last night. We have to produce results, and the faster the better. Caitrin, start by telling us about your meeting with Mr. Baer."

Caitrin put down her cup. She could tell she was being assessed; Bethany was watching her expression and listening to every word she said. "He was curious about the priory."

"Does he suspect anything?"

"I don't think so."

"Not sure?"

"I'm never sure with Teddy."

"You told him what you wanted?"

"Yes, I said it was time to make great changes, and I wanted to be an active participant."

"And his reply?"

"He said, I might wish I had never asked him for help."

"What do you think that means?"

"Teddy says what he means and nothing else," Caitrin said and shook her head. "Desperate times, desperate people, desperate action."

"What happens next?"

"We wait until he contacts me."

"Contact him."

"He has no telephone. Uses a band of Whitechapel native runners to ferry messages back and forth. When he is ready, he'll ring."

Bethany settled back in her chair. "In 512, we take pride in being open and honest with each other. It is the only way to engender trust in an untrustworthy business. It's how we stay alive. With that in mind, I am now being honest. You are keeping something back about Teddy Baer, and it's time to come clean."

Bethany's response was not a surprise; in fact, Caitrin had expected it earlier. "Teddy Baer and I are much alike," she said. "We both come from poverty-stricken communities and had to fight our way out."

"You respect him?"

"No, but I do have a degree of admiration for him. He could easily have become a violent gangster, but he's smarter. Teddy's no Robin Hood, but he has his own set of ethics."

"Are you attracted to him?"

"No," Caitrin said and wondered if that were entirely true.

"Is he attracted to you?"

"Yes." *Or would it be just the conquest he wanted?*

"Would he harm you?" Hector asked. *Good old Hector, such a kind man. Hope you're not making a mistake with him, Grace.*

"Not intentionally, but Teddy has a dream. No, more than that, he has a goal and will not stop until he reaches it. Nothing and no one gets in the way."

"And what is that?"

"It's where Teddy and I differ." Caitrin said and laughed. "I want to tear down the landed gentry, while you want me to save them. Meanwhile, Teddy wants to become one, and probably will. He's following in Benjamin Disraeli's footsteps. That's what I was hiding from you, a poor man's ambition to achieve what he considers to be greatness."

There was a knock on the door; a young woman entered, gave Bethany a slip of paper, and hurried out. Bethany glanced at the note and passed it to Caitrin. "Read aloud, please."

"Have contact. Insist meet Blind Stag. 8:00." She put down the note. "We have our answer. Or will soon."

There was no moon; the night was dark, and the city lay numb and silent under its permanent blackout. Caitrin used a flashlight to find her way up the steps to the Blind Stag front door. It was ajar, and gramophone music, American jazz, filtered out. She pushed it open wider and entered. The pub was dimly lit with just a few oil lamps, and her warning instinct told her to leave. Until Teddy appeared from the shadows carrying a bottle of champagne and two glasses.

"My apologies for the gloom," he said, setting the champagne and glasses down on a table. "My regular candle supplier was bombed. It seems there's a bloody war going on somewhere. Sit."

Caitrin sat as he opened the bottle and poured them each a glass and asked him, "Why the champagne?"

"Why not?" Teddy raised his glass in a toast. "Here's to the end of the war and us not getting bombed."

"I can drink to that," she said, toasted, and put down her glass. "Now, can we not engage in the long dance this time? What do you have?"

"I have a contact that will take you directly to the beacon makers."

"Good."

"But, before I reveal it, I have to ask you one last time: are you quite sure you want to continue?"

"Yes. I'm sure."

Teddy cocked his head to one side. "Are you sure sure?"

"Teddy, in my world, yes means yes. If I said I don't know, that would mean I wasn't sure, while no would mean no. So, yes."

"All right, fair enough," Teddy said, put down his glass and pushed it to one side. "We have different motives. I do what I do for money, while you want to change the world."

"Not all of it, just this country. We've already been through this. Let's not do it again."

He put his hands on the table in front of her, palms up, and said, "Show me your hands."

"Why?"

"Show me your hands. Indulge me, please. The last time we did this, you got your wedding ring back, remember?"

Reluctantly, Caitrin put out her hands, palms up.

"Working-class hands. Turn them over," he said. "Both of us have working-class hands. And—"

She heard a sound behind her, made to turn, but Teddy's hands clamped hard on her wrists and held them firm. A hand swept from behind her chair and pressed a chloroform-soaked pad to her face. She struggled, but for only a few moments, as Teddy kept her hands pinned to the table until the chloroform had its effect. The last thing she heard was him saying, "You did say yes, Caitrin."

Hector could find nowhere close to the *Blind Stag* to park the Wolseley where they would not be seen. With most of the buildings flattened, the only reasonable choice, where they would at least be partly hidden, was behind a burnt-out lorry a hundred yards away from the pub. From that distance, the pub was a slightly darker mass against the ruined street.

Grace, sitting next to him, fidgeted. "You do know Bethany doesn't trust her, don't you?"

"Her?"

"Caitrin. She doesn't trust Caitrin."

Hector snorted a disapproving breath. Recently, Grace was

becoming increasingly irritating. "And just how do you know that?"

"From the way she accused her of keeping secrets about this Teddy Baer."

"Bethany was being direct. That's her way. And Cat was honest; that's *her* way."

They fell silent as an old man wheezed past on a bicycle.

"Perhaps so, but she still doesn't trust her."

Hector bit his lip. There was nothing to be gained by arguing with her.

"I'm not trying to cause trouble, Hector, it's just that—"

"Grace, let's talk about something else. Better still, let's not talk at all for a while," he said and raised his binoculars to scan the pub. In the darkness, he could see little detail through them, but at least it kept him from arguing.

A Chorlton's Bakery, Bread & Cakes van, with ARP painted in clumsy letters over the sign on the side, turned the corner at the pub and drove past them.

"There's a fire," she said.

"Where?"

"On the roof. Look up on the roof."

Hector tilted the glasses to the roof to see bright orange flames curling above the parapet.

"And coming out of the top windows," Grace said.

Hector dropped the glasses, pushed open the car door, and ran toward the pub. Grace followed. They were thirty yards away when the building exploded. The front door blew off and went shearing through the air; wooden boards covering the windows disintegrated into splinters, and bricks howled past like cannonballs. The blast knocked both of them to the ground. Dazed, his ears singing and his face lacerated with cuts, Hector struggled to his feet. The Blind Stag was a roaring, twisting column of flame. He stepped back, turning away from the heat, and saw Grace lying facedown in the street. She was so small; she had lost all dimension.

At the far end of the street, the bread van stopped in the shadows, the window rolled down, and Teddy leaned out to see what he had done. For just a moment, he watched the inferno of the burning Blind Stag, and before it, the silhouette of a man trying desperately to resuscitate a woman who was obviously dead. "Nothing to see here," he said. "A good night's work and a job well done."

The bread van turned a corner and was gone.

31

Bethany sat in silence with Hector in his room. It was early evening, the blackout drapes had yet to be closed, and a soft window light settled across Hector's grief-lined face.

"I forgot to get tea," he said. "I'm so sorry; there's no tea."

Bethany patted his hand. "It's all right, Hector, we can do without tea."

"It didn't happen," he said in a whisper, and louder, "it didn't happen. I keep telling myself that, but it did."

She let him speak without interruption. *It was so much harder being a man. Women could cry and get upset; we could be, and were expected to be, emotional, but not men. They had to maintain a front. It must make them so lonely.*

"We had to park a long way from the pub. It was so dark I could hardly see anything. Grace noticed the fire first. We ran toward the pub, and it exploded, and the blast knocked me over. I was only half-conscious when I stood up and saw her lying on the ground." He stopped. Looked away. The silence rose again. "I lost her."

"It was an accident."

"Now I understand why my father never talked about the war."

"War is about loss. There's no honor or glory to it, just loss."

"We were sitting in the car, watching the pub, and Grace was going on about something that was beginning to irritate me. I was a bit abrupt with her. The fire started. If I had told her to stay in the car and—"

"It wasn't your fault."

"And Caitrin. What about her? The pub was an inferno; no one could have escaped."

"We don't know that for sure."

"It burnt to the ground. You've seen it. Nothing is left."

"When I was little, we used to go to the seaside, and my dad would play games. He'd point to a cottage on the other side of the bay and ask me what color it was. It's white, of course, I'd say, and he'd answer, no, you only see that the wall facing you is white. Which is a long way around of saying we cannot tell for certain she died in the fire. We do know she entered the Blind Stag. That's all."

"Grace kept going on about you not trusting Caitrin. That's what was irritating me. You do trust her, though, don't you?"

"It's the women with strong integrity, the honest ones, who can often fool you. I knew she was holding something back about Teddy Baer, and I'm still not sure she told us everything."

"Now it doesn't matter."

"Yes, it does, perhaps even more. The pub had no electric or gas connections, so the explosion was probably not an accident. Did you see anything at all before the fire?"

"Not much, it was so dark. There was an old man on a bike, and just before the explosion a bread van with ARP splashed on the side drove past."

"What do you remember about it?"

"I didn't get the whole name, just the first letter, C. Bakery and bread and cakes was the sign on the side. That's it."

"Try to remember more, it could be important," Bethany said and stood. "We have work to do, Hector. I'm sure Teddy is still alive, and we'll assume Caitrin's alive until I know she's dead. She might have been killed or abducted by Teddy and the explosion was meant to cover his tracks. Or she might have gone with him willingly. We have to find out."

"How do we do that?"

"She was a policewoman. They will have her personal records, and she was very close to her mother. Perhaps there are letters between them that will offer a clue. You should go to Wales. Right now."

Hector went up into the grimy mining valley on the same train Caitrin had taken months earlier. He walked the same small streets and sat in the same tiny kitchen with her mother, Gwen Colline. Like Caitrin, Gwen had a mass of curly hair, although gray not red, and her daughter's determined face and kind eyes. She sat erect and met his gaze. This was a family of resilient women. Behind her on the kitchen wall was a picture of her four children, now two, with one dead and another missing. Over strong tea, she listened to his description of the night her daughter disappeared and thought him a fine young man, albeit a little out of place, who was struggling but trying his best. Emotions she kept to herself because, no matter what he said, her heart knew Caitrin was still alive.

The letters Caitrin had sent her mother yielded nothing useful. Hector apologized for bringing sad news, thanked Gwen for her hospitality, promised to be in contact the instant there was any new information, good or bad, and left.

There was so much of his life ahead of him, but he had already lost Grace and probably Caitrin. As his train trudged down the valley, Hector glanced through the window at the passing coal tips, the mines and the thin streets, and felt as though he had intruded. He did not belong there. For the first time in his life, he belonged nowhere. This war was gradually whittling him away.

Bethany parked behind Hector's Wolseley, got out of the car, and walked down the debris-strewn, bomb-cratered street toward the Blind Stag. It was a dismal journey. The buildings of what was once a thriving working-class neighborhood had been flattened into great heaps of gray rubble. Scattered around were the remnants of destroyed lives: a broken pram with buckled wheels; a miraculously undamaged china teapot; a dartboard and a red shoe half-hidden under a floral pattern frock. She found Hector sifting through ashes in the far corner of the pub.

"I thought you'd be here," she said.

Hector straightened. "Hello, Bethany."

"Find anything?"

He shook his head. "The fire after the explosion incinerated everything."

And everyone. Her heart went out to him. Hector was drained of life. The shock of losing Grace and Caitrin was corroding him, and he seemed incapable of surviving it. "I just left Winston," she said.

"How was he?"

"Not doing his jolly dancing-bear routine this time, but he was, and I quote, 'exceeding joyous and gleeful.' The Russian army is resisting the Germans, and Roosevelt just seized Japanese assets. It takes some of the pressure off England."

"That would be good."

"Winston has decided he is the man of destiny, the man who will overcome all adversity and save the British Empire, single-handed. And he's probably right. Not the single-handed part, though."

"Some encouraging news at last."

"I'm afraid it's not all good news. Last night, the church at Deersted was targeted. Thirteen hundred years of history blasted and burnt. The Luftwaffe also destroyed St. Andrews in Weirmouth, County Durham, built in six seventy-four, and All Saints Church, outside Bury St. Edmunds, built eight fifty. A grievous loss."

"That cannot be replaced."

"Winston is concerned these attacks will do more damage to the public than the Blitz. They are spiteful bombings to obliterate English history and, if not stopped, will weaken morale. He asked—no, Winston doesn't ask—he demanded to know what we were doing about it."

"What did you say to him?"

"I told him we were doing our best, but had recently suffered casualties," she said.

"And we have no damn clues and no direction to turn," he said. Bethany put her arm through his. Hector needed to be taken from this place. "I'm going to buy you a pint in a decent pub, young man."

She led him back to the cars, but he stopped halfway. "This is where Grace died, just lying there as though she had fallen asleep. I couldn't understand because there was no blood and no signs of injury. The coroner said the brick that hit her chest was traveling so fast the impact stopped her heart. Just like that, beating, alive, stopped, dead."

"Come on."

Hector was planted and did not move. "When I went down to Wales, Caitrin's mother surprised me," he said. "I thought there would be tears when I told her she was missing. But she patted my hand, thanked me for coming, and said, wherever she was, Caitrin was alive. If it were otherwise, she would know. She was so sure of that. A truly remarkable woman."

"With a remarkable daughter."

"Yes," Hector said, and his chin tilted as he fought back a

tear. He glanced over her shoulder at the spot where Grace had died, and farther to what remained of the Blind Stag. Caitrin.

"And you are a remarkable young man." Bethany took both his hands, tightening her grip to bring his attention back to her, and said, "You don't always have to be strong, Hector. For your own sanity, let go."

And for the first since he was a little boy, Hector let down his defenses and wept.

32

Caitrin opened her eyes and saw only darkness. Outside, a bird was singing, and below, some distance away, a voice called out and got no response. She tried to raise her right hand, but it was tied down. So too was the left, and her ankles. She was wearing a nightgown and lying, restrained, on a bed.

"Teddy," she shouted, her voice cracking from disuse. "Teddy!"

A moment later, a door partly opened; a woman slipped in and closed it behind her. "You're finally awake."

Her voice was familiar, but she was hidden in the darkness. "Where am I?"

The woman pulled open a blackout curtain to let in daylight and moved to the bedside. "You're with friends, Caitrin."

"Florence?"

"The very same, risen from the dead," Florence said as she untied the restraints. "Let me get rid of these silly things."

Caitrin tried to rise and failed. Florence sat on the edge of the bed. "You're weak. Take a little time to gather your strength. I'll get you some water. You must be parched."

Florence hurried out and returned with a glass of water. "Here, this'll clear your head."

As Caitrin drank, Florence said, "I'm sure you have a million questions, but let me tell you you're quite safe. Teddy used restraints because he didn't want you coming to and racing off on a wild adventure in the middle of the night."

"You could have just locked the door."

"It's a very old house, and there's no key. And, knowing Caitrin as I do, you would have gone out the window or up the chimney."

"Why don't I fire off a couple of those million questions? Starting with, where am I, why was I brought here, and what are you doing here?"

"I can't tell you the name of the place, but we are in a house out in the country; actually, it's a hunting lodge, although what they hunt I don't know. You're here because that's what Teddy wants, and I'm here for the same reason."

"Florence, you are a damn fool."

Florence shrugged. "We can't all be strong and brave like you. There's a bathroom behind that door, and some of my clothes on that chair. We're about the same size, and they'll probably look better on you. When you're ready, come downstairs."

Florence went to the door, paused, and said, "Now you're awake and untied, there'll be a man outside the door all day and night. He'll bring you down." She left.

Caitrin, bathed, dressed, and alert, opened her bedroom door and recognized the guard in the hall. He was Large Eric, the doorman she had met outside Teddy's New Year's Eve party at the Blind Stag. A dozen lifetimes ago. The one who had called her a popsy in a bad Humphrey Bogart accent.

"Hello, Large Eric," she said. "First Florence and now you. Another resurrection."

Large Eric pointed at the floor and said, "Downstairs. To the kitchen."

"Lead on, Lazarus," she said.

"It's Eric."

She winced a smile in reply and followed him. It was an old country house with the usual admixture smells of damp, woodsmoke, and wet dogs. Too small to be an estate's main home, and, judging by all the still-life paintings on the walls of dead ducks and hares arranged around bowls of fruit, Florence was right; it was either a hunting lodge or a farmhouse. Eric led her into the kitchen, where Florence was making tea and a man sat at a table near a window. He too was a surprise; Ernie, the second of Teddy's guards.

"Yet another hath risen from his icy tomb," Caitrin said.

"Morning, miss," Ernie said, tapped his forehead, and gestured for her to sit.

"Good morning to you, Ernie. We have a veritable cornucopia of lost and found souls here," she said and sat across from him as Florence slid a mug of tea in front of her. "We need only one more to complete the set. What was his name? I think it was Samuel, right?"

"He's Samuel Breen," a man said as he entered and stood next to Ernie.

Caitrin searched his face. He was slightly familiar, but she could not place him. "And you would be?"

"Donnie Thatcher," he said and sat next to Ernie.

"The thief who stole my wedding ring."

"I thought you was dead when I took it off your finger. I wouldn't have done it if I'd known you was alive, honest."

"Honorable."

"I was happy to give it back. To do a thing like that is bad luck."

"I'm still alive, but I heard you were dead."

"I was, but I'm not anymore. Teddy told me I could come back. The bomb wasn't supposed to land on the Café de Paris."

"This is turning into a day of surprises. Tell me more."

"I dropped Sammy off at Leicester Square, which is right next to the café. His job was to put the beacon under the Shakespeare statue in the middle of the park, but there was too many people around for him to hide it properly, so he put it in the café instead because that was close enough."

My Max would still be alive if Sammy hadn't done that.

"I said we had strict orders, and he had to go back and recover it. But Sammy was nervous and needed a drink first. I was also a bit edgy myself. We went to the King's Head on Wardour Street, and time slipped past the way it does sometimes, and then came a bloody big bang, and it was all over."

It was all over, and Max was dead, and all our plans died with him. "And Sammy?"

"Sammy, who knows—?"

"I'm sorry to say Sammy's no longer with us," Teddy said as he entered, took the chair next to Caitrin, and spun it around. He straddled the seat, folded his arms along the back, and said, "So there will be no more questions about him."

"I have questions about other things."

"So do I."

"Me first, where am I?"

"Let's take a walk in the fresh air, just the two of us."

The warm air smelled of summer as Caitrin and Teddy went outside. She glanced back. The house sat in a slight depression, hidden by old beeches and surrounded by fields. There were no other houses or roads in sight.

"A strange-looking place, isn't it?" Teddy said. "The inside doesn't match the outside. Seems her ladyship of that period wanted traditional English cozy, while the pukka sahib lordship had made his pile in India and imagined living in the Taj Mahal. They each got half of what they wanted. We'll take the path to the right. It goes through a very pretty wood."

She noticed he was wearing a half Norfolk jacket, cavalry

twill trousers, and boots. Teddy was, as ever, assiduously re-hearsing being a gentleman until he transformed into one.

"Before you ask any more questions," Teddy said. "I have to apologize for the dastardly drugging and kidnapping of your good self."

"Why did you do it?"

"A lot of things had to happen in order and quickly, so—"

"You decided to have everything done your way?"

"Guilty as charged. But, remember, I did first ask if you were absolutely certain about continuing."

"And I said yes, remember? But obviously that wasn't con-vincing enough for you."

"I didn't want a long discussion, and we had to leave the Blind Stag quickly."

"Why?"

"Because we blew it up. No trail or sign it ever existed has been left behind," Teddy said as they entered the wood. The air was cooler, damper, with the infiltrating scent of decaying mat-ter. "It now all happens here."

"Where is here?"

"I can't tell you."

"Can't or won't?"

"Both. And don't ask me again. Don't ask anyone."

The wood was denser as the path sloped more steeply, and only occasional splinters of sunlight pierced the air. They were quiet for a while, each waiting for the other to speak.

"When you offered to put me in contact with the saboteurs planting the beacons, I didn't imagine it would be you."

"Why not?"

"It doesn't bother you?" she said. "Killing your fellow Eng-lish men and women?"

"I don't kill them. The Germans drop the bombs, not me."

"A distinction without a difference. No beacon, no bomb. And your beacon and a German bomb killed my fiancé."

"It wasn't meant to. I'm sorry."

"How do you choose the targets?"

"I don't."

"Who does?"

"Looks like rain, no? A summer shower, perhaps, good for the rhubarb."

"All right, I get it," she said, and a thought intruded. *The gold sovereigns Hector found on the German bodies on that Cornwall beach were for Teddy and his work. He wouldn't have trusted their paper money because he doesn't trust anyone but himself.* "Neither of us has any loyalty to the Crown or the landed gentry, but do you really want Germans taking over this country?"

"Funny old world. We always seem to end up arguing against our own beliefs," Teddy said. "I'm not as educated as you, but I know what I need to know. The House of Hanover ruled this country for centuries, right up to Queen Victoria, whose tubby hubby and first cousin Albert was German. Along came the family who went to bed one night as the Saxe-Coburgs of Gotha and woke up next morning as Windsors because of the last war. And the Battenberg dynasty instantly became the Mountbattens. So the Germans are hardly strangers here."

"The Nazis don't like Jews. You do know that?"

"Caitrin, please. Do I look like a Jew to you?" Teddy stopped, pivoted to face her, and spread his arms wide. "Do you see the Nazi caricature Jew with the hooked nose, bulging eyes, and blubbery lips?"

"No, I do not. Your blond hair, and," she said and traced a line down her cheek, "that could be taken as a Prussian Mensur dueling scar that would make any Aryan jealous."

"By the time the Germans paddle across the English Channel and roll up here, I will be Lord Daniel de Barr of Whitechapel, tucked safely away from the Nazi horde on my extensive estate. They might even toss an Iron Cross my way for services rendered. A generation from now. it will not matter anyway, and the generation after that, it will all be forgotten."

She could not help but appreciate his relentless drive, an urgency no different from that of the countless landed gentry who had gone before. No English estate was untainted by theft or blood.

"I have a question for you," he said. "You said you work at the Langland Priory teaching feminine hygiene to sad unwed mothers."

"Yes."

"That is a laudable pursuit, to aid the downtrodden."

Laudable. Pursuit. A clumsy sentence, but a year ago he would never have used those two words. Or downtrodden either. There was something darker behind that statement, though, an unseen menace.

"My next question is a simple, yet important one for you," he said and pulled Caitrin's revolver from his pocket. "I found this in your pocket. An unusual weapon is the Webley-Fosbery automatic revolver. Heavy. The cylinder and barrel assembly slide back after each shot. A man, or especially a woman, would have to be quite an expert to use it properly. Are you considered a Webley-Fosbery expert, Caitrin?"

"I try."

"Why would you want this cannon? To teach the poor unwed women how to shoot their perfidious and elusive men?"

Perfidious, elusive. Teddy really is expanding his vocabulary, and I am in trouble. "I'm sure that thought has crossed a few women's minds at the priory. Actually, I bought it off a man because parts of London are not safe at night for a woman."

"Why did you not choose something smaller, more suitable to the, um, delicate female hand?"

"It was all I could afford at the time. Keep it if you like it so much," she said. "Teddy, you offered to help me connect with the saboteurs. That's all I want."

They were deeper in the woods; there was no sunlight, and no sound. The air was damp, and she shivered and glanced at the revolver in his hand. *Was it one lie too many, and is this where it all ends?*

Teddy's eyes met hers, unblinking, assessing. A blackbird sang in a nearby tree, but it seemed to come from a vast distance. He raised the revolver, hesitated, flicked open the cylinder, removed the rounds, and handed it back to her. "Before you start planting the beacons, you need to know how they work. First order of business for you—stay here with the others, learn how to assemble them. And ask no questions, of anyone."

"All right."

"Large Eric and company are a docile flock who have no idea what they are building. There is no telephone here, or postman, so if they were to find out, it could only come from you."

"Not a word."

"Good girl."

33

It was a small bedroom made smaller by Florence's irritating presence. Caitrin had grown up in a tiny row house and was used to sharing a bedroom with three brothers, but not with an untidy woman who prattled ceaselessly about Teddy, the great love of her life: a love that was not at all reciprocated. The bedroom was not without its surprises. A generous stack of new clothes had appeared on Caitrin's bed, including several pairs of slacks and even bib-and-brace dungarees. Rationing had obviously been ignored, and the clothes would have been far too expensive for Caitrin's budget, although they suited her taste. Teddy Baer was an observant man.

"Another day toiling down in the mine," Florence said as she sat at a small vanity table in their bedroom and vanished in a spray of perfume. "Are you ready to take up your pick and shovel and put in an honest day's shift?"

Caitrin coughed as the perfume caught at her throat. Florence had the same morning routine with the same inane remarks, and the thought of her being anywhere near a coal mine was ludicrous. "Don't you ever wonder, Florence?"

"Wonder about what?"

"About where we are?"

"Nah," she said and applied a second layer of scarlet lipstick.

"That doesn't bother you?" Caitrin said, wondering why she bothered.

"My lipstick?"

"No. Where we are."

Florence put down the lipstick, sprayed herself with another perfume cloud and shot Caitrin a pitying look. "I'm living in a posh house in the country with my Teddy. I'm wearing smashing clothes, and so are you, by the way. The grub's lovely, and no one is dropping bombs on me every night. And, in return, all I've got to do is stick a little wire in here and tighten a little screw there. That's where I am, and so what's there to be bothered about?"

"And those little screws and wires. Do you know what you're making?"

"We're helping the war effort."

"Which side?"

Florence stared slack-jawed at her. "What a silly question. For us, of course. Caitrin, you've been alone too long if you're thinking up a daft question like that. Why would we help the Nazis?"

"There's a swastika on the base of the beacons."

"I asked Teddy about that, and he said the wood came from a captured German freighter and we're just reusing it."

"Where do they go once we've assembled them?"

"To do good for king and country," Florence said. "What a question."

Talking to Florence and expecting an intelligent reply was optimistic, and Caitrin went silent.

But Florence didn't and explained in a deliberate, measured voice, "What we're doing here is top secret. That's why we don't know where we are or what we're doing. Do you understand?"

"Yes, I do," Caitrin said.

"Ask Teddy if you don't believe me."

"No need to. I believe you," she said, not wanting Florence to tell Teddy she had been asking questions. "You explained it well. Shall we collect our picks and shovels and go down the mine?"

The drawing room downstairs had been cleared of all furniture, except for a long table running down the center. A few chairs were placed at the table; one end was set up to charge batteries, the middle was filled with clockwork escapements, and the other end was ready for transmitter and final beacon assembly. Assembling the beacons was a slow and laborious process, and they worked in silence. Large Eric took a base that, with typical German thoroughness, had holes already drilled and the component places outlined, screwed down a battery, and passed it down the table. Next, Ernie fitted in the clockwork escapement, after which Florence and Caitrin inserted valves and soldered wires to attach the transmitter. Once that was done, Large Eric tested the system and screwed the cover in place. "Make sure the cover's the right way around," he said. "This hole here has to be right over the clockwork so it can be activated with a screwdriver."

Caitrin's description was apt; it did look like a brick. *So how could they possibly hide it without being seen?*

Large Eric put the beacon to one side and was starting another when the door opened and Charles entered with a tea tray. "Elevenses," he said, and Florence squealed with delight.

Charles had taken over the kitchen and forbade them to enter as he prepared meals that also defied rationing. He put down the tray and said, "Battenburg cake, custard slices, and Florence's favorite, Bakewell tarts."

All work instantly stopped, and Charles watched with pride as they devoured his cakes. "Has anyone seen Donnie?" he asked.

"He went off early in the van to London on one of his runs," Large Eric said. "Should be back before supper."

"Have him come see me when he returns. I need some things next time he goes. Enjoy," Charles said and left.

Caitrin watched Florence demolish a plate of Bakewell tarts and thought, *Donnie Thatcher drives the ARP bread van to and from London to supply them with provisions. There was a way out after all.*

Hector sat in the tower room and stared at the blackboards. He was unaware of Bethany studying him, oblivious to her presence on the other side of the table and the tea tray sitting in front of him. Over his objections, and because she was concerned about his emotional strength, Bethany had chosen one of her female agents, and not him, to accompany Grace's body home to Somerset. *Age shall not weary them, nor the years condemn. At the going down of the sun and in the morning, We will remember them. No, we won't, not really.* Her husband Laurence had been killed on the bridge of HMS *Exeter* almost two years ago when it engaged with the German battleship *Graf Spee* off Montevideo, Uruguay. At the time, the grief and shock of his death were overwhelming, and she wanted to die, but gradually they faded away, taking her memories of him with them. Sometimes now she had trouble recalling his voice, and often the images of him she pulled from memory were diffused, as though being viewed through frosted glass. Details were more diminished every time he surfaced. Eventually, Laurence would be just one person in the long parade of people who faded into the mist as they passed through her life, perhaps standing a little taller and looking back sometimes to catch her wistful eye, while what had been between them would no longer exist. *At the going down of the sun and in the morning, We will remember them. Not true, I will not remember Laurence at every sunset and sunrise, only sometimes, and although the pain and shock are gone, the sadness will remain much longer. But Hector is still entrapped by his grief.*

To her, Hector looked so young and too old at the same time. He was in mourning for two women. She had heard about his relationship with Grace, but knew the deeper affection lay with Caitrin. Except for a matter of just a degree or two, they were so close to being an ideal couple, the kind you envied for having a love that lasted their lives.

"I have the daily report," she said, opening the folder in front of her on the table, and failing to get his attention. "Hector."

"What? Sorry, I was far away."

"I said I have the daily report."

"I already read it," Hector sat straighter. "Wee Adolf Hitler wants to know if he can go on holiday to Blackpool if he says sorry, stops the war, and promises to pay for all the breakages."

Bethany's expression softened. He had taken a small step away from his grief. "I wish, but, unfortunately, it's more unpleasant. There were four beacon bombings last night. Radford Hall in Derbyshire and three ancient churches. The Radford family was killed, as was an air-raid warden at one of the churches."

"These attacks are so damaging."

"Because someone inside the country betrays us by setting the beacons."

"It is a treacherous stiletto in the back."

"And in Europe, the German Sixteenth and Eighteenth Armies, along with the Fourth Panzer Group, are closing in on Leningrad. It seems there is nothing the Russians can do to stop them. As you can imagine, Winston is not at all happy."

Hector's gaze returned to the blackboards. "Both those boards are filled with information, but we are no further along. In fact, now, with Caitrin missing, we are further back."

Bethany said nothing. He was right. Their team was now just the two of them, and any chances of unearthing and infiltrating the beacon organization had died in the Blind Stag explosion.

"There is something else," Hector said. "I look at all those facts and figures written there, but keep seeing only one thing. I see a name: Daniel Teddy Baer. I believe you're right, Bethany; he didn't die in the explosion. He is still alive, out there somewhere. Find him, and I guarantee we find the beacons."

"And perhaps find Caitrin too," Bethany said and immediately wished she had not. It was cruel to offer hope to him, or even to herself.

34

It was late when Florence catapulted out of the bedroom in a pink silk negligee and trailing an exhaust cloud of perfume as she went to serve her beloved Teddy—and left Caitrin lying in bed staring at the ceiling. With Florence gone, the silence was appreciated, but Caitrin could not sleep, got out of bed, and drew the blackout curtains open. A thin moon cast enough light to outline the fields and silhouette the bread van parked below. She could just read the white letters ARP daubed on the side.

There were many questions that urgently needed answers. She had discovered Teddy built the beacons, but what happened to them after that? Who was planting them? What was the criterion for choosing a target, and how did they manage to smuggle in what was essentially a brick without attracting attention?

And finally, what should she do next? The bread van was a possibility. It would be easy to wire the ignition and drive away before anyone knew she was gone. And then what? When she faced north outside the house, there were times when the droning of German bombers attacking London came from her right. That meant the house was somewhere south of the city, probably fifty miles or so, and deep in a darkened countryside. Finding her way back there with no lights or signposts would be impossible, while leaving meant her identity would be exposed. And if she did manage to return, to avoid capture Teddy could simply hide the beacons or shift operations to another location. All contact would be lost. She had no choice but to stay.

The crunch of footsteps on gravel came from outside, and she stepped back a little from the window to avoid being noticed as Donnie Thatcher opened the rear door of the bread van, went into the house, and returned carrying the beacons. Caitrin left her bedroom, slipped down the stairs, and eased the front door open. She watched him load the beacons into the van and drive quietly away. He returned twenty minutes later. She waited until he had left and went to the van. It was empty. So, wherever he had taken them was not far away. She would watch him take the same trip several times over the coming weeks.

She retreated to her bedroom. Donnie and his bread van were still a way of communication with the outside world, even if she had to remain.

There were problems in the drawing room the next morning. Some of the boxes of supplies had been delivered damaged, with broken transmitter valves and a few leaky batteries. It meant pausing building beacons to sort through and test all the parts and discard the useless ones. It was midmorning before they were satisfied work could continue, and Donnie entered just as they started.

"I'm off to London, so last orders, if you please," he said.

"More Truman's Pale Ale," Large Eric said.

"And some Guinness wouldn't hurt," Ernie added. "And twenty Seniors."

Florence held up her lipstick. "I'm almost out. Richard Hudnut's Caressing Crimson."

Donnie made a wry face. "I'll try, but you might have to use red lead paint. Anything for you, Caitrin?"

"No, thank you."

"I'm off, then. See you in the morning."

Caitrin waited until Donnie had left the room before following and catching up with him as he was starting the van's engine. "I almost forgot. There was something, Donnie. Could you post this for me?"

Donnie glanced at the envelope in her hand and said, "More than me job's worth, Caitrin. Teddy won't allow it. Strict rules. More than me life's worth too if I get caught."

"Please. It's to my mam. She's not well, and there's only her in the house. She'll be so worried about me. It's just a few harmless lines. Read it."

She opened the envelope and gave him the letter.

He handed it back. "It's private, and I don't want trouble."

"It just says I'm all right and not to worry," Caitrin said as she put the letter back into the envelope and sealed the flap.

"I don't know. Teddy's very strict about—"

"Post this for me, Donnie, and we'll be even with you stealing my wedding ring. All that put behind us and forgotten."

"All right. I shouldn't, but this one time only," he said and took the envelope. "Tell no one."

"Mum's the word. Thank you so much." She stood back as he drove away. She had taken action, and Donnie was carrying her first line of communication.

"He's getting you something exotic from London, I hope," Teddy said, his voice coming from behind her.

She froze for an instant. *How long had Teddy been there and what had he seen? What had he heard?* She turned toward him, her expression blank. "I had a sudden urge for an orange, but then realized how difficult it would be to find one."

"If anyone could find an orange, our Donnie could," Teddy said, put two fingers to his lips and released an ear-piercing whistle.

To Caitrin's dismay, the van stopped and reversed back to them. Donnie wound down his window and squinted up at Teddy. "What's going on, guv'nor?"

Caitrin interrupted before Teddy could question him. "I was telling Teddy I really wanted an orange and was going to ask you to find one, but it seemed a bit much."

"Not easy nowadays, oranges or virgins, beg your pardon," Donnie said. "But I'll try my best, if you like."

"Would you?" Caitrin said.

"Anything else, Donnie?" Teddy asked, and leaned into the window, his eyes locked on Donnie. "Anything?"

"No. You need anything, guv'nor?" Donnie said and grinned, "Or have you already got everything you want?"

Caitrin was impressed at Donnie's performance. He was a natural, cheeky liar, and needed to be to save his life. And her life too.

Teddy laughed at his impudence. "Bourbon biscuits. See if you can find some of those."

"Righto, guv, Bourbon biscuits for the gent, and a virgin orange it is for the lady," Donnie said, wound up the window, and drove away before Teddy could ask him any more questions.

Caitrin gave a sigh of relief as they watched the van disappear. That was close, too close.

"Once you've finished for the day, I'd like you to take a walk with me," Teddy said. "There are things to be discussed."

"Such as?"

"We'll take a walk, later, just the two of us, and you'll find out then," Teddy said and turned away.

*   *   *

They left the house in the evening, when there was still some light in the sky, and went toward the wood before turning left onto a smaller path that ran down a long slope to a brook. The land was dark, indigo-shadowed, and a rising mist smudged the trees and hedgerows. A bat fluttered by, and a lone bird darted for home. The path switchbacked at the end of a long, low wall.

"See that? I don't understand why they built that wall," Teddy said. "There's no reason for it."

"It's called a ha-ha," Caitrin said.

Teddy shot her an uncertain look. He was sensitive to any insult—real or imagined, intentional or accidental—to the fragility of his knowledge. Teddy might well become a peer of the realm one day, but he would always be a poorly educated one.

"I'm not making it up. It's called a ha-ha."

"Why would they call it that?"

"Supposedly, the son of one of the many French King Louises stood at the top of one and said, 'I am expected to be afraid of this? Ha-ha.'"

"I'd have pushed the bugger over. Bounce-ha-ha-bounce."

Caitrin laughed. "I'm quite sure you would. The wall and the angled banking are designed to keep deer and cattle out of the gardens, and because you cannot see it from the house, it offers an unobstructed view."

"How does a girl from a Welsh coal-mining town know about ha-has?"

"I read a lot."

"Ha."

"Ha."

The chattering of the brook grew louder as the path followed its banks. The light was fading and detail disappearing.

"No moon tonight," Teddy said.

"No bombers either."

Ahead of them a man sat on a stile. He jumped down as they approached and put out his hand. She recognized him.

"Sammy Breen. You're dead."

"No, I'm an actor."

"Resting between shows," Teddy said.

"You set the beacon that killed my fiancé at the Café de Paris."

"It wasn't me."

"Donnie Thatcher said it was you."

"Only a fool would trust Donnie Thatcher."

This fool did trust him, which means my letter is probably wadded up and lying in a ditch somewhere between here and London. "Who did it, then?"

"We'll talk about it tomorrow," Teddy said.

"No, let's talk now, and I notice the Whitechapel Street accent's disappeared. You sound almost posh, Sammy."

"As mentioned, I'm an actor."

"Which accent is real?"

"Neither. I can do Irish, Scottish, German. Would you be wanting to hear about the Blarney Stone, then, or the hunting of the wily haggis, mein schön fraulein?"

"Caitrin, you'll understand better if we wait until tomorrow," Teddy said. "After we finish our little chat here."

"All right," she said, unsatisfied.

"I know you're irritated at being stuck on building the beacons, although Donnie says with those delicate female fingers, you're the best at wiring."

"So says untrustworthy Donnie Thatcher."

Teddy smiled, his teeth showing in the darkness. "They want the targets increased."

"They?"

He ignored her reply. "That means more people are needed to set the beacons. I'd like you to work with Sammy. He doesn't drive, but you do, and people instinctively trust a woman."

"What do I do?"

"Rehearse with Sammy until your story is flawless."

"When?"

"Tomorrow."

Twilight was gone, and only the stars showed the separation between sky and ground. The two men were featureless shapes facing her, hardly distinguishable from their surroundings. No moon, no bombers. Not true. Tonight the Lighthouse beacons would be guiding a few.

35

Bethany dropped a folder onto the table and slumped into her chair. With just the two of them working there, the tower room seemed empty. She opened the folder. "Some grim statistics, Hector. The Blitz so far has damaged or destroyed two million homes. Deaths forty-three thousand, and eighty-six thousand injured."

She glanced up at Hector who sat, seemingly deaf and immobile, in his chair. "You look as though you've been shot, stuffed, and mounted, except for staring at the clock every ten seconds."

"What? Sorry, I'm just not very good at waiting. I'll be all right once the courier arrives," he said.

"He'll be here soon, but what do you expect to learn from the actual letter?" She tapped a sheet of paper on the table in front of him. "This is an accurate transcription, isn't it?"

"Yes, Gwen read it to me over the telephone, and I wrote down every word."

"Then what?"

"I don't know, but there's maybe something, some clue. I don't understand why Caitrin wrote to her mother and not us."

"I'm happy to know she's alive, and in a way, she did write to us in that letter."

Bethany took the paper from him and read aloud, " 'Dear Mam, London has been so hectic I decided to take some time off. I'm staying at a place in the country which is secluded and quiet. Tell Uncle Nigel I'm thinking of him,' " she looked up at Hector. "That would be you."

"Why use Nigel?"

"Because Welsh miners don't call their sons Hector and definitely don't have surnames like Neville-Percy." She returned to the letter. " 'And Auntie Grace too.' She doesn't know Grace is dead."

"No."

"Writing directly to us might not have been safe, which is why she wrote a harmless letter to her mother. Don't forget that Teddy Baer easily found our supposedly restricted telephone number. 'Once this war is over, you and I are going on a long holiday, and we'll spoil ourselves rotten. All my love, Caitrin. PS: Important. Tell Auntie Beth I know the left turn is bothering her, and we'll do something about it soon.' I must be Auntie Beth."

"Left turn? That makes no sense."

"Not yet, but at least we now know she wasn't killed in the Blind Stag explosion and is probably somewhere with Teddy Baer."

"She's working with him?"

"I don't think so. Why else would she disguise us in a letter to her mother?"

"Left turn. What left turn?"

A knock at the door interrupted him.

"The courier, thank goodness," he said, with a great sigh of relief.

The door opened; a secretary entered and said, "Mrs. Goodman, the courier is here."

The courier was not who they expected. Gwen Colline stood in the doorway, both hands clutching her handbag. She wore a plain cloth coat and a felt hat that failed to discipline her curls. Bethany immediately liked her, once she got past the shock of her surprise appearance.

Hector was stunned. "Gwen, Mrs. Colline?"

"I brought Caitrin's letter with me," Gwen said.

"Gwen, I'm Bethany," Bethany said as she recovered, took her arm, and led her to a sofa. "Hector you've already met."

"I'll go get tea," Hector said and hurried out.

"This is unexpected, but thank you for coming all this way. Please sit down."

"Thank you. I don't get many letters from Caitrin, and they're precious to me."

"I understand. How was your journey?"

"Um . . . I . . . uh . . . I don't know what to say," Gwen said.

"Start at the beginning and tell me everything."

"All right. I was having a morning cuppa with my next door neighbor Maureen when someone hammered on the front door. Made us both jump, and she spilled her tea on my new oilcloth. There were two soldiers there, a young officer who looked as though he was wearing his dad's uniform and a private with a rifle. He was no older. They weren't even Welsh, from somewhere near Hereford instead."

"That must have been a surprise."

"The first of many. The boy-officer said he had come for the letter, and I said it was mine and wasn't going to give it to him. He said the letter was going to London, and I said not without me, and he said all right then. He asked if he could come in, and I said yes, but the guns had to stay outside."

Bethany laughed. "That was a surprise to him."

"It was. He said that was against orders and they'd wait outside, but I had only ten minutes to get ready. Maureen was giggling like a brook in the kitchen."

"I'm sure she was."

"I told him I already read the letter to Hector in London over the telephone, and he said they needed to look at the original for clues. What kind of clues, I said."

"Latent clues, madam."

"What's latent?"

"Top secret."

"So I said, all right. I'd never been in a car before, just once, at my husband's funeral, a big black Humber it was."

"Another surprise."

"Yes, but not the biggest. They drove me to an aerodrome and put me in a tiny little aeroplane. I sat in the front and a pilot sat in a seat behind me. It was wide open, there was no roof, and I had to take my hat off and wear a leather helmet with a microphone."

"Were you scared?"

"No."

And there was revealed Caitrin's mother, and the honesty and strength of character she shared with her daughter. She was an admirable woman.

"Go on, please."

"It was noisy, windy, and the pilot said it was the aeroplane they used to train Spitfire pilots. He said I could try flying if I wanted, and just moving the stick backwards and forwards would change the size of Wales. I said I liked Wales exactly the size it was, thank you very much. We flew at a hundred and twenty-five miles an hour, imagine, and after we landed another big car, a Bentley, brought me here." Gwen stopped, out of breath, and looked at the clock. "What a day. This morning I was having a quiet cuppa with Maureen and talking about growing rhubarb, and now, for the first time in my life, I've been in two cars and an aeroplane, and I'm here in London, and all before tea time."

"You've had quite the adventure."

"Yes, I have, and a big one at that."

"The train would have been impossible, slow and crowded."

"What is this place?"

"It's a home for unwed mothers."

"Who run around with pillows shoved up their jumpers. I'm not as daft as I look."

"Daft you are not." Bethany raised her hands in surrender. "And I can see you are your daughter's mother."

Hector entered with a tea tray, and they sat in silence until the pouring and spoon rattling was done.

"We are a clandestine organization called 512, and our role is to hunt down enemy spies and fifth columnists in the country," Bethany said and heard Hector gasp at her admission. She turned to him. "Gwen is Caitrin's mother. How long do you think we could keep up the unwed mother charade with her?"

"And Caitrin is one of you?" Gwen said.

"Yes."

"Have you spoken to her?"

"No."

"Do you have the letter she sent you?" Hector asked.

"Yes."

"May I have it?"

Gwen's hands tightened on her handbag.

"I promise I will give it right back to you. Promise."

Gwen reluctantly opened her handbag and gave Hector the letter.

"She has beautiful penmanship," Hector said as he opened the letter.

"Caitrin loves writing, although she's terrible at writing letters. She was the only child in Mrs. Williams's writing class who would come home with perfect marks and no ink stains on her fingers."

Hector's lips moved as he silently read the letter to himself. "Does left turn in knitting mean anything to you?"

"No, I'm terrible at knitting."

"It's strange that she ran those two words together. Left-turn."

"A spelling mistake, you think?" Bethany said.

"It's the only one on the page, and the two words are perfectly linked," Hector said and grinned. "Caitrin wouldn't make an elementary mistake like that. Leftturn, leftturn. It's not a mistake, you little Welsh genius, you!"

"What?"

"Both of you, repeat leftturn as one word, quickly. Go!"

"Leftturn, leftturn, leftturn."

Hector joined in. "Leftturn, leftturn, leuchtturm, leftturn, leuchtturm, leftturn, leuchtturm. Leuchtturm is German for lighthouse. She's telling us about the Lighthouse beacon." He read a sentence from the letter, "Tell Auntie Beth I know the left turn in her knitting is bothering her—the leuchtturm, lighthouse, is bothering her—and I'll show her the right way soon."

"I told you she was alive," Gwen said.

"She found them." Hector sat back, beaming with pride as Gwen whipped the letter out of his hands and into the safety of her handbag.

"Now all we have to do is find her."

"Knowing my Caitrin, she'll probably find you," Gwen said.

Bethany nodded in agreement. "Is there anything we can do to thank you, Gwen?"

"Just one thing."

"Tell me."

"I'd like to meet Winston Churchill."

"I could arrange that."

"So I can give him a piece of my mind about his terrible treatment of the Welsh miners."

Bethany looked stricken. "Perhaps not."

"I'm teasing you," Gwen said and grinned. "What I would really like is a shop that sells decent knicker elastic. There's none to be had in Wales. Begging your pardon, Hector."

36

Teddy led Caitrin to the back of the house while the others were at breakfast. They passed a black Riley Kestrel parked in the yard and entered the empty stables. Caitrin had an instant mental image of Teddy as the future Lord Daniel de Barr, striding past stalls of thoroughbred horses and trailing a cloud of obsequious grooms and eager stable-lads: the great m'lud, owner of all he surveyed. They stopped at the tack room door, where Teddy raised a hand and pressed his fingertips against the wood.

"This is decision time," he said. "For you. Once through this door, you will need to develop instant amnesia. Everything will be forgotten, except for the work ahead, and not a word spoken about it to anyone."

"That's a bit dramatic."

"It's realistic. Agreed?"

"Memory gone."

Teddy opened the door. Inside, Sammy was waiting for them, sitting feet up with his chair tilted back against a wall of harnesses.

"And a verrah grand morning to you," he said in a music-hall Scottish accent.

"The man of many voices," Caitrin said and was having difficulty hiding her dislike of Sammy Breen.

"And master of them all," Teddy said.

"Is there a real one?" she asked.

"This is it, Taffy," Sammy answered in a soft, southern Irish accent.

Caitrin ignored the slight, and the urge to reply in same.

"Enough," Teddy said. "Business."

"I'd like to know what happened at the Café de Paris the night of the bombing before we begin any business," Caitrin said.

"So you want the true story?" Sammy said.

"I doubt I'll get that, but I've already heard Donnie Thatcher's account, so now you can give me your version."

Sammy lit a cigarette and exhaled a long stream of smoke as he stared at the ceiling. "Donnie and I were supposed to plant the beacon at the Shakespeare statue in Leicester Square, but it was crowded, and there was no way to do it without being seen. So we went to the Café de Paris for a drink, even though it was early, while we decided what to do next." He half-turned to face her. "After an hour or so, I suggested we try again and went to the cloakroom to pick up the beacon. But Donnie was tipsy, lost the ticket, and the girl couldn't find the right one."

"Couldn't find the right one? You left the beacon in the cloakroom?"

"Yes."

"This is confusing. What, with all the other beacons? I don't understand."

"No," Sammy shot her a withering look, stood, took a gas-mask bag from a hook, and threw it to her. "We carry the beacons in these."

"A perfectly anonymous hiding place," Teddy said. "Because everybody in the country carries one slung over their shoulder. They also forget them, especially after a few drinks. The cloakrooms of London's clubs and theaters are filled with hundreds of forgotten gas masks."

"Donnie was worried the girl might uncover the beacon as she searched through the pile, so we left. End of story."

No, that's where the story began, and it ended when the bombs dropped and my Max died. Beacons hidden inside gasmask bags—another question answered. And Donnie might have been lying, so what happened to my letter? She kept her silence.

"Now, down to business," Teddy said. "You work as a team. That means from the moment of leaving here to the time you return, you are always together."

"What if I need to go to the lavatory?" Caitrin asked.

"I'll be a gentleman and avert my eyes, until the tinkling of falling rain or the plop plop of solid matter ceases," Sammy said, and Caitrin disliked him even more.

"No separation, until you return," Teddy said. "Sammy will introduce himself as MI6 Senior Officer Samuel Lockhart, and you are now Field Officer Catherine Walters. Sammy has your identification. Rehearse the story before you leave. You will drive because Sammy cannot. But Sammy is armed; you are not."

"Why not?"

"Because I trust Sammy. I do not yet trust you," Teddy said, as he shrugged, gave her his little boy smile, and left.

"There's a challenge for you," Sammy said. "Earning Teddy's trust."

"You can try earning mine."

"Teddy tells me you're a red-hot Welsh socialist. Is that why you want to blow up the English aristocracy?"

"It's a good enough reason. Why are you doing it?"

"Beggorah, I'm Irish, am I not? What other reason would a leprechaun need to beleaguer the English toffs?"

Caitrin fought an overwhelming urge to stop the funny voices by smacking him square in the mouth. "I suppose we all have our own reasons. Are we the only ones setting beacons?"

"We're not alone. That's all I know."

"What is the plan?"

"Our targets for today." Sammy pulled an envelope from his pocket, took out a card, and read: "St. Mark's church, Canterbury. It dates from five ninety-seven; Swarton Manor, eleventh century; and Pett Bottom Hall, tenth century. All fairly close to each other and not very far away."

"Who chooses these targets?"

"Were you not warned about asking questions? It's not your business."

"All right. Harmless question, then. What do we do?"

"We drive up, and you stay in the car, facing away from the building."

"Why?"

"Because if something goes wrong, we can get away quickly. I will introduce myself and explain to them there are reports of German fifth columnists in the neighborhood and their place might be on the target list. Just to be sure they are safe, I will suggest making an inspection of the property. Then you join us and use your womanly charms to seduce and distract while I set the beacon."

"Unbutton the blouse and lean forward sort of thing?"

Her sarcasm was wasted. "Whatever you think works best, Field Officer Catherine Walters. I'll leave that up to you. Time to load up."

They placed three beacons in gas-mask bags on the rear seat of the Riley, and Sammy covered them with a blanket. "We have to be careful because the transmitter valves are delicate. The slightest shock can break them."

"What if the beacon fails?"

"Then it fails, and we abandon it. We never return to the same location."

Caitrin slid behind the wheel, and Sammy sat next to her with a map spread across his lap as they drove out of the yard. For Caitrin, the world was bright and open after being sequestered in the hunting lodge. It was high summer, the air smelled of freshly mown hay, and the hedgerows teemed with birds and butterflies. The country was running on double summertime, which extended the day so twilight stretched far into the evening. It seemed so bizarre to her that, while they were driving through such beautiful countryside, people were dying fifty miles away in London, and more would die tonight when the Luftwaffe returned. And the next night. Meanwhile they were carrying beacons that would ensure more deaths.

Sammy gave her precise directions, and it took a little while for Caitrin to realize he was taking them on a deliberately circuitous route down country lanes. All signposts had long since been removed because of the threat of invasion, and it would be almost impossible for her to find the way home alone.

"How far away are we from the first one?" she asked.

"St. Mark's church. It's on a hill on the outskirts of town and about ten minutes away."

Caitrin followed a road that narrowed and was bordered by greystone walls as it curved uphill to the church. She turned around with some difficulty at the lych-gate and switched off the engine.

Sammy gazed through the windscreen at the church. "It's supposedly one of the oldest churches in England. Built on a Roman foundation. Are you by any chance a religious lass?"

"No."

"Me neither. Nice church, though. Oh well, pity, but all good things come to an end. Come on, we'll do this one together."

He gave her one of the gas-mask bags. "Sling this over your shoulder. Women are better at obeying orders than men."

"That's why we live longer."

They walked through the lych-gate and toward the church. The ancient graveyard, with its tombstones at all angles, reminded Caitrin of where Max was buried in Kirton-in-Lindsey in Lincolnshire. *Visiting his grave was so long ago, when I was young. Or a different woman with a different story.*

A boy pushing a lawnmower stopped as they approached, straightened, and mopped his brow.

"Hello," Sammy said, and added in his public school accent, "rather warm work for a chap on a day like this."

"Aye."

"What's your name?"

"Andy."

"Is the vicar around, Andy?"

"This time of day, he'll be out doing his rounds," Andy said with a crooked-toothed grin. "Probably saving souls at the Crown and Cygnet about now."

"Is it all right if we take a look inside? My girlfriend here loves old churches."

"Aye," Andy said and went silent, having exhausted his vocabulary.

The church door quivered on its hinges as Sammy pushed it open. Inside it was cool and dark.

"All churches smell like churches," Sammy said. "The dust and deceit of ages."

He found a hidden corner behind the altar, took the beacon from the bag, and activated it. Caitrin glanced back at the rows of dark-wood pews and imagined the devastation this beacon was about to bring. For centuries, generations of people had prayed here, in good times and bad, for forgiveness or in gratitude, and they were all connected to each other through the ages by this building. Heritage was nothing more than memory, and that was contained in and guarded by the church. A people without a memory could not endure.

"Job well done. Let's go," Sammy said as he took her arm and hurried out.

The lawnmower was abandoned and Andy gone when they left. Caitrin caught a glimpse of him as she drove away. He was pissing on a monument near the church wall and blushed as he saw her looking at him. But then she winked, and he felt better.

"Turn left and straight on for about a mile. Then right," Sammy said. "I wish they were all that easy."

"What's the next one?"

"Swarton Manor, eleventh century."

Swarton Manor might well have been eleventh century, but its Victorian owners had spent considerable time, money, and trouble to erase any style or grace from the building. Even on this bright and eager day, it looked as though it were sulking. The bricks were made of melancholy. Caitrin turned the Riley around on the gravel drive so it faced the entrance. They got out and gazed at the building. It was deserted, with all of the windows shuttered.

"Two thousand acres of prime farmland, a half-dozen tenant farmers, and bugger all to do every day. What a gift," Sammy said. "That's the Saunders-Bricklett family's life for you."

An Austin Shooting Brake crunched up the gravel drive and stopped next to them, and a portly man who looked as though he had interrupted an afternoon of drinking got out. He seemed to be annoyed, but seeing Caitrin mellowed him. "Hello, may I help you?"

Sammy put out his hand and, with his best old-boy accent, said, "Hello. Terribly sorry to bother you. I am MI6 Senior Officer Samuel Lockhart, and this is Field Officer Catherine Walters."

"Major Bevan-Broad, the estate's agent. How do you do. What brings MI6 here?"

"How do you do, Major. We have reports of German fifth-column saboteurs in the area, and Swarton Manor might well be on their list."

"Damn."

"Would you mind awfully if I gave the place a quick once-over. Damn clever, these Jerries."

"The place is closed up. Where's the family?" Caitrin asked. "The Saunders-Brickletts."

"Bermuda, for the duration," Bevan-Broad said. "Lady Anne has a delicate constitution, and the war has been so wearing on her."

How terribly rotten for the poor dear; how she must be suffering. With difficulty, Caitrin kept her mouth shut.

"Field Officer Catherine here can explain more while I scurry around and make sure the place is safe," Sammy said as he snatched up a gas-mask bag and hurried away before the Major could reply. Caitrin tightened a grim smile as Bevan-Broad, with hope in his eyes, even though he didn't much like women wearing trousers, tilted a little off axis toward her.

Caitrin accelerated away, skidding a little to pepper the major in a shower of gravel as they left. Sammy glanced in amusement at her.

"Two down, one to go. Pett Bottom Hall, tenth century," he said. "Where there are, hopefully, no drunken majors."

"Lady Anne has a delicate constitution and the war has been so wearing on her," Caitrin mimicked Bevan-Broad. "The English are such hypocrites."

"The last one is Pett Bottom Hall, tenth century, with a huge ancestral home and ten thousand acres. Owned by the—"

"Petty Big Bottoms."

"One can only imagine. No, the Fraser-Greenwoods. Perhaps they are in Bermuda too and the place is empty."

Pett Bottom Hall was not empty. A half-dozen cars and an army ambulance were parked outside, while nurses with patients strolled the expansive grounds. Caitrin stopped short of the entrance.

"This is a convalescent home now," Caitrin said. "For wounded soldiers."

"Wounded *English* soldiers."

"They're just boys. Sammy, I won't let you go in there. They've been through enough."

"*You* won't let *me*?"

"No, I won't."

Sammy took out his automatic. "And what will you do to stop me?"

"I'll raise the alarm."

He pressed the muzzle against her temple. "Not dead you won't."

Caitrin slammed her hand on the horn, and a half-dozen nurses and patients turned in their direction at the sound. "Go ahead, shoot me now they're all looking at us. You can't drive, remember? How are you going to get away? Teddy won't like that."

Sammy lowered the gun, sat, and stared at her for a long moment. For the first time since she had met him, he gave her a genuine smile, reached to the back seat, and picked up the remaining gas-mask bag. He took out the beacon, hammered it against the dashboard, and, in an exaggerated upper-class accent, said, "I say, old girl, that was jolly careless of you, dropping the darned thing."

"I was clumsy, sorry."

"It probably has broken valves now, so we will have to abandon it—"

"And, of course, we never return to the same location."

"Yes," he said, and was Irish again, and serious. "You get one, and that was it. You owe me now, and we don't ever talk about this, understand?"

"Yes, Sammy."

"Two out of three is a good day's work. Good enough. Drive us home."

Caitrin drove away from Pett Bottom Hall. Things had changed. Now she had an ally in Sammy Breen. Or did she? Sammy, like Donnie Thatcher and Teddy Baer, lived and survived in a mean, friendless world, and would betray her instantly if it kept him alive.

37

The rational part of Bethany's mind assured her nothing lasted forever, and that sooner or later everything, good or bad, changed. But often her experiences overrode the rational. The days were very much alike now: she woke early, ate breakfast, picked up the morning's briefing, and went to meet Hector in the tower room. Judging by his weary expression, he probably felt the same way too. She sat and opened her briefing folder.

"Not good news, I'm afraid. Barbarossa, the German advance into Russia, has been overwhelming. On the first day of the invasion, the Russians lost over twelve hundred aircraft. The Germans captured three hundred thousand troops and then a further three hundred thousand a bit later. In Kiev, they trapped and captured four hundred and fifty thousand troops."

"Those are hard numbers to comprehend."

"Winston fears the Germans will sweep through Russia in a few weeks and can then turn their full attention on us. Our forces are not yet recovered enough from Dunkirk to face such an onslaught."

"Let's hope and pray Hitler does a Napoleon."

"We'll need more than hope and prayers," she said and slid a document across the table to him. "This also has him worried. Last night, three successful Lighthouse beacon attacks in Leicestershire, all ancestral homes, and two in Canterbury, one estate and a church. They're increasing."

"St. Mark's," Hector read the description.

"And utterly destroyed. Winston is very concerned about these attacks. He says they are being seen as personal, malicious, and people with influence are voicing alarm. And we have very little to show him in return."

"You've heard nothing more from Caitrin?"

"No. Winston is worried that, with the increasing success of Lighthouse, the Germans will turn to larger targets. That could create panic," she spread her hands and shrugged. "And we have no clues."

"I have one—it's small, but a clue. The bread van that passed us the night the Blind Stag blew up. I remembered only C, the first letter of the bakery's name, and made a list of possibilities in and around London. They all turned up blank; either no vans or no more bakeries after the Blitz. All except one, Chorlton's Bakery, in Putney."

"And?"

"They had three vans. Two were destroyed when the bakery was bombed, and the third vanished."

"Apparently not."

"The bakery is back in business, but greatly reduced," he said and offered her a sheet of paper. "And, here are the vehicle details."

"Thank you. I'll pass this on to the police," she said, and put a folder of photographs in front of him. "And talking of police, Sergeant Goodwillie sent these over. Large Eric Ambrose, Ernie Wood, Donnie Thatcher—all believed dead, but you never know—and Samuel Breen. And not forgetting Florence Simmonds. They all worked for Teddy at one time or another, but have also disappeared, presumably with him."

"What's our next step?"

"I want you to go to Canterbury, inspect both targets, and see what you can find."

"All right," Hector said and stood. "On my way."

"If you would like someone to go with you, I have several bright recruits who are—"

"No. I'd rather do it alone, if you don't mind."

"I understand."

Hector smelled the church long before he saw it—the cloying scent of burning wood and paper extinguished by water. He drove the narrow, winding road uphill and parked at the lych-gate, where an ARP warden was waiting for him, an elderly man in an ancient uniform, sitting on a deck chair beneath the gate, reading a ruined bible. He looked up as Hector approached.

"Good morning, young man. You'll be the secret fellow I was told to meet."

"Good morning. I suppose you could call me that."

The old man put down the bible and gestured to the church behind him. "It's a crime what they did last night. A crime against human beings is what it is."

Hector nodded in agreement, but the old man was not finished.

"I was married in that church, and my boy and his boy after him was christened there. My wife, Phyllis, God rest her soul, is buried in that corner over there. It was a criminal act."

"Do you mind if I take a look?"

"Not at all. There isn't much to look at. I'll stay here if you don't mind. My grandson Andy's down there cleaning up. He was here yesterday mowing the grass. That was a waste of time."

Hector left him and went to what was left of the church.

Most of the tower remained, although the door was gone, and the far wall still stood, minus its stained-glass window. There was nothing in between. The high-explosive bombs had blasted off the roof and shattered the long walls, to let the following incendiaries consume centuries of bone-dry wood. The linked memories of countless generations were gone. The headstones close to the church had been flattened, and several larger monuments that remained standing were seared black by the flames. He saw a boy trundling a wheelbarrow between the graves, stopping frequently to pick up bibles and hymnals scattered by the blast. He would inspect each one, wipe them clean with his sleeve, and drop them in the wheelbarrow.

"Good morning. You must be Andy," Hector said.

The boy straightened and wiped at his face. "How'd you know that?"

"Your grandad told me."

"Oh, aye."

"That's a job and a half you've got."

"Aye. Don't know why I'm doing it, though. Not much point, really. What can you do with a wheelbarrow full of burnt bibles?"

"You're doing a good thing for the congregation, Andy. Your grandad tells me you were here yesterday."

"Aye. The church was in one piece then."

"Did anything unusual happen yesterday?"

"Unusual around here? That would be different."

"Were there any visitors?

"Just two, a man and a woman."

"Can you describe them?"

"The man was tall and built like a rugby prop forward. Posh voice."

"The woman?"

"Lovely she was, and had all these shiny red curls. Pretty."

Hector caught his breath. "Curls?"

"Aye. Head full of red curly hair."

"Was she posh too?"

"Don't know. She didn't say anything."

"Do you know their names?"

"No, they didn't give any. He said his girlfriend liked old churches and wanted to look inside. I said they could, and so they did."

"Did you go with them?"

"No, my boots were too muddy to go inside, and I had no reason to anyway."

"Thank you, Andy. Was there anything else unusual?"

"No, just the bomb going off woke me up. Blew up my lawn-mower too," Andy said.

"If you think of anything else, call me," Hector said and gave him a card.

"I don't have a telephone."

"Try the police station. They'll have one."

Andy screwed up his mouth, thought for a moment, and said, "I would, but the Canterbury police told me they don't ever want to see my face in there anymore."

Major Bevan-Broad was sad and sober when he met Hector in front of a still-smoking Swarton Manor. The window shutters were strewn across the driveway like discarded playing cards, the roof was gone, and the chimneys had collapsed into the building.

"I don't know what I'll tell the family," he said, close to tears.

"The Saunders-Brickletts?" Hector said, reading from his notebook. "They are away?"

"Bermuda. The war has been so unkind to Lady Anne's nerves."

"Yes, it would be," Hector said, failing to hide his sarcasm, but the major was too involved in his own misery to notice. "You were here yesterday, Major?"

"One of our tenants noticed a car driving through the gates and notified me. We were not expecting visitors."

"And who were they?"

"A couple. A tall man, well-spoken, and a young woman, wearing trousers of all things."

"What did she look like?"

"Quite charming, in a city-pale sort of way, with a veritable crown of red curls. Extraordinary, really. Welsh accent, but a pleasant enough one."

"Why were they here?"

"He said they were from MI6, mentioned German saboteurs were in the area and Swarton Manor might be a target. He looked around the building for suspicious activity," the Major said and risked a glance at the smoking ruin. "He was right."

"Names?"

"I'm so bad at names. Field Officer Samuel something. She was Catherine, I forget the rest. This is tragic, so tragic."

"Do you remember what kind of car they drove?"

"I do, because the family has one. A Riley Kestrel, black."

"Number plate?"

"I didn't think to take notice."

"Of course not. Thank you, Major."

"This will shatter Lady Anne. What will I tell the family?"

"The truth? Tell them there's a war on," Hector said, shook hands with the major, and left. He drove home, confused. Caitrin had sent a letter saying she would be taking care of Lighthouse, but now, apparently, she had helped plant two beacons. Whose side was she on? And where was she? His heart and mind wanted to trust her, but his training had taught him to trust no one.

38

Several families in London were living in the dark because Teddy Baer had all their candles. The lodge dining room glowed amber with them. There were burning candelabras on every shelf, mantelpiece, table, and sideboard. The dining table at the center of the room was a masterpiece of Irish linen, silver cutlery, fine porcelain, and crystal glass. It too had a candelabra. Teddy sat at one end in his informal best, a soft-collared shirt under a cream cricket jumper, with Caitrin at the other.

"I had them shorten this ridiculous table," he said. "Because I hate shouting and like to see who I am dining with."

Dining with. The Whitechapel Teddy would have said eating, or noshing with. "That was a very good idea."

"The toffs are strange people," he said and picked up a piece of silver. "This, for example. They call this a gravy boat. Why a boat?"

"I suppose because it looks a bit like a boat."

"Fair enough, but what about this?" He showed her another piece of silver. "A dredger, a salt dredger. I ask you, where the hell did that come from?"

Caitrin shrugged. "Perhaps it's ye olde English for thing that holds the salt and needs a short name starting with D."

He put down the dredger and wagged a finger at her. "Clever, you're very clever. And I hope hungry too. Charles has been slaving away in the kitchen all day. Beef Wellington, he tells me. I hope it's not meat in a rubber boot."

"Teddy, you do know there's a war on, with severe food rationing?"

"So I heard, but it can't be everywhere. Champagne?" He poured them each a glass. "This is a bit like the good old Blind Stag days. I miss that pub, but only sometimes."

Caitrin raised her glass. "Here's to the Blind Stag."

"The Blind Stag." Teddy sipped his champagne, sat back, and wiped his lips. "I've been thinking about you a lot. What is it that's different about her, I asked myself. Then I finally got it. You're me if I was a woman, and a much kinder person."

"You have been thinking."

"The problem is when I'm dealing with you, I'm dealing with another me. Me wouldn't trust I, and I wouldn't trust me."

"You have to find solid ground to stand on at some point."

"I have it. Me, on the top of the mountain."

"Lonely."

"Safe."

"You don't trust the others?"

He snorted in amusement. "Large Eric and Ernie are foot soldiers, and Florence is a lost bird looking for a safe perch. Donnie Thatcher is honest in his way, an honest mercenary loyal to the money."

"Sammy Breen?"

"Irish and an actor, which is really the same thing. He thinks he's bright, but it's a blackbird brightness. Nothing behind it. That leaves just you."

"Now I feel lonely."

"No, you don't. Sammy said you did well out there."

"Except for dropping the last beacon."

"It works out for the best."

"What do you mean?"

"What's the phrase about the mother of invention?"

"Necessity is the mother of invention."

"War's the father. The beacons have changed, and we just put in a different transmitter."

"What's different?"

"Before, the aircraft flew high, which sometimes made accuracy difficult, even with a beacon. With the new planes, they fly low and fast, drop their bombs right down the chimney, and disappear in seconds. You're taking one of the new ones back to the target you missed."

"I thought we never revisited the locations?"

"Usually not, but Sammy said you stopped at the entrance when you saw the nurses and patients. So you never really went in there. No one met you."

She stared at him in horror. "It is a convalescent home for wounded soldiers."

"It's on the list."

"What list? Who makes the list?"

"I don't."

"Teddy, they're just boys, some of them terribly wounded. Working-class boys."

"They know that."

"This is monstrous."

"I hear most of them are badly hurt, so you'll be doing the boys a favor."

Caitrin sat back and glared at him. "What an outrageous thing to say."

He shook his head. "No, it's not. See, I'm not the smart one in the Baer family, not the really intelligent one. That was my big brother Isaac. Isaac was patriotic, went off to war for his country, and the Germans blew him up. He was still alive when they brought him back to England, but his arms and legs were left in France."

Teddy was talking to her, but he wasn't there. "He was in a convalescent home in Scotland. All the way up there. I went to see him. I was seventeen, and he was twenty-three. It was a big house on the bank of the River Clyde, just outside Glasgow. It was a sunny day when I got there, and they said he was outside in the gardens enjoying the view."

"Teddy."

"I went outside. My big brother Isaac was lying in a wicker basket. They had wrapped him up in a sheet, and he looked like a large baby in a crib with Isaac's head on top. Enjoying the view—all he could do was look up at the sky."

"That must have been awful."

He didn't hear her.

"His voice was damaged, so he couldn't speak very loud. I leaned over him, and he whispered, 'Teddy, help me leave here. You know, you know how.'"

Teddy stopped, was motionless, and silence flooded the room. Caitrin could hear the candles burning.

"You know, you know how?" she murmured.

"Isaac was a butcher, kosher of course, and he showed me what to do, how to sever the arteries so the animal dies quickly. I went to the local village, bought an open razor, slipped back into the gardens, and helped Isaac leave."

Caitrin saw what she had never seen before, tears in Teddy's eyes.

"As you said, they're just badly wounded working-class boys, Caitrin. You'll be doing them a favor. They always put the officers in the best rooms, and the enlisted men and badly damaged ones are in the back, out of sight. Donnie goes with you."

"He can drive. You don't need me."

"I need you to go and do it. I need to discover if I can trust you. To find out if you're me." The tears were gone, and Teddy was alone again on his mountaintop. "Donnie and Sammy will be armed; you will not be. Either one will put a bullet through your head if you fail me."

* * *

Cat drove in silence. Sammy sat next to her with the map, his directions perfunctory, while Donnie lay sleeping across the back seat. She stopped a hundred yards short of the entrance.

Donnie sat up and said, "What are you doing?"

"Teddy thinks I'm a female version of him and wants me to prove it. I'm going to do just that. Give me the beacon and a screwdriver."

"Do you know how to set the trigger?"

"I assembled them, Donnie."

Donnie hesitated, glanced at Sammy, who nodded, and handed over the gas-mask bag. Caitrin got out of the car, opened the bag on the bonnet, and used the screwdriver to activate the beacon. She sat behind the wheel again and pressed the bag to Sammy's ear. "Hear the clockwork ticking? It's activated. Hold it carefully."

Sammy held the bag as she started the engine and drove up to the house. She took it off him as they got out, slipped the strap over her shoulder, and said, "Use your charm to get us inside, and I decide where it goes."

A nurse came out, and Sammy did his charming upper-class gentleman routine. She took them to meet the matron, Mrs. Winterburn, who agreed that with so many people coming and going daily, a saboteur could well have slipped in unawares, and naturally they were welcome to inspect the house.

"It was a grand home once," she said, and whispered, "but I hear the lord of the manor had a bit of a gambling habit. The family had to surrender the property to pay taxes."

"We all have our cross to bear," Sammy said.

"Yes, especially nowadays," the matron said and led them into what had once been the library. It had tall open windows and some flower arrangements. Walls of books remained, but the room was lined with well-spaced hospital beds. In one corner, officers sat on a sofa and several easy chairs grouped around a table, smoking and playing cards. "This is the officers' ward, and the other ranks are—"

"In the back?"

"Yes, how did you know?"

"Wild guess," Caitrin said and turned to Sammy. "Field Officer Samuel, why don't we inspect the other ranks' ward?"

The enlisted men's ward was different. The room was larger, windowless, and smelled not of flowers, but disinfectant and ether. It had a mortuary silence, with the beds much closer together, and most of the men were badly injured. While Sammy stood at a distance, she sat at the bed of a soldier whose head was bandaged. His chart said he was nineteen, Private Llewellyn Meredith from Harlech. "How are you, Llewellyn bach?" she said in Welsh.

He groaned and answered in Welsh, "I thought I'd die before I'd hear Welsh again."

"You didn't, though, did you?"

"Thank you. I can't see you, but I know you're lovely."

"So are you. Dewch yn dda, Llewellyn, so you can go home," Caitrin said and slid the beacon under his bed. She rose, touched his hand. "You'll hear Welsh again, soon." She left.

No one spoke on the drive home, and Sammy kept shooting glances at her until she asked, "What is going on, Sammy?"

"What you did."

"What about what I did?"

"Calmly putting the beacon under a wounded soldier's bed."

"A badly wounded, blind soldier with not much of a future in front of him. I did him a favor."

Sammy was so shaken by her answer he forgot to navigate a complicated way back to the lodge, and finally Caitrin had a sense of where she was.

"The bomber might not get there in time," Donnie said in hope. "The weather's been a bit changeable recently. You never know, the coast could be fogbound."

* * *

The coast was clear as Luftwaffe Hauptmann Karl Trautloft flew his Heinkel 111, named *Lotta* after his mother, low and fast above the waves. Karl loved his Heinkel almost as much as he loved his mother. It was a stable machine to fly, but not without faults. The Junkers Jumo engine exhausts were close to the cockpit, and headsets did little to silence the deafening roar. The nose was made almost entirely of perspex, and there was no floor, so the crew could look directly down at the land below. Many aircrew disliked the cockpit because they felt exposed and vulnerable. But not Karl.

This would be a different kind of attack. Usually they bombed from altitude, but this flight would be at ground level. Flying at night, at two hundred miles an hour so close to the ground, needed Karl's full attention. The slightest error would be fatal, but he was not the kind of pilot who made errors. There were supposedly no tall obstructions on their planned route, but the British loved their antiaircraft balloons as much as he hated and feared them. They popped up like malignant mushrooms and, with their aircraft-snagging cables, were invisible at night.

Heiko, the navigator/bomb-aimer, voice crackling in his headset, gave him a heading. "Turn zero five zero over reservoir ten miles ahead."

Karl banked the Heinkel onto the new heading above the reservoir and saw moonlight catch the port wing. He shivered as his mind sent him a warning. British night fighters would be in the air, and although flying so low made his aircraft difficult to see against the dark ground, a quick flash of metal was all they would need to find him. He leveled off as Heiko settled behind the *Lotfernrohr* bombsight.

"Ten miles to target," Heiko said. "Pett Bottom. Silly name."

"Silly English," Karl said as he steadied the aircraft. They would soon hear the *Leuchtturm* beacon transmitting and have just seconds to release their bombs.

"Five miles."

They should hear the beacon now.

"Two miles."

Heiko turned to him and tapped his headset. Karl shook his head. No beacon.

"Past the target. No beacon."

Karl throttled back and banked hard right. They would go around and try again. Moonlight caught the raised wing, and he watched with dread fascination as bullets stitched holes toward him across the metal surface. Cannon shells struck the port engine and sheared off a propellor blade. He instantly throttled back before the unbalanced prop shook the engine to pieces. Smoke trailed as he turned away, desperate to reach the coast. He dare not climb on only one engine and could not go lower.

"Come on, *Lotta*," he muttered.

The glass nose shattered as cannon shells swept the aircraft, and Heiko was in two pieces at his feet. Karl kicked at the rudder to keep the aircraft straight, but the control cables were gone. Flames blossomed from the port engine, and he knew the night fighter was close behind and he was about to die. This time his beloved *Lotta*, named after his mother who loved him, would not be taking him safely home.

39

Bethany sat on a bench overlooking the pond. She had a thermos of tea at her side and was parsimoniously sharing a few rich tea biscuits with the ducks. It was a clean, sharp day, and she closed her eyes, exhaled a long, calming breath, and relaxed. A thrush sang high on a branch above, ducks squabbled at her feet, and Hector came pounding up the path toward her. He stopped, hands on hips, fighting for breath.

Bethany opened her eyes. "Hector, you look as though you're being chased by someone's husband."

"I have news."

"And I have tea," Bethany patted the bench. "Sit and pour yourself a cup."

He did as he was told and opened his mouth to speak, but Bethany raised a hand to stop him. "Tea first. Calm."

Hector stirred his tea.

"Ducks."

"Ducks?"

She threw the remaining biscuit to the ducks. "The ducks

think I'm being altruistic by sharing my few precious biscuits with them. I'm not. If this rationing continues much longer, I shall be fattening up one of them for Christmas."

"With only a few biscuits, perhaps you should concentrate on feeding one particular duck."

"Ducks are identical, so how would I tell them apart?"

"Caitrin once said all ducks should be numbered."

"Good idea," she said.

"Come in, number five, your time's up," Hector called to the ducks. "Now, about the news."

"I came out here to relax, to get away from sitting in the tower room with Teddy Baer's name glaring at me from the blackboard. It's like one of those paintings where the eyes follow you around the room. Out here it's pleasantly Baer-free."

"Yes, it is."

"I feel the touch of a cooler month approaching. Autumn is near, and with it comes conker season. Did you play conkers as a little boy?"

"Everyone did, no?"

"I thought perhaps the wealthier classes had a footman do it for them."

"You're sounding like Caitrin."

"I'm not as quick," she said and shivered. "It's definitely cooler. My ancient bones serve fair warning."

It was quiet for a moment.

"You missed a golden opportunity there, Hector."

"For what?"

"Flattery. When I mentioned my ancient bones, I gave you the opportunity to be shameless to your superior officer by saying, surely not ancient? Wise bones, perhaps."

"I'll remember next time," Hector said and sipped his tea. "This conversation has wandered off on the strangest tangent."

"Let's bring it back. Tell me your news."

"Someone saw the Chorlton's Bakery bread van."

"Who?"

"A constable in the Elephant and Castle noticed it driving down Newington Butts. He followed it, but couldn't keep up on his bicycle."

"We'll get him. Just make sure they don't stop him. Follow, not arrest. Is there anything else?"

Hector grinned, and she knew there *was* something else, something much bigger. "After the two attacks in Canterbury, I sent the police photographs of the beacons and also one of Caitrin. They got a call from a Mrs. Winterburn, the matron of the Pett Bottom convalescent hospital, who told them a man and a woman, who said they were from MI6, inspected the building because they were concerned about German saboteurs."

"And the woman was Caitrin?"

"Yes, she identified her. Mrs. Winterburn was a little suspicious and wrote down the make and number of their motorcar."

"Well done, matron. The man?"

"Tall, well-built, with an educated accent."

"That's not Teddy."

"It seems while the matron was showing the officers' wards to the man, the woman went to inspect the enlisted men's quarters."

"That sounds like Caitrin."

"But this doesn't. She put the beacon directly under one of the wounded men's bed."

"That's cold-blooded. There was no bombing last night, so what happened?"

"Last night an RAF Beaufighter shot down a Heinkel 111 close to the hospital."

"So it never got a chance to locate the beacon?" she said, stopped, and peered at him. "You have a little secret, don't you?"

"As soon as I got the call, I hared off to Canterbury and collected the beacon before the police or MI6 could collar it. The reason the bomber didn't locate the beacon was because it wasn't transmitting. One of the wires had been disconnected from the battery."

"An assembly error, perhaps?"

"I don't think so. The battery contact was unscrewed all the way and the wire bent back at a right angle. It was deliberate."

"And mysterious."

"No mystery." Hector picked up a piece of biscuit at his feet and tossed it to the ducks. Next, he brought a rectangle of wood from his pocket, rubbed his fingers in the dirt, ran them across the wooden surface, and held it up at an angle to catch the light. "This is the beacon cover, with something scratched on the surface. See?"

"CC," Bethany said, reading the initials raised by the dirt.

"CC for Caitrin Colline. She disabled the device and knew it wouldn't work when she put it under the soldier's bed. The bomber being shot down was just a coincidence. It was probably wandering around searching for the beacon signal when the night fighter struck."

"So Caitrin is still out there, doing her best to send everything over the edge. I admit I doubted her."

Hector's face clouded. "You're not the only one. So did I, a bit."

"So you should. Doubt everyone in this business, including yourself, especially yourself."

"What's our next step?"

"I don't know, but Teddy Baer isn't the mind behind all this. He's cunning, but this requires more than that. It needs organization and knowledge. Someone who knows the aristocracy and the country well. The attacks are increasing, and now they're after hospitals. We have to find the master organizer, Mr. Beacon himself, and Caitrin is not at all safe until we do."

40

Caitrin was sitting across from Florence in the drawing room, assembling beacons, when Donnie Thatcher entered, tapped her on the shoulder, and whispered, "Teddy wants to see you in the library."

She followed Donnie down the hall, but stopped him halfway. "Donnie, I have to ask you about my letter."

"What about it?"

"Did you post it for me?"

"Yes, but don't ask me to do it again."

"Did you really post it?"

"Yes. No more. He wants you." Frightened, he pointed to the door and hurried away.

She entered the study. It might well have shelves of books, mostly about hunting foxes, shooting pheasant, or the healing of myriad horse diseases, but calling it a library was an exaggeration. It was a study. Teddy sat behind the study desk, wearing a brightly embroidered dressing gown. "Good morning, Caitrin."

"Good morning, Teddy. You look like a skinny Winston Churchill in that dressing gown."

"I do?"

"He has a wide selection of them."

"How do you know that?"

She had made a careless, and possibly dangerous, mistake. The Caitrin Teddy knew would never have met Churchill and wouldn't know about his dressing gowns. She recovered. "So I have heard. Shouldn't gossip, I suppose, especially about our Winnie."

He showed no obvious reaction, waved at a tea tray on the desk, and said, "Tea?"

"I just had breakfast, so no, thank you."

"You don't mind if I do?"

"Please."

Teddy poured himself tea, sipped it, and put the cup down. He tapped a finger on a copy of the *Daily Mail* on the desk in front of him. "This war creates great tragedies."

She said nothing as he opened the paper and read aloud, "The President of the Board of Trade has informed the members of the Flushing Cisterns and Copper Balls Association that in future, and I quote, 'No more copper balls, I'm afraid. From now on they will have to be made of plastic.' What do you think of that?"

"I'm speechless."

"And rightly so. When I first read it, I thought he said, 'no more *coppers*' balls.' Not that it would make much difference to the London Constabulary."

"Won't affect you, though, because yours are brass, right?"

He grinned and showed all of his white teeth. "Right you are. There's a bigger tragedy than coppers' balls. Do you know how many different kinds of biscuits are made in England, Britain?"

"No idea."

"Guess."

"Forty-seven."

"Three hundred and fifty. Because of rationing, that has now been reduced to guess how many."

"Forty-six."

"You're not trying. Twenty."

"Oh, horror, I swoon, and the Empire crumbles."

"But wait, all is not lost," Teddy said and waved his finger in a well-rehearsed gesture. "Look behind you."

Caitrin looked around at several tall columns of cardboard boxes stacked in a corner.

"I have rescued two hundred of them. After this bloody war is over, the country will thank me for saving their biscuits. That building in Trafalgar Square, the one with the moldy old portraits . . ."

"That would be the National Portrait Gallery."

"They will chuck out all the pictures of ancient dead geezers and display the wonders of English, British, biscuits. And all because of me," he said and spread his arms wide. "Above the entrance it will read, Lord Daniel de Barr's Museum of English Biscuits. What do you think?"

"I think you're spending too much time on the mountaintop alone. And the bunch you've got working here will eat them all by the weekend."

"Then we'll display the empty boxes. Sammy said you were insistent on planting the beacon in the convalescent home."

There it was, the reason for the meeting, slid right into the middle of idle chatter to catch her off guard. It did not.

"Sammy's right, I was insistent."

"And he said you placed the beacon under an enlisted man's bed."

"I did. He saw me do it."

"That was cold-hearted, and unexpected, coming from you."

"The soldier was Private Llewellyn Meredith from Harlech,

North Wales. Llewellyn was nineteen, blind, and seemed unaware he was missing his feet. What kind of future would a boy
like that have? I thought of what your brother Isaac said to
you, 'Teddy, let me leave here. You know, you know how.'"

Teddy was quiet.

Caitrin rose, saying, "If we're finished, I have work to do."

"We're not finished, sit down," he said. "No matter where
you put the beacon, there was no bombing last night."

*Guilt will fill silence, so as much as you want to speak, say
nothing. Wait.*

"The battery will be dead by now, and probably someone
has found the beacon," he said. "Which means there's no returning to that location. It also means you got what you wanted."

"I did everything as you wanted," she said. *Don't over-
explain.* "I armed the clockwork mechanism and had Sammy
listen to prove it was working, so I don't know what happened."

"No? I do. I know exactly what happened, Caitrin."

*Stoic. Bethany's favorite word. Let no emotion show. Let the
situation unfold, but be ready to fight. And don't be the next to
speak.*

Silence rose.

"Don't you want to know?" he said.

The instant he moved, she would be ready to leap over the
desk, snatch up the letter opener lying there, and bury it in his
eye. "Tell me," she said, her voice distant.

"The Brylcreem boys saved the day. The bomber was shot
down by an RAF night fighter close to the hospital."

She relaxed, a little. "Told you it wasn't me."

"But you do get a second chance. The next six targets." He
slid a sheet of paper toward her.

She read the list. "Apart from one, they're all hospitals."

"Yes."

"Teddy, isn't this too much, bombing innocent people?"

"I'm not bombing them."

"You're instrumental, partly to blame."

His expression clouded. "Where's the blame supposed to lie, huh? The gunmaker, the bullet, the soldier who's only obeying orders, the officer who gives the orders? The finger that pulls the trigger or releases the bomb? Or the mothers who let their boys go off to war without stopping them, or the dads proud of seeing their sons in uniform? The English adore Florence Nightingale, their glorious Lady with the Lamp, but her family supported her with a fortune made from their cloth mills and lead mines, supplying the troops with uniforms and bullets."

His face was tight, jaw set. "Who the bloody hell is instrumental? Who is to blame? Who are the innocent? You tell me."

Caitrin sat back in her chair and let his rage settle. "I'll do what you want, Teddy."

"The others will set those targets. There is a list of three on the back for you. Read that one."

She turned the page over. "Shifton Manor, Mathurst Down, and . . . Ramilton Woods? I thought that was going to be yours after the war?"

"I'm just giving the customer what he wants. You and Sammy will take those targets; they're closer."

"Rupert Ramilton knows me."

"Not as much as he wanted. He doesn't know what you do and wouldn't care anyway. Searching for saboteurs means you're doing him a big favor. Stay in the car if you like, just as long as he sees you."

"A female distraction?"

"And a fetching one," he said, his expression softening. "Don't tell me it doesn't work."

Caitrin and Sammy left early next morning in the Riley. He did his usual baffling circuitous navigation to the first target, Shifton Manor. The butler showed them in, and Sir Reginald

Shifton, a charming man, listened with great concentration and readily agreed to let them inspect the house. It took only a few minutes, but Caitrin got the feeling he was lonely and would have been happy to have had them stay longer. The second one, Mathurst Down, was secluded and neglected. The driveway was weed-covered and the grounds untended. Sammy hammered on the front door and got no reply. As they were turning away, a rattling on glass caught their attention. An old woman, Medusa-haired and wild-eyed, and wearing only an open dressing gown, was staring at them through a front window. She shouted something that made no sense and scratched again and again on the glass until a woman with an apologetic face took her arm and led her away. Sammy left the beacon under a bush.

Driving up to Ramilton Woods was unsettling. Caitrin had never imagined returning there. Rupert came out of the house as soon as she stopped, saw her, and tugged the car door open. "My goodness, the Welsh firebrand. How marvelous to see you again."

"Yes."

"Emma's away. She'll be so disappointed not to see you."

Sammy saved her from being rude with his oleaginous and insincere charm. "Sir, I am Senior Field Officer Samuel Lockhart, MI6."

Caitrin noticed Sammy's accent had shifted from educated upper-class to the clenched-teeth, squeezed diction of the Midlands.

Rupert turned back to her. "MI6? Cloak and dagger now, are we? How thrilling for you."

"Not me. I'm just the driver."

Sammy explained to him what they were doing. Rupert listened and gave them permission to inspect the house. "I'll be in my study," he said with a professional smile. "Caitrin knows her way around."

Sammy found a good location, took the beacon from his gas-mask bag, and hid it securely. Rupert was a gentleman as he waved them goodbye, and Sammy again led them on a winding path home. Although were no signposts, Caitrin remembered a particular cottage, a tree, a gate, and was building a local geography. Donnie had posted her letter—she had to believe him— which meant someone in 512 must have worked out her leftturn puzzle by now that told them she was alive. And perhaps they had also discovered her initials scratched on the hospital beacon. Perhaps.

"You didn't like him much," Sammy said. "That fancy Ramilton geezer."

"I did not, and I don't want to talk about it."

"All right," he said. "But if it's worth anything, with that beacon placed right in the middle of his house, Randy Rupert's going to have a very sleepless night tonight. It might be his last."

41

Hector entered the tower room to see Teddy Baer's name had been erased from the blackboard and replaced, in large block capital letters, with MR. BEACON. All of the accumulated thoughts, names, and clues had also been erased and rewritten in orderly columns. Teddy's name, now much smaller, was at the head of the first column.

"Good morning, Hector," Bethany said. "Sit down, and we'll get to work."

He sat opposite her at the table and said, "You look serious."

"I am. Last night there were nine Lighthouse attacks. Three near Birmingham, three outside Manchester, and three south of London. Four of the first six were hospitals, the three local ones all ancestral homes. Winston is furious at the increase."

"Understandably."

"We have no clues. Caitrin is, we pray, still inside the organization, but where and for how long is a mystery."

He gestured to the blackboard behind her. "Is that why Teddy has been dethroned by Mr. Beacon?"

"Teddy is dangerous, but only Whitechapel smart. Windsor or Hampton Court would be a foreign land to him, but Mr. Beacon is more sophisticated. He appears to know his landed gentry well, the ancient churches, and especially hospitals. We have to track him down. These tip-and-run bombing raids are causing terrible damage and upsetting lots of people who are not used to being upset. They do not like it."

"Do you have any ideas?"

"MI5, MI6, Scotland Yard, and probably the Salvation Army, along with the Ilkley Ironworks brass brand, are trudging all over the Midlands. I want you to go to the three local targets and see what you can find."

"That doesn't seem like much."

"It's not," she said, picked a sheet of paper, and read, "Shifton Manor, Mathurst Down, and Ramilton Woods."

"I will." He half-rose when she stopped him.

"You're not going alone."

"What?"

"One of my agents is coming with you."

"I'd rather they didn't."

"This is a 512 operation, not SOE."

"I understand, but—"

"But what?"

Hector slumped in his chair. "I really don't want to be responsible for another woman's death."

Bethany slammed her hand hard on the table, and shocked, he flinched. Her expression was hard, angry. "Responsible for another woman's death? Who are you, just who the bloody hell do you think you are?"

"What?"

"Grace Baker was a fine agent, who knew what she was doing was dangerous and died in the service of her country. When the Blind Stag exploded, it sent debris in all directions. A brick flew past you at a million miles an hour, struck and killed her. Did you harbor some fantasy of buckling on your armor, picking up your sword and shield, and in a millisecond defending Grace, the poor damsel in distress, from flying bricks?"

"It wasn't like that at all."

"Exactly. Now I'll tell you a secret. From the day 512 was born, we *girls* got together every morning, early, and said how wonderful it would be to have a strong man take it all over and save us from the big bad world. Which is utter, bloody male nonsense." Bethany was angry now, the words biting out as she rose to her feet and leaned toward him. "You are working here only because Winston Churchill doesn't have the balls to admit he doesn't trust women to do little more than type his letters. It was his idea, not mine. Any one of my women can shoot better than most male agents; they speak two or more languages and are probably more intelligent. So don't you dare tell me we need a man to be responsible for us. The Crown Jewels would be on display in Fatty Göring's Karinhall right now if a woman, our Caitrin, hadn't saved them, and did so damn near alone. Remember that?"

"Yes, I do."

She dropped into her chair with a long sigh. "I will not have the courage and endeavor of my agents diminished in people's eyes simply because they are women. Men have done it for far too long. It's embedded in their masculinity, and they're not even aware of doing it."

"I consider myself chastised, corrected, and contrite. And promise to do better in future."

"I know, and we appreciate you and your work. If only you were a woman."

"Not sure how to do that without some painful reconstruction. Who is coming with me?"

"Evelyn Despenser."

"That's a very English name."

"Isn't it just?" Bethany picked up the telephone and asked

for Evelyn to join them. A moment later, the door opened, Evelyn Despenser entered and obliterated any mental images Hector had of the woman with a very English name. She was slender, poised, and Indian.

"Lord Hector, I've heard so much about you," she said, shaking his hand.

"It's Hector, please, and I'm afraid I know nothing about you."

"But you're thinking: English name, Indian woman. My real name is Nimrata. Nimrata always brings images of agile rodents to mind, so it had to go. And Despenser was my husband's name. He's dead, but no suttee for me because he was English."

"I'm sorry."

"The war broke out, Roland got patriotic, we left India, and he dumped me with his mum in Bournemouth. Bournemouth— oh, the ribaldry, the giddy excitement, it was all so overwhelming—"

"Bournemouth?" Hector said.

"I jest; it's a bloody cemetery. Then he toddled off to join the few to whom it seems we owe so much. His Spitfire was shot down the first time he went up, and I became a widow. What a loathsome word that is."

Her direct confidence fascinated him. There was such a concentration of character to her. Her eyes were like an owl's in that, no matter how she moved, they stayed trained on him. But they were friendly eyes.

"Now you two have met, you can get to work. I need facts. Report to me this evening," Bethany said. "Off you go."

Evelyn moved closer, gazed at him with her steady eyes, and said, "We're both the same height, Hector."

"Equal," Bethany said.

42

Sir Reginald Shifton sat at a garden table in the center of the south lawn and studied the remains of his home, Shifton Manor. The west wall was mostly intact, but the rest of the house was a still-smoking, blackened ruin, with the occasional dart of flame. Reginald wore striped pajamas and had a black-and-yellow Brasenose College Boat Club scarf wound around his neck, even though the autumn morning was warm; he had an ancient French kepi on his head and a glass of amontillado sherry in his right hand. To one side, and a discretionary step in the rear, stood butler Burton Bisby, hands clasped behind his back and dressed in his butler's black coat over butterfly patterned pajamas. Both men were shoeless, but dignity shod their feet. So intent were they on surveying the ruins, they hardly paid attention to Hector and Evelyn's arrival.

"Good morning," Hector called out as they left the car.

"Good morning," Sir Reginald answered. "I hope you haven't come to buy the place, because we're in the middle of renovations. Come back on Tuesday."

Hector laughed. "No, sir, we're here to find out what happened to your house. I'm Hector Neville-Percy and this is Evelyn Despenser. We are from 512."

"Is that a club, like the 400?"

"No, it's an anti-espionage and counter-saboteur agency, like MI6 but much smarter."

Sir Reginald waved his sherry glass at the house. "Could have done with you yesterday. Now it's a bolting the stable door after the horse has buggered off sort of thing."

"Yes, in a way I suppose so."

"Excuse me if I don't get up, but I scorched my bum fleeing the holocaust."

"Would you mind telling us what happened?"

"Simple, really. I was fast asleep. There was this bloody great crash, and Burton here saved my life. He dashed into my room, snatched me out of bed, tucked me under his arm like a rugby ball, and hot-footed it out of there. Bloody hero, if you ask me. Hector, Lysander, and our Burton Bisby."

Burton's head made the slightest inclination toward modesty.

"Off he galloped, dodging and swerving like a mad Baa-Baas fly-half past all sorts of burning horror, and got us out completely unharmed, apart from my bum. Managed to grab a few things, most of which I'm wearing, and a decanter of my best sherry and a glass too. You do know Wodehouse modeled Jeeves on Burton?"

Burton coughed, and murmured, "Come come, sir. Hardly that."

"If he didn't, he bloody well should have," Sir Reginald said and turned to Evelyn. "Indian?"

"Yes, sir."

"From where?"

"Pondicherry and then Nandidurga hill station."

Sir Reginald brightened. "The Nandi hills, home of Tipu

Sultan of Mysore and an impregnable fortress, until Cornwallis took it and kicked his arse down the mountain."

"Yes, sir."

"I made my pile in India as a young man and came home before malaria got me. Good country, good people, bad diseases for the white man. Now, what precisely are you doing here?"

"It wasn't an accidental bombing. You were deliberately targeted with a Lighthouse homing beacon," Hector said. "Did you have any visitors yesterday?"

"Don't usually get many. A man and a woman, who said they were from MI6, turned up and wanted to check for possible saboteurs."

"They were not MI6, and they planted the beacon. Do you remember their names?"

"No."

"Senior Field Officer Samuel Lockhart," Burton said, "and Field Officer Catherine Walters. They were driving a black Riley 9, number plate SAX 873."

"See what I mean?" Sir Reginald said. "A veritable Jeeves."

"Thank you, Burton," Hector said. "Would you recognize them from photographs?"

"I should imagine so."

"I'll get the folder," Evelyn said and went to the car.

Sir Reginald watched her go. "I don't like to see women wearing trousers, so un-English, but I must confess that she is the most charming creature. Damn, it's good to have an empire."

Evelyn returned with a folder, opened it on the table, and spread out the photographs.

Sir Reginald jabbed a finger at a picture of Florence. "She looks like a murder victim, and the others probably knocked her off."

"That one," Burton said, sliding the photographs apart. "He's definitely the man, and that is the woman."

"Samuel Breen," Hector said.

"Caitrin?" Evelyn asked, and Hector nodded in reply.

"You know them?" Sir Reginald said.

"Yes, and now we have to catch them. Thank you."

"You don't seem very upset about your house burning down," Evelyn said.

"Centuries ago, the Shifton family won the estate at the point of a sword, along with the usual rape, ravaging, and obligatory uncivil behavior," Sir Reginald said and shrugged. "But I'm tired of living out here alone with a hundred moldy old ancestors staring down from the walls at me. The house was a shambles, leaking roof, draughty rooms, damp walls. I hated growing up here. It was primitive, and I'm glad it's gone, but there's still the land and the farm rents to see me through."

"It must be an expensive loss, though."

"Not when you have Burton Bisby as a butler. I forgot about insurance, but he didn't."

Burton tried to blush but failed.

"I'm going to my place in Belgravia, if it's not knocked down. Close to my clubs, but Burton won't be happy. My housekeeper has spent so much time there alone she imagines it belongs to her."

"The Claw," Burton said under his breath, but Sir Reginald heard him.

"Yes, the Claw. Miss Havisham with teeth and talons."

"May we give you a lift to the nearest train station?"

"No, thank you. By good fortune, the Bentley was being serviced at the local garage. They're bringing it up this afternoon."

"All right," Hector said and turned to Burton. "You might want to get those burns looked at. Hands are very delicate."

Surprised, Burton pressed his hands behind his back. "Thank you for noticing, sir."

*   *   *

Their second stop, Mathurst Down, looked as though it had been derelict for centuries. The roof had collapsed, all doors and windows were gone, and the surrounding trees had been seared by the blast into crippled silhouettes. A lone police constable appeared from behind the building, buttoning his fly as Hector and Evelyn drove up. Hector showed him his identification.

"Not much to see here, sir," the constable said. "Lady Beatrice is gone, and our Gladys was lucky to get away with her life."

"Gladys?"

"My neighbor, Gladys Pope. She was looking after her. Sad it was, so sad."

"What was?"

The constable glanced over his shoulder, although there was no one in miles to hear him. "If you don't mind me saying, Lady Beatrice was a bit, a bit daft like, and getting worse recently. When the bombs dropped, she went off the deep end. Gladys grabbed her hand and led her out. But she stopped at the door, screamed, got free, and disappeared back into the house. Nothing Gladys could do; it was falling all around her. That was the last she saw of Lady Beatrice. Shame, really."

"Is Gladys all right?" Evelyn asked.

"My missus gave her some of her cherry brandy, and she'll be right as rain soon enough."

"Did she mention if anything unusual happened yesterday, before the bombing?"

The constable took out his notebook and leafed through the pages. "She said a man and woman knocked on the front door, and it agitated Lady Beatrice. Gladys didn't answer because visitors can upset the poor old lady for days. She thinks they're her children, see? Who never come to visit. Shame that."

"Descriptions?"

"Just a man and a woman was all she mentioned," the constable said and turned toward the house. "Gladys thinks Lady Beatrice is going to haunt this place. I wouldn't be a bit surprised if she did."

On their third and final stop, Evelyn took the long sweeping drive up to Ramilton Woods. She stopped outside the front entrance and stared in surprise at the house. She turned to Hector, who also looked bewildered, and neither believed what they were seeing. It had been a day of strange events, but this one was the strangest of all.

43

Florence was snoring in her bed, the rest of the house was sleeping, and it was now time for Caitrin to leave. She nudged open the bedroom blackout curtains onto a moonless night and waited for Donnie to return in the bread van. Earlier, she had watched him load up the week's production of beacons and drive off. Wherever he went, it was not far away. She had intended to stay longer and learn more about Teddy's operation, but being directly involved in planting beacons, especially the aborted one in the convalescent home, weighed heavily on her. The thought that her actions might have inflicted the same carnage she had experienced in the Café de Paris was horrifying. Also, the newly designed beacons were much more accurate, production had increased, and she needed to be with 512 to combat them. With no telephone, newspapers, or wireless in the lodge, it was impossible to know what was going on in the outside world.

The slit of a single yellow headlamp bobbed up the driveway; Donnie had returned. He parked the van, got out, put the keys in his pocket, and winced as the muzzle of Caitrin's Webley-Fosbery revolver dug into his neck.

"The night is young, and so are we, Donnie. Let's go for a moonless drive, just the two of us."

"You can't scare me. You wouldn't do it. Pull the trigger? Nah."

"Desperate girls do desperate things, so don't test me. Keys, please."

He handed her the keys; she pushed him behind the wheel, went around the nose of the van, took the passenger seat, and handed them back. "Now we're all safe and comfy."

"Where are we going?"

"London."

"I just came from there this afternoon."

"So even in the dark you'll know the way," she said and poked him in the ribs with her revolver. "Drive, Donnie, drive."

She waited until a few minutes had passed before asking him, "Where do you take the beacons?"

"Selfridge's."

"Try again."

"Shoot me now and get it over with, because I'll never tell you."

She jabbed the revolver hard into his knee. "I don't have to kill you."

"No, you don't, but Teddy will. He'll off you too."

"He'll have to find me first."

"London is Teddy's town. He'll find you."

"I could move to Birmingham."

"That's the same thing as being dead." Donnie risked a half-smile that faded as he said, "What are you? I can tell you're not a copper."

"I'm just a girl who doesn't like being locked up in the middle of the sticks."

"And I'm Queen o' the May."

Donnie turned off the country lane onto a main road and headed north. They drove in silence for a while. The road was deserted, except for an occasional army lorry. On the distant horizon, searchlights etched the night sky, followed by the faint rolling sound of antiaircraft guns.

"The bombers are still coming," Donnie said. "Not like before, but they haven't stopped."

Caitrin was about to answer when the van lurched as the engine sputtered and died. Donnie rolled it into a lay-by.

"The fuel gauge is wonky. We're out of petrol."

"What do we do?"

Donnie leaned back against the door, folded his arms, closed his eyes, and said, "I don't know about you, but I'm going to catch forty winks until sunrise. The night is all yours."

Caitrin took the keys from the ignition and got out of the van. "Thanks for the lift, Donnie."

He wound down the window a few inches. "Good night to you, Caitrin—who and whatever you are—Colline. Can I give you a little advice as we part and go our separate ways, never to meet again this side of the grave?"

"Why not?"

"In future, if you're going to threaten people with that great big gun of yours, make sure it's loaded. Good night now." He wound up the window and closed his eyes.

Caitrin rattled the keys to get his attention, dropped them, turned toward London, and vanished into the night.

44

Bethany went early to the tower room. The quiet hour before the others arrived gave her time to reflect on the day ahead. She picked up the current information report to transcribe the latest beacon strikes onto the blackboard. The list was getting longer, they were no closer to preventing the attacks, and Winston was justifiably furious. People died, ancient buildings were destroyed, and they still had no clues or direction.

"How can you possibly work this early in the morning without a cup of tea?" Caitrin said from the doorway.

Bethany spun to face her. "My God, Caitrin."

They embraced.

"I can't believe it's you. You look exhausted."

"I am. My feet are killing me. I walked almost all the way here."

"Come sit down."

They sat at the table.

"Walked all the way from where?"

"I don't know. Some place in the country a few hours south

of London, somewhere off the Purley, South Croydon Road. I'd kill Hitler for a cuppa."

"Wouldn't we all?" Bethany picked up the telephone. "Tea for four, please, and any biscuits if you have them. Is that really all that's left? I suppose they will have to do. Thank you." She hung up.

"Do you know how many kinds of biscuits are made in Britain?" Caitrin said.

"Three hundred and fifty. But now it's down to twenty."

"How on earth did you know that?"

"I like biscuits," Bethany said as she sat across from her at the table. "Are you all right?"

"I'm fine, but to save me telling the same story twice, shouldn't I wait for Hector and Grace?" She caught the change in Bethany's expression. "What's wrong?"

"Grace is dead." Her heart sank at seeing Caitrin's reaction. *This shitty, ugly, bloody war.*

Caitrin sat without moving. *Grace dead. Dead, gone, forever. Grace.* "What happened?"

"She and Hector were on surveillance duty outside the Blind Stag, just in case you got into trouble. They ran toward the pub when it caught fire, it exploded, and Grace was struck by debris. She died instantly."

Died instantly. Alive, click, dead. "Teddy had me bound and blindfolded in the van. I heard the explosion. We must have passed them."

"You did. Hector saw the van leave."

And, at that moment, for that moment, Grace was still alive.

A secretary came in with a tea tray, put it on the table, and left as Hector and Evelyn entered. He wrapped Caitrin in a tight and long embrace.

"I can't breathe, Hecky."

"Sorry, so sorry," he said releasing his hold and becoming an Englishman again. "I was just so, so surprised. And delighted."

"Me too," Caitrin said and turned to Evelyn. "I've seen you around here, but I don't know your name."

"Evelyn Despenser."

"It's good to meet you, Evelyn."

"Tea?" Bethany said. "I'll be mum. Oh, dear, Lorna Doone biscuits. Is that all that's left? I really hate Hitler."

They sat at the table and made the tea to their own taste. Bethany wrinkled her nose at a Lorna Doone biscuit and said, "Caitrin, why don't you tell us of your grand adventure?"

"Teddy kidnapped me to a remote place in the country. His motley crew, Large Eric—"

Bethany gave Hector a piece of chalk. "Write them down in your lovely handwriting. Go on."

"Large Eric Ambrose, Ernie Wood, Donnie Thatcher, and Samuel Breen. And not forgetting Florence Simmonds. We assembled the beacons, and every so often Donnie would take most of them away. Where they went to I have no idea."

Hector scribbled the names on the board.

"I eventually got into Teddy's good graces enough to be allowed to go out with Samuel and plant the devices."

"How did you get them into the buildings?" Evelyn asked. "The beacons are not exactly small."

"Gas-mask bags. It's so obvious if you think of it. We asked everyone who had been bombed what the people looked like and if there was anything unusual about them. There was no mention of the bags in their descriptions because everybody carries one. There are over forty million of them out there. Harrod's and Selfridge's sell fashionable bags if you really must."

"Before you go any further," Bethany interrupted, "we got your letter. Your mother didn't want to let it go, so we flew her and it up to London."

Caitrin grinned. "My mam. I bet she enjoyed herself."

"She had a grand time, and Hector worked out the leftturn, leuchtturm puzzle."

"Well done, Hector; you've become a part of 512."

"Thank you," he said. "We also got the beacon with your initials scratched on the lid. You disconnected the battery so it wouldn't activate?"

"I did. I was lucky the German bomber was shot down because if it hadn't been Teddy would have been suspicious of me when it failed to locate the beacon." Her expression tightened. "I still had to set three beacons that I could not disable."

"Shifton Hall, Mathurst Down, and Ramilton Woods."

"How did you know?

"Sir Reginald Shifton said, 'One of them was a pretty woman with masses of red curls.' That sound like you?"

"He was a nice man, and I felt terrible planting the beacon in his house. I wanted to stay with Teddy and get more information, but I couldn't plant beacons to bomb innocent people anymore. I had to leave."

"Just so you know, Sir Reginald hated his place and was pleased to see it burn down, while his butler, the remarkable Jeeves–Burton Bisby, insured it, so he's happy. Lady Beatrice at Mathurst Down was a tragically unhappy woman, and it was probably a blessing for her."

"Ramilton Woods is the strange one," Evelyn said. "The bombs missed by a half mile. It was completely untouched. I took these." She sent photographs of the bomb site across the table to Caitrin.

"That is odd," Caitrin said. "The new beacons are highly accurate, and I was with Sammy when he planted one right in the middle of the house."

"And when we asked for a description of the visitors, Rupert Ramilton said he couldn't identify you," Hector said. "Neither could his wife."

"That is strange, because I saw a lot of them," Caitrin said with a shiver at the memory of that weekend.

"You said most of the beacons were taken away," Bethany said.

"Teddy is not the leader of Lighthouse. He is a supplier."

"We've named the leader Mr. Beacon," Bethany said.

"Sammy plants them in groups of three, but only locally. The rest go somewhere else, to Mr. Beacon. And I don't know who or where he is." The thought crossed her mind that the Ramilton beacon might have malfunctioned. *If so, with no guidance, how did the German bombs land so closely? Perhaps Ramilton Woods escaped bombing because Teddy still wanted it for himself. He knows if the first strike fails, they never go back for a second attempt, and that rendered Ramilton Woods safe.*

"There is no possibility you could find your way back to Teddy's operation?" Hector said.

"There are no road signs anymore; we took circuitous routes down narrow country lanes, and traveled mostly at night. It's a featureless landscape of fields and hedges."

"You should all know this, before we go any further," Bethany said as she rose, took the chalk from Hector, and wrote one word in large letters: SPUCKANGRIFFE. "Spite Attack. The Blitz was intended to force Winston to negotiate. If he agreed to talks, the bombing would stop. That simple. But these beacon bombings are called *Spuckangriffe*, Spiteful, because they have no reason and no end. I hear they were Göring's idea after his beloved Luftwaffe was badly humiliated in the Battle of Britain. He just wants to hurt us by hitting undefended civilian targets. We have to stop him, and Winston badly needs a win to convince the Americans they should enter the war."

"You said it was a featureless landscape with no signposts?" Evelyn said.

"Nothing but fields and hedges."

"That's from the ground. What about from the air? Could you possibly recognize the building from above?"

"Perhaps."

"Identify the building from the air, and it will be easy to trace the roads leading to it."

"Good idea," Hector said. "Bethany?"

"I can try, but getting a pilot and an aircraft at short notice is almost impossible."

"I can do it," Evelyn said. "I have a friend who works at Fairey Aviation on the Great West Aerodrome at Heath Row. He'll lend me his aircraft."

"Lend?" Caitrin said.

"Yes, and we don't need a pilot. I'll fly it," Evelyn said with a confident smile. "Of course, unless you're reluctant to fly with a woman."

"I'll go." Caitrin grinned in reply. "And it's about time."

"But not today. First thing tomorrow morning," Bethany said.

"Why?"

"Because I'm going to London to placate Winston. If he shuts 512 down, we all go home, and Langland Priory closes," she said and patted Caitrin's hand. "And you are about to fall asleep into your teacup, Caitrin. Off to bed with you. Fly tomorrow morning."

Caitrin was too tired to protest.

In honor of his friend Luftwaffe Hauptmann Karl Trautloft, who recently had been shot down by an RAF night fighter, Gustav Hohner volunteered for the hastily scheduled flight. Shortly after midnight, Gustav flew his Heinkel 111 bomber low across the Channel, over the English coast, avoiding the cities, and headed north. Ernst, the navigator/bomb-aimer, was tracking their progress on his flight chart and was amused by English place names; Gustav was not.

"Climping Sands," Ernst's voice cackled in his headset. "Fittleworth, Balls Cross, Wormley—"

"Just keep us on course, Ernst," Gustav interrupted. "And make sure we stay well away from London."

There was little chance a single, low-flying aircraft at night would be picked up by the English, but he had no wish to stray anywhere near London's prodigious barrage-balloon and anti-aircraft defenses. The X-Gerät homing signals would direct him close to the target, and then they would hear the distinctive sound of the *Leuchtturm* beacon.

"Twenty miles directly ahead," Ernst said as he put down his chart and wriggled into the bomb-aimer's prone position beneath Gustav's feet in the aircraft nose.

The first ping came, soft but growing louder, and Ernst raised his hand to tell Gustav he heard it. Louder now, almost a steady tone, and Gustav throttled back. For many pilots, there was something unsettling about slowing down over enemy territory, but he wanted to be accurate the first time and not have to make a second pass. The *Leuchtturm* beacon was warbling; they were close. He could see little below, dark squares that were fields with no detail rushing past. The beacon was steady, loud, and Ernst released the bomb load. The Heinkel bucked and lifted now it was freed from the weight, and Gustav banked hard. Usually, they would put the nose down, open the throttles, and bolt for home. Not this time. He wanted to see the results of their attack. For a long moment, there was nothing. Until sharp edges of flame cut through the darkness. That would be the high explosives. A moment later, a blue flash shot across the landscape and illuminated the building and surrounding fields. It vanished as orange clouds of flame roiled up from the building's center. The incendiaries had ignited.

"Direct hit!" Ernst shouted. "Right in the middle!"

Gustav held the bomber in a circle around the target. The *Leuchtturm* had done its job well.

"Good work; now let's go home," Ernst said, as Gustav leveled off and turned the bomber south. He had finished the task in honor of his friend Hauptmann Karl Trautloft. The target, whose English name did not amuse Ernst, no longer existed. Langland Priory was gone.

45

Winter was coming, the night air cool, and Caitrin pulled her coat tighter as she walked through the woods toward the pond. A full moon made the path a steel ribbon, silvered the beech leaves, and printed impenetrable shadows on the ground. Although she had been exhausted on arriving at the priory, going to bed so soon was a mistake. Now, close to midnight, she was wide awake while the world slept. The priory was dark and silent when she slipped out. Bethany was away in London, but Hector and Evelyn were asleep in there, and Caitrin wondered if they were in one bed or two. Mugs, the priory cat, saw her and froze, one paw raised, suddenly two-dimensional. Caitrin took a step forward, and he transformed into a sleek shadow that raced across the grass, flowed up and over a wall, and was gone.

She reached the pond and sat on a bench overlooking the water. The surface was so still it reflected the sky, an intimate copy, and when she tilted her head to one side, the pond became a hole in the earth that let the stars shine through. Little creatures rustling in the undergrowth fell silent as an owl announced the hour.

Imagine Mam in her best coat flying to London in an open-cockpit aircraft. She'll never stop talking about it. And Dafydd flying secret operations he cannot talk about, while the baby, Gareth, is somewhere out on the deep waters. And I wonder if we'll ever be together again? "I miss my family," she said aloud, and the night snatched the words away.

She heard a faint sound, a lone distant aircraft, and remembered Dafydd telling her about the German Luftwaffe. The Dornier 17 bomber made a strange rattling sound, while the Ju88, a fast aircraft, had a steady smooth tone. Unlike RAF pilots, who, Dafydd insisted, commanded their aircraft with complete authority, the Germans could never get the Heinkel 111's two engines synchronized, so they always sounded clumsy, awkward.

The aircraft was closer, although she could not see it. But she heard its engines, unsynchronized, growing louder. And finally, she saw a black sinister shape, moonlight glinting off the glass nose as it raced low over the fields. She could tell where it was going and ran, stumbling through the tree shadows toward the priory. The aircraft engines changed pitch as it slowed, and for a moment, Caitrin thought perhaps she was wrong about its target. Until a blast stunned the earth, flames slit open the darkness, and a blue flash exposed the priory surrendering to a swelling inferno. The aircraft insolently circled, and she screamed at it. Indifferent, it leveled off and flew south.

She stopped a hundred yards away from the building. The heat would not let her get any closer. She stood and watched, awed and frightened. Within the priory walls, only the greedy fire was alive.

A low morning mist surrounded the blackened shell of the priory to protect it from outside view as Caitrin stood in the driveway, watching firemen rolling up their hoses. Several fire engines, a police car, and an ARP van had already left. She rocked a little on her feet, exhausted, drained.

An ARP warden tapped her shoulder. "We can take you into the village, if you like, miss, so you can have a lie-down. You look completely worn out."

"I'm all right."

"Sure? Nothing you can do here. There's nothing left."

"Thank you anyway."

As he left, Bethany's car arrived. She got out, strode toward what was left of the front door, and glared at the ruins. "We failed, dammit. *I* failed and let them walk right in."

She went to Caitrin. "Are you all right?"

"I really don't know."

"Who escaped?"

"No one."

"Yesterday afternoon, while you were sleeping, Billy Donnelly and the other instructors took the recruits to Tain for outdoor survival training. They're chasing capercaillie and wild haggis all over Scotland by now, so thank God there was hardly anyone left here."

"Hector and Evelyn were in there."

Bethany squinted at the priory. "Perhaps not. Do you see that little MG sports car of hers anywhere?"

Caitrin scanned the courtyard. "No. But I hear it."

Evelyn raced up the driveway, skidded to a stop in a hail of gravel, and joined them. "This is awful."

"Where were you?" Bethany asked.

"Seeing a friend. We got a bit tipsy, so I— "

"Hector," Caitrin said, as she saw him trudging up the driveway. This time it was her embrace that was tight and long.

"And where were you?" Bethany asked.

Hector looked sheepish as he fumbled for an answer, so Evelyn replied for him. "He was with me."

"I am so very surprised," Caitrin said, but was not.

"I dropped him off at the corner, so we wouldn't be quite so obvious."

"Obviously," Bethany said.

Caitrin gestured to the ruins. "Teddy did this because I left."

"He knows about 512?" Bethany asked.

"He probably doesn't know about 512, but suspects, and I've seen his operation. That was all he needed."

Bethany turned toward the smoking ashes. "It doesn't matter now. When Winston heard about the bombing, he said it was a blatant signal that 512, with its glaring lack of success, should finally be closed down."

"Will he really do it?" Evelyn asked.

"As from this morning, we no longer exist." She faced them. "Hector will soon get orders to return to SOE, and we ladies are heading for a life of typing, filing, and making sandwiches."

"I won't go," Hector said. "We've worked too hard."

"No making bloody sandwiches for me," Caitrin said.

"Or me," Evelyn said. "And my typing in English is criminally bad."

Bethany held back a tear as she gazed at them. *So young, so brave.* "And what do you propose we do?"

"Fly and find," Evelyn said. "Caitrin spots the building; we land and cause trouble."

"What type of aircraft?"

"De Havilland Leopard Moth."

"Which takes one pilot and two passengers. I'm going too," Hector said.

"Always room for a handsome young chap like you," Caitrin said.

"We sort them out and stop Mr. Beacon, once and for all," Hector dodged the compliment.

"And prove to Winston he made a silly mistake that can easily be corrected so 512 lives again," Caitrin said.

"That's the answer I was expecting," Bethany said. "The local vicar has a small office we can use."

"Which church?"

"St. Peter's."

St. Peter's. Peter Derwent, the aspirational apprentice vicar, the Lincolnshire lad from Boothby Graffoe, just up the road from the cathedral. The mental image of him calmed her. There were a few sane people in this lunatic world. "We have to act now because Teddy will not stand still," Caitrin said. "And if he leaves, we'll never find him again. Let's go to church."

46

The office in St. Peter's was a small storeroom behind the altar, packed with the detritus of decades of church activities. In one corner stood a wooden thermometer showing the funds needed to repair a leaking roof; it never reached the top. A large black-and-white Tombola board leaning against a wall was half-covered with a hand-painted banner that read: CHURCH FÊTE; the rest of the room was filled with broken furniture, music stands, and boxes of unloved donations from countless jumble sales. Hector noticed the desiccated corpse of an unfortunate mouse caught in a trap in one corner of a box.

Hector found and unfolded a card table. Bethany wedged a piece of cardboard under a leg to stop it wobbling and began the meeting, only to be interrupted by Doris, the vicar's housekeeper, fussing in with a tea tray, which she placed in the middle of the table. On it, along with the tea things, was a small plate with four custard-cream biscuits precisely arranged into a four-pointed star.

"Those came from the vicar's personal hoard," Doris said,

whispering and jabbing at the biscuits. "He's so naughty and can be a bit parsonmonius with them."

"Thank you, Doris," Bethany said.

Caitrin noticed the tea cozy was hand-knitted in a camouflage pattern. "Did you knit that?"

"Oh, yes, there is a war on. It's me doing my little bit. We all have to, don't we?" Doris said, gave them a knowing smile, and left.

"Does she know she said parsonmonious?" Hector asked.

"I doubt it, but don't ever correct her. The British Empire thrives on tea and vicars," Bethany said.

"And their housekeepers," Evelyn said.

"To business. Officially, 512 no longer exists, so we can expect no help from anywhere, or anyone, other than from ourselves."

"The priory burning down with everything we own in it doesn't help much," Evelyn said.

"What resources do you have on hand?"

Caitrin put her Webley-Fosbery revolver on the table. "All I've got. No ammunition, though."

Evelyn ejected the clip from a Mauser HSc. "Eight rounds 38." She flicked four of the rounds free and rolled them to Caitrin.

"Thank you."

"Hector?" Bethany said.

Hector put his Browning Hi-Power automatic on the table. "One magazine, ten rounds 40 calibre."

Bethany slid a stiletto from her sleeve and placed it next to her teacup. She noticed their startled expressions. "I'm sensitive to loud noises."

Hector stared at the stiletto. "I'm always wary of Caitrin and Evelyn, but now terrified of you, Bethany. Have you ever used it?"

In one unbroken movement, Bethany speared a biscuit, dropped it onto her saucer, and with a silken whisper of steel, slid the stiletto out of sight. And said nothing.

"We have to get moving, before Teddy disappears on us," Caitrin said.

"Agreed," Bethany said. "Evelyn, call your friend now and see about the aircraft."

Evelyn nodded and left.

"The vicar has a map of the area we can use. Don't fly directly overhead or make too many passes in case you alarm them. If you find the place, mark it on the map, come straight back, or land where you can ring me up."

"We could lose valuable time doing that," Caitrin said.

"These are short days, and if you're not successful, you won't find them from the air at night. We need to know the area and the access roads," Bethany said. "And don't forget, Teddy sent a bomber to obliterate the priory, with you in it."

"And thinking you're dead, he might not be in such a hurry to pack up and vanish," Hector said.

"And if he is getting ready to leave, they're not assembling beacons. If we can't catch him, we will at least keep him on the run and disrupt the supply," Bethany said and pushed a piece of paper in front of Caitrin. "This is the church telephone number. I'll be waiting. Good luck."

Evelyn entered. "Got an aircraft. We have to go. Now."

Bethany dropped them off at the Fairey Aviation factory on the Great West Aerodrome at Heath Row, just east of Windsor Castle. It was much busier than they expected. "This is a veritable beehive," she said. "And a very loud one."

"The Fairey Company bought the land off the vicar of Harmondsworth ten years ago," Hector said. "Good old vicars again."

"How did you know that?" Caitrin asked.

"Men know things."

"Oh, really? Where are the thirty-nine steps?"

"I thought you had them."

"Stop it, you two," Evelyn said.

They watched as completed Barracuda torpedo bombers were pushed out of the factory, while others roared low overhead on test flights, and RAF Hurricane fighters constantly landed and took off again. Bethany said her goodbyes, and Evelyn led them down a row of bombers to a bright yellow de Havilland Leopard Moth at the end of the flight line. Unlike the all-metal, brutal Barracudas, the high-wing monoplane Moth was small and delicate, made of wood and fabric, with the name SUZIE written in pink ornate script on the nose. It sat low on the ground and looked much like an actual moth next to a row of large vultures.

"This is Captain de Havilland's favorite aircraft. You have flown before, I take it?" Evelyn asked them as she circled the aircraft in a preflight check. Hector and Caitrin said they had as they followed her. "We have only enough petrol for an hour flight, along with a warning to stay clear of London and all towns. Being bright yellow is no guarantee we won't be shot at."

"We could start searching halfway down the South Croydon Road," Caitrin said. "That's well away from London, and there is nothing there but fields and villages."

"All right. There is one other thing I should mention to you. Now the Blitz is fading, the Luftwaffe is sending over single-seat fighters, 109s and Focke Wulf 190s, in tip-and-run nuisance raids. They come in low, carry only one bomb, drop it anywhere, and flee for the coast. We would be an easy and tempting target for one of them as we make our way home."

"Sounds like we're all going to have a jolly good time up there," Hector said with a brave grin. "You have flown one of these machines before, I trust, Evelyn?"

"Me? I thought you were the pilot?"

"Me?"

Caitrin opened the aircraft door. "Maybe there's a driver's guide in here somewhere."

"All right, teasing over. Get in," Evelyn said. "There are binoculars in the back seat."

Hector and Caitrin climbed into the rear, where Hector spread the map across his lap, while Evelyn sat in the central pilot's seat. It was a snug fit. They slipped on their headsets, Evelyn finished her preflight check and started the engine. The Moth trembled and the shaking got stronger.

"What's wrong?" Caitrin asked.

"Not us, our bigger brethren." Evelyn pointed to her left where a pair of Hurricanes rumbled past the nose of the Moth to the takeoff point. The shaking died as they passed. "You can't see it, but if I get too close to them, their propellor wash could blow us over, so we'll wait until they're gone and the turbulence has settled."

The Hurricanes were dots in the sky before Evelyn taxied out and took off. She stayed low, flew southeast, found the South Croydon Road, and turned. "I'll throttle back and fly a quadrant based on the road," she said. "Let me know if you see anything you recognize."

"Everything looks the same from up here," Caitrin said as she peered down. "There's no perspective, and one green field looks like another."

"Which also makes this map just about useless," Hector said.

"But at least we can see the roads. That helps. We'll keep going as long as the petrol holds out," Evelyn said as she banked into another turn. "I'm going to stall the aircraft."

"Why?"

"Trawling up and down might seem a bit suspicious to someone on the ground, so I want this to look like a training flight. Don't worry; we won't fall out of the sky. It'll just feel that way. Hold tight." Evelyn closed the throttle and eased back on the stick as the aircraft slowed. The nose rose higher, Hector and Caitrin were pushed back in their seat, and the rush of airstream over the wings slowed and then stopped. The Moth was hanging vertically in silence as they stared straight up at the sky.

Gravity asserted itself, the nose dropped, and they were staring directly down at the ground. Evelyn opened the throttle, the engine note increased, and she eased the aircraft up into level flight.

"That was different, I must say," Caitrin said. "An aerial roller-coaster."

"Fun, in an odd sort of way," Hector said.

"Ha-ha," Caitrin said.

"Yes, ha-ha fun."

"No, look over there to the left. You see that wall? That wall's the ha-ha built on the property. Turn right, Evelyn."

Evelyn banked right.

"There it is, that's the house! We found it!"

Evelyn turned west.

"Where are you going?"

"Back to Heath Row, to call Bethany."

"No!"

"She said, once we know where Teddy is, we'll have him on the run so he can't make any more beacons."

"She's wrong about him," Caitrin said. "I know Teddy better than she does. Why do you think the police can never pin anything on him? He's too smart. He's not going to run; he'll leave this house and find a place to hide or, more likely, join up with Mr. Beacon and keep churning them out. We have to land and catch him right now, or we'll never get him."

"Caitrin, we have specific orders."

"Land and drop me off, then."

As the aircraft turned onto its new heading, something on the ground off to her left caught Caitrin's eye. "That black scar ahead, isn't that the—"

The roar of an engine at full throttle drowned her voice as a German FW-190 fighter flew overhead just feet away. The concussive propellor blast tilted the Moth onto a wingtip, and Evelyn fought to regain control and almost got level until a second aircraft, a pursuing RAF Spitfire, howled past even closer. Empty brass shell casings rattled on the Moth and ricochetted off its propellor blades as the Spitfire fired its guns at the vanishing German. The propellor blast inverted the Moth, and it stalled and spun toward the ground. Evelyn kicked hard at the rudder and got the Moth upright, but they were too low and slow to recover. The right wingtip crumpled as it clipped a tree, and the aircraft spun into the ground. Its fuselage snapped in two, as the fuel tank ruptured and sent petrol into the cabin. A short-circuited wire supplied a spark, flames bit into the dope-impregnated fabric covering, and in seconds, the Moth was ablaze.

47

As the Moth spun in, its tail wheel scored a deep arc in the soil, torsion splintered the aircraft's wooden airframe, and Caitrin was sent hurtling through a broken bulkhead. She tumbled over and across the ground before coming to rest on her back with the sky swirling above. She lay still for a moment, settling, surfacing, and assessed her injuries. To her surprise, they appeared to be little more than cuts and bruises. She sat up and shook her head to clear it.

"Cat! Help me!" Hector shouted as he tore at the aircraft door. Caitrin got to her feet and stumbled to his aid. Evelyn was inside, half-conscious, with her right foot trapped under a bent rudder pedal. Petrol ran down the control panel and ignited as Hector tried to free her.

Together, they wrenched at the pedal until the metal fractured and Evelyn's foot was loose. Hector lifted her out of the cockpit and, with Caitrin's help, carried her away from the flames to safety.

"Are you all right?" Hector asked, as he settled her on the grass.

"Shaken, and I . . . my ankle is broken," Evelyn said.

Evelyn whimpered in pain as Caitrin knelt and examined her ankle. "I don't think it's broken. More likely a bad sprain, but your hand is burnt. There's a village just a few fields away to the south. Bagsby."

"How do you know that?"

Caitrin pointed to the sky. "Because, thanks to being up there, I finally know where we are, and where everyone is. Can you two manage to get to the village?"

"I think so," Hector said.

"Teddy's house is on the other side of that hill."

"Then you should go," Evelyn said. "You and Hector."

"No," Caitrin said. "You need medical attention right away. Hector will get you to the village."

"You want to catch him alone?" Hector said.

"I want Evelyn to be looked after, and I don't want Teddy disappearing again. Call Bethany from the village. Sorry about Suzie, she was a good 'un." She left, running up the hill before Hector could reply.

The house was farther away than Caitrin realized, and she was exhausted as she reached the last hilltop. She lay flat to regain her breath and scrutinized the building. There was no activity, at least not in the back of the house or the stables. She waited a few moments longer, saw no signs of life, and hurried downhill. The stables were empty; she crossed the yard, slipped through the back door, and searched the ground floor. There was no one; even Charles and all his utensils were missing from the kitchen. The bedrooms upstairs were also empty. She was too late. Teddy and his gang were gone.

There was a noise outside; perhaps not everyone had left. She went to the window and peered down at Florence and Donnie Thatcher loading suitcases into the bread van.

"Don't let me get in the way of you leaving," Caitrin's voice stopped them as she stepped out of the front door with her automatic trained at Donnie.

"Just like a Wednesday, you're back again," he said.

"We have unfinished business to take care of," she said, and held up her gun. "This time it's loaded. Where did everyone go?"

"On holidays to Skegness with their bucket and spades."

"Suggestion for you. Stay a small-time villain and leave the comedy alone, Donnie. It's not what you're good at, and you'll live longer," she said and glanced at Florence. "And dear Florence, why don't you go find a nice milkman in some town like Macclesfield, marry him, settle down with a half-dozen kids, and let yourself go?"

Her eyes locked on the gun in Caitrin's hand, Florence said nothing.

"Don't worry, I'm not going to shoot you. But I might take aim at him. Take me to Teddy, Donnie, and I'll let you go bullet-hole-free."

"No, I won't, and you're not a killer."

"True, but I could easily be a wounder, and you could end up with a permanent limp or a squeaky voice. Not much of a choice, really, in that."

"If I don't tell you or take you, you won't know where he is."

"Not true. He's with Mr. Beacon at Ramilton Woods. I now know exactly where that is, so I could just shoot you and take the van. I'm being kind."

"If you don't mind me saying so," Florence found her voice, "you look a bit, um, a bit bashed about, Caitrin."

"It's been a sort of up-and-down day, Flo. Shall we go, Donnie, or do I take the van and drive myself? Don't think too hard; you're not good at that either."

Teddy watched through the Ramilton Woods drawing-room window as Donnie came up the driveway, turned a half-circle, and reversed the bread van to within feet of the front door. It was an odd maneuver, especially as he did not get out but sat behind the wheel, his face obscured by reflections in the glass. Teddy went out to see why he was acting so strangely.

"The rear entrance, Donnie," he called out. "You know better than to come to the front."

In reply, Donnie wound down his window, stuck out an arm, and waved. "In the back, guvnor."

Puzzled, Teddy opened the van's rear door and took a step away. Inside, Caitrin was sitting on a box with an automatic in her hand. She gave him a thin smile that had no warmth, but did notice how much he had changed. To show how well he was doing in life, the old Teddy would have been dressed in new, expensive, and brightly colored clothes. This Teddy wore old corduroy trousers and a comfortable jumper with leather elbow patches. Standing in front of the ancient building, he fit perfectly into his surroundings. Daniel Teddy Baer's metamorphosis from Whitechapel slum Jew to English country gentleman was almost complete.

"I was assured you were dead," he said.

"Whoever told you that was mistaken, and what kind of man bombs a home for unwed mothers?"

"What kind of woman works for a secret organization that hides behind those poor mums?"

"Who told you that?"

"That's not the kind of information I could ever find," he said and gestured to the house behind him. "But these ancient families are connected and look out for each other, all the way to the top. 512, right? All women. Fascinating."

She stepped out of the van, closed the door, and tapped on the side. "Off you go, Donnie."

The engine started, and the rear wheels spat gravel as Donnie drove away.

Teddy waved a dismissive hand at Caitrin's automatic. "Put it away. I'm not armed and it's just me here. Come inside so we can lie about everything in comfort. Tea?"

They sat across from each other in the drawing room and

had hardly settled when Charles appeared with a tea tray. He placed it on a low table between them, whispered greetings to Caitrin, and left. She kept the automatic at her side.

"Biscuits," Teddy said as he pointed to a plate on the tray. "From my collection of those no longer being made."

Caitrin smiled to herself. *I've got more than you, I'm not supposed to have it, and I don't care. That is the old Teddy.*

Teddy inspected her. "You look as though you've being fighting a battle with a badger."

"You should see the badger."

"I'm really not that curious, but I suppose I should ask how you found me."

"I saw the lodge when we flew over it and then the burn scar from the bombs that missed this house. They're close together, and I'm guessing the lodge belongs to the Ramilton estate."

"It does, and a fine secluded spot too for my work."

"Why did the Germans bomb Ramilton Woods? You're on the same side." Caitrin tapped her forehead. "Silly me. To deflect suspicion, right? I mean, how could you and Rupert possibly be involved with the Lighthouse beacons if the Germans were bombing you? The beacon Sammy and I set here should have brought the bomber right overhead, but somehow it missed by a half mile."

"That's because Sammy told Rupert where it was—unactivated, of course—and he moved it to the field after you left. You are clever, Caitrin, but that's very dangerous in a woman."

"You're just the assembled beacons supplier. Remember the gas masks we delivered here, supposedly for the villagers? Rupert Ramilton is Mr. Beacon."

"Mr. Beacon?"

"That's the name 512 gave the head man."

"That's a bit melodramatic, no? Sounds more like a shady character from a Hollywood B film."

"He had to be called something."

Teddy took a biscuit and dipped it in his tea. He yawned and asked, "Now what?"

"You stop creating beacons."

"Or?"

"Teddy, you're killing your own people."

"I'm eliminating the old money, and isn't that what you want? Cut out the dead wood to give the average bloke a chance. And who cares about some old churches? No one goes to them anyway."

"They're a place of solace for some. And the hospitals?"

"Part of the deal." Teddy frowned. "But, to be honest, I don't like doing that much."

"No? You made me go back to that soldiers' convalescent home, twice."

"And the bomber that was going to attack it was shot down by a night fighter who knew he was coming. I wonder who told the good old RAF? But they won't give me a medal for that."

"I disconnected the battery wire anyway. If you gave up, it would—"

"Enough of this nonsense," Teddy said and leaned toward her. "You come here alone to talk to me about giving up. You're filthy, ragged, with an antiquated revolver."

"This old thing?" Caitrin raised her automatic, fired, and Teddy's teacup exploded in a mist of porcelain and tea.

He shrank back, startled, recovered, and sat upright. "So now you're Annie Oakley, but with no idea what you're doing, which makes you a serious liability. So I might as well give you to him."

"Him?"

"He means me," Rupert said from behind the chair as he pressed the muzzle of an automatic into the base of her neck. "Don't even imagine moving, and drop the gun. But do imagine this: my right index finger is curled around a trigger. If I squeeze said trigger, it fires a bullet into your neck. The bullet would cut your spinal column and leave you alive, but paralyzed from the neck down. Imagine, just the tiny little movement of one finger of mine and it's a very different and very painful rest of life for you."

Rupert unknotted his tie and threw it to Teddy. "Tie her hands behind her back."

Teddy quickly tied her hands.

"And move the tea things; we don't want to make a mess."

Teddy moved the tea tray to a side table.

"Now, my little Welsh spitfire, on your knees," Rupert said and pushed her to the floor before she could react. He bent her over the table. "Let's finish that weekend we had together, shall we?"

She fought against him.

"Don't move." He pressed his forearm to the back of Caitrin's neck to stop any struggle as he knelt behind her. "Damn, women and their stupid trousers."

Teddy heard a sound outside, glanced through the window and saw a Daimler pull up. "Emma's here."

Rupert took no notice as he struggled to undress Caitrin. The front door opened, closed, and Emma's shoes sounded on the wooden floor as she approached. "Hello, Teddy."

"Hello, Emma."

"Rupert, darling, do stay still for a moment, would you?"

He ignored her.

"Rupert, please."

"Shut up."

"Rupert."

"Not until I've had this slut. Damn trousers."

CRACK! A shot shocked the room. Rupert straightened, grunted, collapsed over Caitrin, and slid to the floor with a neat hole in his left temple.

"I did ask nicely, darling. You really should have listened."

Caitrin rolled off the table and looked up at Emma holding a Walther pistol. She undid the tie and pushed Caitrin into a chair as Teddy picked up the automatic. "That was his favorite regimental tie. He must really have wanted you. Thank goodness for trousers. *Virtus incusum, if not integra.*"

Caitrin stared at her, trying to make sense of what had just happened.

"You look scruffy, my dear," Emma said as she sat on the arm of Teddy's chair. "But, then . . ."

Caitrin ignored her. *There is a little voice in your head you must learn to listen to,* Bethany had often insisted during Caitrin's training. *Something will be said and the voice tells you to take notice, remember. All too often we don't.*

Through his family contacts, Rupert could easily discover country estates suitable for targets, perhaps with additional help from researching Debrett's, and old churches were not hard to find. But Caitrin's little voice recalled Teddy saying Rupert's wife spent her life running around to hospitals, *showering her grace and charity on everyone.* Teddy was ambitious and Rupert an ugly soul, but Emma Ramilton chose the target hospitals. She ran Lighthouse, not her husband. She was the monster.

"Are you with us now?" Emma said. "You look a bit dazed."

"I'm with you," Caitrin said and knew she had little time left if Emma wanted her dead.

"I always had a strange feeling about you. The Germans call it Fingerspitzengefühl, an intuition at your fingertips. We'd say a sixth sense."

"Know a lot of German, do you?"

Emma gave her a thin smile in response.

"I came with two other agents. They will have contacted London by now."

"Two agents from a now-defunct organization." Emma lowered the hammer on her pistol and put it in her pocket. "Admirable, but to what end, dear?"

"They'll find Florence and Donnie and the others in London."

"No, they won't," Teddy said. "I can, but your people won't, and they would say nothing anyway."

"Sammy Breen and I planted—"

"Which Sammy? He's an actor, a man of a dozen characters, none authentic, and he's back in Dublin," Emma interrupted. "Getting drunk in Toners pub and telling everyone how he taught Shaw to use the semicolon." She laughed, and her hand affectionately brushed Teddy's hair. "Then, drunker, he'll confide to everyone that he knew Maud before W. B. did and later, sober, be absolutely baffled that there are no roles for him at the Abbey."

Caitrin glanced at Teddy. He was sensitive about his poor education, and she wondered how much of that he understood. Emma sat opposite Caitrin and said, "Teddy and I are going to leave now, but first I will give you a choice. After we're gone, and I emphasize *after*, you can use the telephone in the study to call your superior and say you have solved the case, but sadly Mr. Beacon committed suicide. Rupert was left-handed, which is why I shot him through the left temple. Tomorrow morning at six, his men will be here to pick up the next batch of beacons. Arrive earlier and you will nab the whole lot."

"Or?"

"You and Rupert got into a gunfight, and shot and killed each other. Not much of a choice, is it? But the best I can do in the circumstances."

"I had the beacons assembled at the lodge and delivered here so Rupert's men never met me. Emma is rarely here, so there is no connection to either of us," Teddy said. "There is only Rupert, he is their Mr. Beacon. And—"

Emma interrupted him. "You and your irrelevant all-girls team are a little late. The beacons are no longer active."

"Why?"

"Because of this." Emma took a coin from her pocket and flipped it to her. Caitrin caught it.

"A gold sovereign. One of thousands in payment from Germany. Keep the coin. I will be right back," Emma said and left.

Teddy shifted in his chair and held Caitrin's automatic loosely on his knee, the muzzle pointed at her. He shrugged and said, "C'est la vie," with the French accent of a Whitechapel spiv. It was so ludicrous she almost laughed, but Emma returned, with her right hand hidden, and said, "Put the coin down there."

Caitrin's fingers had barely placed the coin on the table when Emma brought a meat cleaver from behind her back. She swung it in a vicious arc, burying the blade deep in the wood and cutting the coin in two. "Inspect, if you please."

Caitrin picked a half of the coin. It had a thin, outer layer of gold, with a thicker, dark grey center.

"Gold sovereigns," Teddy said. "They are exactly the same dimensions as a real one, but made with a lead center. Almost worthless, and so there will be no more beacons for the Third Reich."

Now Caitrin did laugh. Teddy had been outsmarted. "Oh my goodness, Teddy, what kind of world are we living in where we cannot trust Adolf Hitler?"

"How true. And once the beacons are gone, interest will fade, and this episode will vanish into the greater madness of the war. Well, made up your mind for you, have we?" Emma said, and Caitrin nodded.

"You have made the right decision, very wise," Emma said as she went to Rupert's body, wiped the Walther clean of prints, and pushed it into his hand. "After we've left, you can use the telephone."

"Where are you going?" Caitrin called after them, and even as she spoke, it seemed a ludicrous question to ask them. To her surprise, Emma stopped and turned. "There's nothing to hide.

We're going to Crentock Hall, the Fairbirn estate in Cornwall, my family's home, where I spent most of my time away from Rupert. It's along the cliffs near Sennen Cove, where the dead Germans washed up a while ago. I'll wait there, prepared to be shocked at the tragic news of my husband's death. Even though we were estranged because of his cruelty and drunkenness, still, some residual affection remains for such a poor, tortured soul. You must come visit for a weekend sometime."

"Or perhaps for our wedding," Teddy said.

"Yes, that's a splendid idea. You really must come to the wedding. I'll send you an invitation," she said, turned away, and they left, hand in hand.

Caitrin waited a few minutes, went to the study, picked up the telephone, and called the church.

"Wixton 550, St. Peter's Church, this is Doris speaking," the housekeeper answered.

"Doris, this is Caitrin Colline. Is Mrs. Goodman there?"

"She's a very happy woman; the vicar just gave her a chocolate finger," Doris said.

"Lucky Bethany."

"I'll get her for you."

Bethany was eating when she came to the telephone. "Caitrin, Hector just called. Are you all right?"

"Yes, I am, but I think you had better get a cup of tea and sit down. This is going to take a while."

48

A light snow fell overnight and hid the town's scars and blemishes. The coal tips were perfect white cones, and the parallel rows of slate-roofed, terrace houses became the fossilized ribs of some fabulous creature. It was a black-and-white landscape, save for the occasional bursts of orange flame from open furnaces in the ironworks. Caitrin sat on a stile set into a drystone wall high on the southern hill, below St. Illtyd's church, and gazed out over the valley, her valley, where she had grown up. The thought crossed her mind that she might not return to sit there many more times. Ties were loosening, and there was only her mother left as a reason to visit.

The letter. She turned it in her hand. The envelope was battered, one corner torn, and covered with a half-dozen scribbled-over addresses. The last legible one was her mother's address.

"Tea and vicars may help the British Empire thrive, but it's the tenacious Royal Mail that stitches it all together," she said to herself and opened the envelope. The letter inside was written in a strong, plain hand.

Dear Caitrin,

When I got married, I looked forward to taking the road with my wife, together with our Max. Along the way, we'd meet Max's wife, and his children, and if we were blessed, perhaps even a great-grandchild or two. I knew that when my road came to an end, Max's would continue on with his own family. My son would not travel through life alone. But my wife died young, and now Max is gone, and there will be no family for him, or me. I still cannot understand how that came to be.

I have ordered a drum kit from Sears and Roebuck. When it comes, I will set it up in the barn. And yes, it's a red barn. I will buy a half-dozen ducks and have them numbered. Galvan up the road a ways has a donkey we can borrow for as long as we like, and he doesn't care if you call it Derek. We have dogs, male, but calling one Fiona won't matter to him. Everything you talked about with Max will be here for you, ready and waiting. As will I.

I also understand if you don't want to come. It is a long way. Be safe in this terrible war. Losing Max was the deepest cut to my soul. I don't want it to happen again. And finally, if between now and the time you visit, you happen to get married, bring your husband along too. The road is wide enough for us all.

Your American Dad,
Hywel Evarts

She folded the letter and slipped it back into the envelope. At the right time, she would reply to Hywel, but it would not be soon. The war had made her a realist. Today she was going back to London for the last meeting of 512.

49

Doris entered the storage room, carrying a tea tray high as though it were a grand trophy at the head of a victory parade. She placed it on the card table, whipped off the tea towel covering it, and stood back and waited for applause.

"Chocolate digestives!" Caitrin, Bethany, Evelyn, and Hector said, almost in unison.

"The vicar's done you proud on your last meeting," Doris said.

"He has indeed," Bethany said. "Thank him for me. I'll come and see him later."

In reply, Doris gave an odd flouncy curtsey and left.

"Evelyn, please be mum while I start the meeting."

Evelyn shifted her cast-enclosed foot and reached for the teapot. She poured everyone a cup of tea, and they each added what was deemed necessary to suit their taste.

"Here is the news," Bethany said. "512 is being absorbed into the SOE. We will have offices in Baker Street and retain our name."

"Will it still be all women?" Hector asked.

"And Hector," Caitrin said.

"Yes, but, in future, we will be working in Europe rather than England."

"There is no possibility of remaining independent?" Evelyn said.

"I'm afraid not, and Winston has far greater issues to deal with. They are good ones, though. Rommel is retreating in Africa, the Germans have been stopped outside Moscow, and of course the big one—after Pearl Harbor, the Americans are now in the war." She helped herself to a biscuit, dipped it in her tea, nibbled, and continued. "And, as he puts it in his forthright manner, 512 did not exactly cover itself in glory in the Lighthouse operation."

"That's outrageous," Caitrin said. "I infiltrated them. I watched them build the damn beacons and even went out on a planting operation. We tracked them to Ramilton Woods and almost got killed in a plane crash. Did he not read our evidence reports?"

"He did, but shall I read what Teddy Baer had to say in reply?"

"You've interviewed him?"

"He was a most willing participant," Bethany said and opened a folder in front of her on the table. "He said, 'Caitrin Colline was a pushy little popsy who came, uninvited, to my New Year's Eve party and was a pest. Later, she became a damn nuisance, always chasing after me. One night, I had enough and told her to go away. She got angry and, when my back was turned, set fire to my pub.'"

"What bloody nonsense," Caitrin said.

"'When the fire erupted, she tried to run out, fell, and cracked her head. I picked her up and took her to friend's house in the country. I thought she could recover and relax there. My friend is Lady Emma Ramilton. To pass the time, we made wooden toys for Lady Emma to take to children's hospitals. She is such a selfless and loving saint.'"

"And I'm a cute and adorable Hermann Göring," Caitrin said.

"'Perhaps Caitrin got confused and thought we were making something else. Then one day she disappeared.'" Bethany put down the report. "Lady Emma corroborated his story."

"She would," Evelyn said. "What do they have to say about dead Rupert and the men we swept up the following day?"

"Teddy insisted he hadn't seen Rupert in weeks and Lady Emma hadn't spoken to him in months. They were estranged. She thought the suicide tragic, naturally, knew Rupert was heavily in debt, but had no idea he was working for the Nazis. Also, there were photographs of other things."

"What other things?"

"Things men do with other men, I suppose."

"He *was* a public school boy," Hector said.

"So were you," Caitrin answered and instantly wished she had not as Hector blushed fiery-red and went marble-statue-mute. She mouthed a silent apology.

"I'm not Oscar Wilde and have no witty response," Bethany said. "Not a word of what Teddy said is true, I know, but that doesn't matter because the operation is finished."

"Just like that?" Hector said. "Over?"

Caitrin felt anger rise. "Teddy was created by the Whitechapel slums. He would cut you for a tanner, but there is also a strangely moral character in there somewhere. But Lady Emma shot her husband in cold blood and visited hospitals, knowing full well she was choosing them as targets for German bombs. She is an evil creature, and I cannot just let her go free."

"Caitrin, it's your word against theirs. You will be a little Welsh popsy fighting the Establishment. Not only will you never win, but you will lose what you already have."

"Then what should I do?"

"Accept, and move on to the next fight. Fate has its way." Bethany sat back in her chair and sighed. "Lady Emma was a Fairbirn when she married Rupert Ramilton. The Ramilton family is not an old one, but the Fairbirn family has many branches and goes back centuries. A few are ardently pro-Nazi and active members of Die Brücke."

"So arrest them."

"Some are in government, while others are close to senior members of the Royal Family. Need I say more?"

"We need a bloody big revolution," Caitrin said.

"Would you like my biscuit instead?" Evelyn said and squeezed her hand.

Caitrin's expression softened. "McVitie's could stop a revolution singlehanded with a chocolate digestive."

"We made a grievous error," Bethany said. "We assumed Emma could not be in command solely because she was a woman."

"I automatically saw Rupert as Mr. Beacon and ignored the possibility she might be involved," Caitrin said and sighed in frustration. "There's such a long way for we women to go, and a lot to learn, isn't there?"

"Yes, but we'll get there. I do have some fascinating information for you, though," Bethany said. "Teddy and Emma are getting married."

"I know. I got an invitation," Caitrin said.

"You did? Are you going?" Evelyn asked, eyes wide and grinning. "We could all go and sit on Teddy's family side."

"And Teddy would love that, but no," Caitrin said and shook her head.

"It was announced in *The Times*—she, as Lady Emma Fairbirn of Crentock Hall, Cornwall, and he, as Daniel Barr, an influential London businessman," Bethany said. "'In a modern twist, their intention is to combine the two names into Fairbirn-Barr.'"

Hector laughed. "I would call that a morganatic marriage, but I'm not sure which one is the inferior partner."

"Sir Daniel Fairbirn-Barr. He did it. Teddy finally got his country estate," Caitrin said. *I hope it turns out to be what he wants.*

"Each of them has what the other wants. She brings land and position; he brings money or knows how to make it," Bethany said. "An ancient story, and not always a happy one. Enough. There are two weeks before the new year, when we will become part of SOE. Go take a holiday and put this nonsense behind you."

"Yes, dammit!" Caitrin shot to her feet and almost knocked over the table as she headed for the door.

"Are you going somewhere in particular?" Bethany asked.

"Yes, I am." Caitrin grinned. "I'm going to Lincoln Cathedral to see a certain apprentice vicar and ask him to save my weary soul." The grin widened. "Or mayhaps blacken his."

50

Clementine Churchill watched Winston with affection as he sat across from her at tea reading his newspaper. Uninterrupted moments together were becoming rare, and their beloved home, Chartwell, was considered too dangerous to visit because, being easily recognizable from the air and close to the coast, it was a tempting target for Luftwaffe bombers. Ronald Tree and his beautiful wife, the decorator Nancy Lancaster, had offered them Ditchley Park estate for their infrequent retreats from London. The house was surrounded by trees and hidden by dense foliage, which made it difficult to identify from above.

"Loos," Clementine said, to see if she could get his attention. She could and did.

"Loos?" He peered over his newspaper at her.

"Yes, Loos. When you were in the front line and had to address punishing one of your men for some misdemeanor, you first asked if he had fought at Loos."

"I did."

"And if he said he had fought there, your punishment was

light or nonexistent. I'm told that, once the other men heard that, from then on everyone brought before you on a charge insisted he had fought at Loos."

Winston chuckled at the memory. "Never underestimate the ingenuity of the British Tommy."

"We few, we happy few, we band of brothers. A touch of St. Crispin's Day?"

"A touch." His smile faded as he rattled the newspaper. "Liverpool has been bombed for seven nights in a row, the center of Swansea is just rubble, and Malta has been attacked by the Luftwaffe a thousand times. In the past, wars were fought between armies in the field, soldier against soldier, regiment to regiment. Go gloriously off to war and return with your shield, or on it. Not anymore; that time has gone. It has now become a people's war, and the battlefield is on the streets of the towns and villages. Young, old, men, women, children, guilty and innocent alike. Everyone is on the front line. It will cause such distress to some."

"Are you thinking of anyone in particular?"

"Yes. Our young Welsh tigress, the fearless Caitrin Colline. I often wonder what the war will do to her in the years ahead."

"Caitrin will survive, of that I am quite sure, and at least she's a credit to Wales, unlike her countryman Lloyd George, who is a shabby little tike."

"He's a good friend."

"Only in public."

Winston laughed. "Clemmie, what would I do without you?"

She gifted him a knowing smile. "Buy even more silk dragon dressing gowns?"

Her soul saved, or at least refurbished well enough to be tucked safely away and forgotten for the moment, Caitrin took the train back to London. The compartment was filled with soldiers, so she wore her female invisibility cloak and stared out of the window. The young soldier sitting opposite her was reading the *Daily Mail.* He finished, folded the newspaper, and offered it to her. She was about to refuse when a headline caught her eye: NEW YEAR HONEYMOON TRAGEDY. She thanked him, opened the paper, and read the report. The tragedy occurred when newlyweds Sir Daniel and Emma Fairbirn-Barr were walking in the moonlight along a path bordering a sea cliff on their Cornwall estate. Inexplicably, and despite Daniel's heroic efforts to save her, Lady Emma slipped and fell to her death. There was a delay in emergency teams reaching her because a telephone call had been made to the police station about a bomb at the farthest end of the village. By the time they had discovered it was a false alarm and arrived at the estate, it was high tide and impossible to reach Lady Emma. The Sennen Cove lifeboat retrieved her body the next day. Sir Fairbirn-Barr was grief-stricken and had to be restrained by three police officers from throwing himself off the cliff after his beloved wife. Through his tears he was heard to say, "Now it's just me."

Caitrin folded the paper and looked again at the headline as she handed it back to the soldier. Sammy Breen might have been an actor, but he was a rank amateur compared to Teddy Baer/Daniel Fairbirn-Barr. *'Now it's just me.' Not as long as I'm alive, Teddy.*

Author's Note

A Beacon in the Night is set in 1941 and based loosely on the Luftwaffe's Baedeker Raids of 1942. Forgive my slight chronological shift. The name Baedeker comes from a series of German guide books, which included detailed maps of selected cities. The Royal Air Force bombing raids on German cities were proving to be very effective, which understandably outraged Adolf Hitler. He wanted to respond in kind, but most of the Luftwaffe had been directed to the Operation Barbarossa campaign against Russia.

Therefore, instead of mass bombing, it was decided to destroy civilian morale by attacking the British cities of historical and cultural value mentioned in the Baedeker guides. They were called terror attacks, the splendid German word for them being *Vergeltungsangriffe*. Cathedrals, churches, and historical buildings were struck in London, Exeter, Bath, Canterbury, Norwich, and York. The attacks continued until 1944, but the Luftwaffe losses to British night fighters became too heavy, and they ceased.

The Germans did have *Knickebein* and *X-Gerät*, which were accurate radio navigation beams to locate a target at night, but the devastating *Leuchturm* (Lighthouse) beacon in the novel is solely my invention. Thank goodness.